Chance Lost

BY

Jo LaRue

To Jenna! Congrats on your Goodreads win! ♡ xoxo Jo LaRue

CHANCE LOST
Copyright: Jo LaRue
All Rights Reserved
ISBN: 1492333131
ISBN 13: 978-1492333135
Published: CreateSpace.com

Find out more about the author and upcoming books online at https://www.facebook.com/AuthorJoLaRue or @JoLaRueAuthor or email me at AuthorJoLaRue@gmail.com.

I dedicate this book to my mother,
Marilyn Carver, who has been my greatest
supporter, best friend, and without
whom, I would have been lost long ago.

You have always been there, even when
times were tough. I love you more than
mere words can ever express.

Prologue

1500 AD –

"Awaken now, my son, it is time for your journey to begin."

He awakens from what feels like a dream with no memories of what has come before. He is standing in front of a man and a woman. It is his maker who is speaking to him: his mother, Lachesis, one of the three Fates.

"Your father, Zeus, and I made you because you are needed by the human world below us. There are others, similar to you, who are killing innocents. The humans cannot know Immortals exist for our own safety. Throughout time, Immortals have been slaughtered for being different. Now, because of the Crusades, a few Immortals have been taking advantage by mating with humans. Even worse, they have been killing them. If this continues, another slaughter will happen. We created you to stop it from happening yet again."

His father spoke up then; his deep voice commanding attention. "Son, I have given you the gift of life so you can stop these foolish Immortals from bringing us attention we do not wish. I have given you a special gift, one that only you will be able to use. You have the ability to shift into any form an Immortal takes. You are our warrior, our enforcer. Your duty is to protect humans from us and keep the balance between our worlds. All Immortals will answer to you."

His mother reached out to caress his cheek before leaving. "You will not always be the only one of your kind, my beautiful son. In the future there will be another, a mate. She will be made known to you only when the time is right. My sisters and I will be watching over you and will be there for you, should you need us. Go now my son, and be the great warrior that we know you are."

His name is Sylas Taiken and he is The Enforcer.

Present day, 2013 –

It was always the same dream. The black leopard runs through the forest, the smell of rich brown earth thick through misty morning. It hung in the air like an intoxicating drug. It was easy to avoid trees and fallen limbs. The vision of the leopards piercing green eyes was sharp and so were his reflexes.

A sleek, black female leopard comes from the clearing. His other half, all lean muscle, and thick fur – her eyes mirrored to the green of his own. She rubbed against him, her scent lingering on his fur and vice versa. They belonged to each other, they were made for each other.

Rumbling purrs of joy from deep within their core echo through the forest as they play amongst the trees, chasing and wrestling each other down. A silver wolf comes from the brush. There's a familiarity, a kinship, and no threat to be had. They greet, and in silent consensus, run through the thick brush, the scent of prey having found its way to their keen noses.

The pursuit doesn't take long, not with three of them, and the deer comes down easily. They gorge themselves until their bellies can take no more, the scent of blood mixing with the earth. Sated, they make their way to the river to clean themselves, and then lay in the warm sun, relaxed in each other's company. Dusk approaches and the wolf gets up, stretching with a yawn … his fangs sharp and bright even in the dim light. The wolf takes off into the forest, howling with his departure.

Before long it's time for the leopards to shift back, to become their human counter parts and welcome the night by making love. The dream fades, and the fog between sleep and awake, steals the images of their human faces before they can be seen.

Chapter 1

"Hi! My name is Chance Cadens, and I've had a craptastic day!" She chuckled at her best friend Gus who was busy working away on a mainframe.

This was their normal way of greeting each other. Almost like being in a support group. It worked for them and that was all that mattered.

"You out, Chance?" Gus looked up and smiled while pulling some wiring loose from the servers.

"Done and shut down now, sweet cheeks! I hope your evening goes better than my day went," Chance leaned her hip on the doorframe.

"Yeah. It was a rough one, I'm glad it's almost over. You sticking with the company now that they're shutting this office down?"

The company had decided to downsize. If people were sticking with the company, they were being relocated. Chance had no such desire, but because she and Gus hadn't had time to catch up recently, she had no idea if her best friend was staying or going.

"We're still in negotiations, but I'm thinking it won't be an issue. It'll give me an excuse to fly my plane more." He pulled more wires from the server and laughed. "We haven't talked in a while, girly. I was wondering if you're staying around here or moving?"

Over the years, Gus had broken her out of her self-imposed shell, with his nerdy quirkiness. The man lived and breathed computers. He stood right at 6'4 and with her at 5'9" with no shoes on, Chance still had to look up at him.

"Sorry about the no talk, Gus. Been sort of busy. To answer your question… Yes, and no. Long story, but I'll be calling you soon to help me set up my own system. I haven't told anyone here, but I bought some property up near the state border a few weeks ago and

I'm planning on going totally self-sufficient up there. Think you can handle the job, Gus?"

"What do you mean by self-sufficient exactly? Where is this place and should I be worried about you being alone?" Gus gave Chance his complete attention. Self-sufficient could mean a lot of different things, but knowing her, this might be something for him to worry about. Gus sat on his stool, crossed his arms over his chest, and frowned at her.

"Like I said, long story, but I promise to fill you in soon, Gus. Just be looking for my call in a few weeks. Besides, you know I can't go long without texting my BFF" She handed him an envelope prepared the night before. In it was a check written out to him for five thousand and a list of what she was looking for.

"That should give you enough to start and if you need more, well, you know how to reach me. If I don't answer, it means I'm out of cell range, but I promise to call back as soon as I can. I'm sorry this is all mystery filled, but everything will make more sense when we have time to talk."

Gus looked up at her after looking in the envelope, "Chance, this is a lot of money. Are you sure this is what you want and can you even afford it? You really are starting to worry me."

Taking Gus' hands in hers, Chance pulled him into a sisterly hug. Lowering to a near whisper, she replied "Let's just say I got lucky with some numbers on a lotto draw recently. That check in your hand is just a drop in the bucket. This is between you and me and no one else. Gus, you are the only person I trust at the moment to do what I need done. I promise, I will explain later, but not here and not now. Text you soon. Take care of you, okay?" Giving him another hug, she turned to leave. Secrecy was not a strong point with her, but necessary right now. Gus wouldn't fail her.

Walking out of the building for the last time was freeing. Looking up at the blue Georgia sky, she laughed. A huge weight came off her shoulders and, for once, she actually felt like celebrating. Her new, midnight blue Wrangler 4x4, sat calling her name. It was her only extravagance until buying the property in north Georgia, and couldn't wait to give it some major trail time.

The jeep unlocked with a beep. Chance threw her shoes in the back, pulled the top back, and got into the driver's seat. The engine started smoothly. She lowered all the windows, put her thick black hair into a braid, cranked the stereo, and left the parking lot. Wind from the road could turn even the silkiest hair into a rats nest and tonight was not a night for fighting with her mane over who was dominate. Tonight was a night to get her groove on and it was past time to get moving on just that very thing.

Chance arrived home to her modest three-bedroom ranch shortly after six. Friday traffic in the Atlanta suburbs has always been a nightmare for the traffic squeamish and she definitely despised it. It was another reason to move out to the middle of nowhere. No more noise, no more nosy neighbors, and no more drama.

The mailbox was full of nothing but junk, per usual. Chance went inside, tossed it on the table by the door, and stripped off her work clothes. Those, along with her other ones would be boxed up and donated. From now on it would be jeans, t-shirts and/or her beloved bike leathers. She was a biker at heart and a country girl down to the depths of her soul.

There was a new biker bar on the other side of town and she was interested enough to check it out. If it were a true biker hangout it would be equipped with pool tables. One of her ex-foster dads was a beer drinking pool hustler. Chance learned quickly, and her foster dad saw an opportunity in her youthful face. Part of her education was learning how to play other people. It wasn't enough to just play the game. Before long her skills were honed, and Chance learned how easy it was not to starve. Darts were a strong bet as well… and most biker bars contained one or the other, if not both.

Standing in her bedroom, she studied the reflection in the mirror. This was a daily ritual. Chance could never understand what it was about her body that made men faun. The girl in the mirror was 5'9", with not much fat, but still curvy. Thick, jet-black hair that fell below her butt when loose and dark green eyes were the only things she could see that might make a man interested. All she saw was butt and boobs, which she hated. She had golden skin and a classic rounded face with high cheekbones. The latter was still a mystery she vowed to research in the future. Removing the rubber band from her braid to run her fingers through the strands, she sighed and gave in. A hot shower beckoned and it was a call not to be ignored.

While standing under the relaxing spray of the showerhead, she reflected on her past. Chance never enjoyed much of a normal life. Her parents gave her up when she was a baby and she spent all of her young life in foster homes. Her foster parents over the years either used her like a slave to do their cleaning or they were abusive, mostly the latter. Thankfully her virtue was still intact, due to a lot of kicking, biting, scratching, and a down right refusal to be used. More than once she was called a hellcat bitch on steroids, and she wore it like a badge.

As soon as she was able, she got a job, started paying her own way, found an efficiency apartment, and went through the courts to be emancipated from the court and foster care system. It wasn't easy but it taught her to be tough and streetwise.

Chance met a woman, Sensei Kiku, who owned a Dojo just down the road from the diner where she worked after school let out. She was abused in her young life as well, and knew and felt the symptoms herself. Back then, Chance would not look anyone in the eye and would flinch when anyone would try to touch her. Sensei offered her free classes in exchange for helping her with clean up, keeping her books and a promise she would finish high school. That was 9 years and a fourth degree black belt ago.

Chance turned her thoughts over to Gus. Knowing he wanted them to be more than friends kept her at bay. She loved him, but not in the way he deserved. Friends were all she could ever see them as. Chance wanted more, needed more than this bare existence. She needed family and someone who took her breath away with a glance. Being in her mid-twenties and alone was no longer tolerable. It was time to trust and let down the walls that shielded her heart. Gus simply was not the gateway to that path.

Finished with her shower, and stepping to her closet, Chance pulled her black leathers out. Taking a moment to breathe in the scent, she was reminded of sitting in the Jeep for the first time. It was a new car smell and delicious in an odd sort of way.

Yep, tonight was a leather night. Pulling her favorite low-slung pants on was almost orgasmic, especially since she decided to go commando tonight and feel the leather everywhere. Next came a leather bustier that didn't quite make it to her waist. This allowed her to show off a crystal belly ring... always an eye catcher, especially when trying to distract male pool players.

Chance put on the barest makeup possible, a bit of mascara and blush to boost her complexion. Shoes were always last. These boots were made for her and contained steel toes, hidden pockets, and a hidden switchblade in the toe if needed.

When it came to protecting herself, Chance preferred to use body and hands. Since she was a fourth degree black belt, weapons were mostly unnecessary, but she was registered to carry as well. Under normal circumstances she would not take weapons with her, but when it came to gambling, biker bars, and past experience... well, a girl just had to be extra careful. Chance slipped an extra switchblade in her left boot and a .22 in her right. Grabbing her pool stick case and long black leather duster, she headed out to the garage to the other baby.

It was a gift from a biker friend she'd saved in a bar fight two years ago and it was the best gift ever received. All chrome, and all hers. The Harley-Davidson Sportster gleamed in greeting when she flicked on the light switch. *Hey baby, ready to go have some fun?* She crooned while braiding her hair again.

Putting the cue case in one of the sidesaddles, Chance donned her coat, helmet, and stepped over the seat. Pressing the garage door opener on her key chain, she cranked it, relishing the feeling of power and the low rumble. *A girl could almost get off just riding one of these bad boys down the road!* As soon as the door was open, the kickstand was up and she was out for a night of fun on the town.

Chapter 2

Sylas pulled into the parking lot of The Den Bar & Grill. It wasn't much to look at, but it belonged to his best friend, Jack. Neon lights in the windows blinked invitations of cold beer and pool tables to anyone passing by. The bar touted some of the best food in town and business was steadily growing since it opened.

Jack was a shifter Sylas knew from long ago. Even in past times it was hard to find friends that were trustworthy. On more than one occasion, Jack proved he was worthy of the title. Sylas was in a funk and Jack was the one person he knew who could brighten his day without even trying. Five hundred years of waiting on a mate was taking its toll.

The Fates created him to keep balance between humans and the Immortals. The only one who could shift into any species on the planet that he wanted. His primary animal was a black leopard and where he felt most at home, even over his human form. Being immortal, lonely *and* bored, well, that was never a good combination.

The Fates threw another wrench into things before he even got started looking for this mysterious mate. He needed to be her first if she was to become his true mate. If anyone else got to her before he did, the deal was off; no mate and she would only be able to shift into her original primary animal. The Fates could be real bitches when they wanted to be. The only other person that knew about his problem was the man he was here to see. After Sylas saved his ass twice in the past, Jack promised to always have his back, and he meant it.

Balance was all that mattered to the Fates. The scales between order and chaos could easily be tipped, and when Sylas slacked, they had no problem reminding him of his job. It was hard to keep the world balanced when he couldn't do it for himself. He slammed the kickstand down a bit too hard, and had to lean over to see if he damaged his Harley.

A distraction was needed, but he was second-guessing whether this was the place to get it. Right when he thought better of being there, Jack stepped outside the bar. He noticed Sylas right off and was walking his way. *Leave now and piss off one bad ass puma? Think I will stay,* he told himself, standing to greet his best bud.

"Hey, Sy! Glad you could make it, man." Jack reached out for a fist bump. "The place is rockin', but not too crowded. I had to come out for some fresh air."

"Noise getting to ya, Jack, or is it the smoke I saw rolling out when you opened the door?"

Jack gave him a lopsided grin. "Just the noise, as usual. What was I thinking when I put in those pool tables? Damn racket! Pun intended!"

Sylas gave him a quick punch in the arm and smiled. "You'll live, pussy cat. The money always wins in the end." They walked inside and went to the bar. "You're buying, right?"

"Usually do, my man, usually do."

Jack went behind the bar and slid a beer to Sylas. The immortal moved to a corner table keeping his back to the wall. From this angle, Sylas could see the entire bar. Unfortunately, his eyes brought notice from humans, and he didn't need or want it. Eyes that glow and change color kept him behind sunglasses when around them. Habit kept him in corners and out of sight.

A group of werewolves walked in and immediately staked claims on two pool tables in front of him. The humans paid them no mind, thinking they were just a bunch of drunken bikers. Sylas could smell their animals. The werewolves were obnoxious, rowdy, and the alcohol didn't help the cause. Their Alpha started a money game on the table closest to him. Sylas signaled for another beer. If things kept on like this, Jack would probably ask Sylas to help bounce them, as he had in the past. Werewolves weren't a job for human bouncers and Jack wouldn't want them to get hurt. A fight would happen sooner or later, and he needed to boost his calm. He huffed and smirked. *Just my luck, a drunk Alpha on an ego-trip. Maybe the night won't be so boring after all.*

The front door opened and the whole bar went quiet. The pool balls smacking against each other seemed loud in the silence. A woman walked in and didn't notice the stir she caused, or if she did it, was commonplace enough for her to ignore it. She was tall and dressed all in black leather. Sylas couldn't see what was under the full-length duster she was wearing, but he could tell she had curves. The noise level started notching back up a little when she turned towards the bar and asked for a beer. Her long, jet-black hair caught Sy's attention. Even braided, it fell past her ass.

The woman walked by scouting tables. Sylas breathed in deeply, catching her scent... human. A slightly floral and spicy scent followed her and Sylas caught no hint of another male on her. Shifting in his seat, he willed more of her enticing aroma into his nostrils. She removed her coat, passing it to Jack, and Sy's breath caught in his throat. The woman had curves in all the right places. It was all he could do to stay in his seat. His instincts told him to get up and cover her with his coat. *His mate and for his eyes only...* boomed through his head.

My mate? Where the hell had that come from? She's human, not shifter. What the hell is wrong with me? She watched the gambling among the tables intently, and moved to the two where the werewolves were playing. She walked gracefully and confidently over towards them and asked if she could join the game.

The wolves were all over her joining them, and the Alpha was looked at her like dinner had just been served. Sy was not going anywhere now. He was not going to leave her alone with this pack. *Nuh-uh.*

Jack walked over from behind the bar. He looked at the pack and then back to Sy. He leaned on the table with his back to the wall. "Gonna have trouble, I can smell it."

"Yep, it's thick."

Sy's shoulders were rigid, his gaze never wavering from the scene by the pool tables. If he clenched his teeth any harder he was going to chip a tooth. "Ease up. I got you and this. Whatever this is." He swept his hand slightly towards the tables and the Wolves.

"Not sure what this is either, but I know you have my back."

"Her name is Chance. She gave it to me when I took her coat." Sylas nodded, still mesmerized.

Jack walked back to tend bar with a promise of another beer on the way. Sylas hadn't moved since she walked in. Taking a long swig, he got comfortable. This was going to be a longer night than anticipated. He relished every minute watching her. Chance sized up the wolves and their game. To her, they were just some drunken bikers, but he knew better. They could and would tear her apart if provoked... with no effort and not think twice about it after.

Chance took out her cue and put it together. Sylas rolled her name around in his head a few times. *Chance. Chance. Chance... Could she be the one foretold? Not possible, she's human. Sexy as hell, but human. Could the Fates be messing with me still?* Probably, but could he afford to not take this seriously? The only answer he could come up with was a resounding no.

Chapter 3

Chance sat at her table ignoring the pompous leader of the biker gang as she watched them play. *Just like a man,* she thought to herself smirking. He was strutting and puffing out his chest like a peacock, a cute one, but still full of himself. It was exactly this type of man she'd hoped to find around the tables. This type of drunk was easy to take advantage of. She wanted in while the stakes were low and right now it was a dollar a game.

Having experienced her fair share of sloppy drunks brought no fear when dealing with them. It was the other types, mean and intent on doing physical harm that she needed to steer clear from. Shivering from the memories that wanted to overtake all her senses and shut everything down, Chance glanced around to see if anyone noticed. Her head felt like something had escaped the zoo and was pacing around in it with the same restlessness that was keeping her awake at night. Shaking it off and gritting her teeth, Chance pulled back into the game.

When her turn came up she walked over to rack the pool balls, and made a show of it. Bending lower than necessary to get the rack, the bikers got a clear shot of ass and boobs. The strutting peacock had won, as she had hoped.

"Game and stakes?" she asked when done, dipping lower to put the rack back under the table.

"What you want to play for, honey? I'm liking call all shots and you as the prize."

"Hmm, well that sounds good for you, but what if I win? I think I prefer a money game instead. Call all and five dollars a game?" She drawled out in her best southern girl accent.

Guffaws and high fives sounded behind him and from somewhere in the back she heard a loud, "Whoa, Craven! BURN!"

Craven bristled and shot a dirty look behind him at whoever shouted. The other men quieted down under his scrutinizing gaze. He turned to glare at her and said, "Fine!"

Chance lost the first game by one and the eight ball. The second by three and the third by two again. As she racked for the next game, she looked up at Craven asking if he would mind upping the stakes so she could, "win some of her money back". Thinking he had an easy mark, he upped it to twenty a game and she agreed.

Still wanting him to think her an easy mark, she paid him the money owed and then proceeded to lose the next two by purposely missing the eight ball. She paid out and racked again.

Time for some magic, she smirked to herself.

He broke and ran all but one and the eight. On her turn she ran all but one and the eight, and in the process, placed the eight in the corner, right behind his ball. He had no way to make a clean shot with his level of skills, but in his drunken state there was no doubt he was going to try.. When he sank the eight and missed his original shot, she crooned at him, "I am so sorry! It sucks to lose that way!"

Craven glared at her, but paid out the twenty and just as she suspected he would, he asked to up the game to fifty. She shrugged and said it was okay with her. To make it look like she sympathized with him, Chance ordered a round of shots, their choice, and another beer for herself.

She lost the next two, but Craven's game was declining from the added alcohol. She won the next three games straight knowing the loss of his profits from her would tempt him into upping the stakes again. Feeling bold, Craven raised the stakes to a hundred. She lost the first and won three more, two by sabotaging his eight ball twice. She now had some of his money and it was not sitting well with him.

"Tell you what, Craven, how about one more game for five hundred and we call it a night?" Her voice was sickly sweet with sugar and southern drawl. "We can even get a neutral person to hold the money?"

Craven nodded his head in agreement, his face turning several shades of red from his apparent anger issues. He was too flustered apparently to speak aloud

Chance could feel the weight of someone's gaze on her. She looked over at the man in the corner. He didn't turn away when she saw him. The corner was cast in shadow, but lately, Chance's vision had seem to have gotten better when it came to seeing in the dark.

She walked towards him slowly. "Would you mind holding the stakes for the game, mister….."

"His name is Sylas." The voice behind her made Chance tense. She'd been so focused on the man in the corner that she hadn't been paying attention to much else.

The bartender walked over to the other side of the table and handed them both a cold beer.

"Names Jack, by the way. I own the place."

Some owners didn't like gambling in their establishment. Chance frowned slightly, unsure of the situation that was about to arise.

Jack sipped his beer and smirked. "Don't worry, I don't mind the gambling." He winked at her. "It's too entertaining not to allow. Sylas however, tends to be too uptight to get involved, so I'll hold the money for you."

Chance could tell they were friends by the quick glances that passed between them. Even though Sylas wore those strange sunglasses, she could see his head move slightly in Jack's direction. A perfect, but barely noticeable, tell. She knew body language from street smarts and through training with her Sensei. Sensei taught her many things over the years and this was just one of many lessons she retained from all the years of learning how to survive on her own.

"I wanted to watch the game anyway. Might be the highlight of the evening," Jack said with a genuine smile that reached all the way to his golden eyes. Bar lights were always dim and had neon signs. They tended to change hues on clothes, eyes, and everything else.

Looking between the two men, Chance compared their looks and liked what she saw in both of them. Both were tall and well built, but where Jack was fair with golden locks and looks, Sylas was dark with a thick jet-black mane. The two were polar opposites and both handsome in their own way. If it were a contest over who had the better looks, Chance would have to lean towards Sylas and his bad boy attraction.

Chance felt, rather than saw Craven walk up behind her. Jack's lips pressed into a thin line with his obvious dislike of the man. She studied Jack for a moment before stepping farther back, so Craven could hand him five bills. Sylas immediately went from semi-relaxed into stiff and fierce... almost catlike. She pictured him bristling like one and felt the anger emanating from his body. What she couldn't figure out was if his anger was directed her or her opponent. At least she knew Jack didn't like Craven either, since it was written all over him. That fact alone made him all right in her book.

Chance gave Jack her best smile, and turned to go back to the game. Her thoughts were still on the two men behind her, and had to shake her head to get mentally back in the game. Still she could not get Sylas out of her mind. What was it about this man that was getting to her? When she noticed Craven trying to give her a bad rack, she shook off those last thoughts and back into what was in front of her.

"Calling bad rack, dude. Try it again. The lead ball is loose," she called over the table.

Craven glared at her and she could swear she heard him growl like a dog. "You trying to call me a cheat?"

"Nope, just calling it a bad rack. No harm, no foul."

Chance took a long pull off her beer and put it on the table. Picking up her cue and scuffing the tip, she walked back over to the table, glancing down at the rack Craven had redone. Satisfied it was tight she walked to the other end of the table. Looking up at him, she smiled and chalked her cue.

"Thank you. Much better!"

His glare became more pronounced.

There was no flirt left in her now. She smiled to herself. *Fine, got you where I wanted you anyway. This is my game and my time. Done deal.*

Chance took a deep breath, taking in all the smells around her. Smoke, leather, and alcohol had a calming affect on her. Leaning over the table, she looked down the shaft of her cue, gave it two strokes and moved forward as her arm swung in the same direction, putting all her weight into the break. Time seemed to slow down as the cue ball rolled forward.

Craven made a huge rookie mistake. When racking the balls he placed all solids on the each corner of the rack. All three seemed to go in slow motion towards the pockets and then they fell in. Another ball fell in, a stripe. The eight moved towards the top right pocket with a stripe right behind it. They both stopped right before falling in with about an inch between the stripe and the eight. Time moved back to normal and a hush fell over the room.

Everyone in the bar moved to watch the game in anticipated silence.

"I call solids, seven ball, one rail, side pocket." She lined up the shot and where she wanted the cue to stop and executed it. Perfect shot. "Calling four ball, no rails, corner pocket." She called as she walked around the table studying her next shot and chalking her cue. She pointed to the corner she wanted so there could be no mistake. Another perfect shot. She heard another small growl, but didn't look up. She knew where it came from and besides, he couldn't rattle her. Not when she was in the zone.

"Calling two ball, three rails, same pocket," pointing again to the pocket she had just sunk the four ball. If she hit this one right, she could call safety on the next one. If he messed up at all, the eight would fall out of turn. Chance bent down and sent a silent prayer to the pool gods. *"Get this shot right and it will be my game."* She aimed putting some hard right bottom English on the cue, wanting to pull the cue back after contact. It would place the cue in the middle of the table and straight on into a side rail with the last ball for the safety. She executed the shot with accuracy and both balls went where she intended.

"Safety," she called out to everyone listening. Hitting the last ball to the rail, with the cue ball resting behind it, Chance stood up, looked at Craven and said, "Your shot."

Chapter 4

Chance played the wolf for all he was worth. Sylas smiled when he realized she was sharking the poor fellow. Not that the fool didn't deserve it. Jack even chuckled a time or two from his side of the table as he figured out her game. Not many could get the old fart to smile, much less laugh, and she did both in under an hour. Sylas didn't notice he was sitting forward in his seat until she called the safety. It was the wolf keeping him and Jack, on edge. It didn't help his pack was egging it on by growling and making snide comments. Chance went back to her table to take a tug on her beer. Sylas relaxed enough to sit back and study her some more.

Sylas rested his arm on the table and ran his fingers over the rough beard stubble on his chin. He smiled when she smiled, delighting in it as it seemed to light the whole room. Her teeth were dazzling white and straight, surrounded by full red lips that begged to be kissed. Watching her chew on that luscious bottom lip drove him crazy with lust. Her eyes were green like his and he wondered if they glowed when she became passionate.

A wolf growled from the pool table, grabbing instant attention. Sy tore his eyes away from her to watch the game, on edge again. He took a quick glance over at Jack. He subtly nodded at Sy, indicating he'd heard the growl as well.

The Alpha had worked himself into a corner. The cue ball rolled too far and now sat behind hers. He would have to hook it to even call a safety. If he missed at all, she would have a ball in hand play. Stealing a glance in her direction again, he saw the tiniest uplift in the corners of those luscious lips while she leaned slightly forward. That tiny quirk and her body language said this play was planned.

The Alpha called for a short cue so he could make his shot. He was rushing it. With more thought, he could make it count. The wolf aimed, holding the cue stick up to make the hook and missed. Chance stood up, put down her beer, and started chalking her cue. She was not rushing her play like the wolf. She walked over to the table and picked up the cue ball. Placing it just in the right spot, he heard her call out, "Six in the side pocket, eight in the corner off the thirteen," and then pointed to both pockets. Chance lined up the shot. The bar went silent in anticipation... the pack included.

Chance took her shot. The balls landed in their pockets breaking the silence like a clap of thunder.

All hell broke loose.

Craven growled in angered and lunged at Chance. One hand wrapped around her thick braid and the other grabbed her wrist for leverage. "You *bitch!* You fucking, lowlife, cheating *bitch!*"

Chaos erupted. The humans were trying to stay out of the line of fire. The pack was backing up their Alpha, and Sylas was about to break Craven's arms for daring to even touch her.

"You have once chance to let go of me or you will regret it." Chance said the words in a deep, controlled tone through clenched teeth.

Craven was either too crazed with anger or he was deaf. He yanked on her braid, attempting to pull her away from the table. Chance flipped over the grip he had on her arm driving her legs up and over with one boot catching his temple. He lost his grip and dropped straight to the floor.

Craven's pack rushed over to tackle her at the same time Sylas and Jack got there. Sylas put his back to hers as the pack surrounded them. Jack was already in a scuffle on the backside of the table. The other patrons moved out of the way into the bar proper.

The pack began to circle them. Sylas caught the glimmer of knives in a few hands. Chance moved to watch them, and so did he, staying at her back. She never looked to see who was behind her, but she seemed to know it was an ally. Sy growled loudly, asserting his authority over all shifters.

Jerking his chin towards the Alpha he said, "You boys need to go pick up your man and leave now. I can't promise you'll leave here unharmed if you don't."

The pack attacked. Chance, Jack, and Sylas worked together like dancers, taking them down, one by one. Knives were thrust and knocked away. Punches were thrown and returned. Right when they thought it was over the Alpha stood back up, blood seeping down his face from where her boot caught him, ready for more.

Sylas stepped forward to take him on when a hand on his arm stopped him.

"He's mine, stay back," Chance said quietly.

It wasn't in his nature to allow a woman to be in danger, but she seemed determined and capable of taking care of herself. He backed off and so did Jack after she gave him a look. Jack shrugged; a silent gesture that he was ready to take action if this went south.

Craven rushed her but didn't get far. Her hand flew out when he was close enough and she caught him in the throat with a stiff fingered hand, nails first. Craven had too much momentum going and couldn't stop. She grabbed both shoulders when he tried to slow down and kneed his groin. Craven doubled over and she finished with a sharp elbow to the back of the head, knocking him out cold.

She was seething with anger. It rolled off her so thickly he could literally taste it in the air. Sylas admired her fearlessness.

She stood over Craven and whispered, "No one touches me, *no* man touches me and your lowlife ass will *never* touch me again." Then lower, so low that Sy thought he had imagined it, he heard, "Never without my permission." Bristling, she walked back to her table, sat down, and downed the rest of her beer.

"What the hell was that all about?" Jack looked over at Chance shaking in rage.

"I haven't a clue, but I'm going to make it a point to find out."

He helped Jack escort Craven and his pack out of the bar. Jack told all of them they were no longer welcome, but not before he collected all the money he was owed.

Sylas pulled off his sunglasses and walked over to Chance's table with a fresh cold one. She didn't look up but nodded her thanks. Sylas wanted to lift her chin so he could look in her eyes.

Catching his hand halfway there he thought better of it. Instead, he sat down and waited for her to break the ice. No need to spook the woman before he even got to speak with her. Chance took the beer bottle and placed it against her cheek and neck in an effort to cool down. He quickly became jealous of the bottle, wanting to caress that silken cheek.

After a grueling ten minutes of silence, she finally looked up. Sylas hadn't taken his eyes off her "Thank you. It's been a long time since anyone had my back. I'm not quite sure how to react. I'm glad I didn't hurt you. That would've been… bad." He nodded once, not sure of what to say. She smiled at him and Sylas forgot how to breathe. Baffled by his reaction, he told himself to wake up. He couldn't help but smile in return.

Jack walked up to hand her the winnings and started laughing when he saw the look on their faces. His laugh was infectious and then they were all laughing deep, tension relieving belly laughs. When they could laugh no more, Jack made formal introductions.

"Chance meet my best friend, Sylas. Sylas, this is Chance. If you both will allow me, I'm ready to lock this place down. Fights always make me hungry. Late dinner on me, okay?"

Sylas waited for Chance to decide. She looked up and seemed unsure. Her emerald eyes had the tiniest bit of a spark to them, not quite a glow, and they glittered in the light. He smiled and shrugged one shoulder, hoping it was enough to entice her.

With obvious mistrust, she grudgingly said, "I guess I could go. I'm suddenly very hungry."

Sylas was pleased. He still didn't understand what was happening with this woman, this human, but he wasn't going to waste time double guessing himself.

Never in his five hundred years had he known a woman such as her. She was self-sufficient, self-assured, and unafraid. There was a hint at some kind of great sorrow in her life. It showed in the tiniest of things, but mostly he caught it when he looked into those emerald eyes.

Sylas asked what Jack needed help with. They spent an hour cleaning up the bar before they were satisfied to close it up for the night, and headed out.

Chapter 5

While waiting for Jack to finish up, Chance thought back over the fight. Something wasn't quite right with the events that had taken place. She'd had been caught off guard when she felt Sylas at her back. It wasn't one of the bikers – instinct told her that, and while she was grateful for the help, it also meant she was responsible for his wellbeing. After all, Chance was the one who wanted to hustle the men even though she had the money from the lottery. There wasn't really a need for it, other than she wanted to have some fun. Letting Sylas take the hit for that wasn't right.

Sylas was all muscle, stealth, and danger. He wasn't an innocent, and probably fully capable of protecting a woman, but Chance could take care of herself. Past experience taught her that relying on men lead down a dark path. With all the growling and posturing that had been going on before and right after, Chance recalled feeling nervous, as if they were predators and she was the prey. The feeling had put her immediately on the defense, not to mention her body feeling as if it was answering some kind of predatory call. It was in this singular moment that she knew that Sylas had brought on those strange feelings.

Chance remembered the moment when she was able to take a closer look at him. He sat down on the stool in front of her while she cooled down. His smile had taken her breath away. If she thought Jack was good looking, then she needed to check her mind in at the local psycho ward. Jack paled in comparison. Sylas had dimples in his cheeks that only showed themselves when he grinned. He sported a shadow of beard that her fingers itched to touch. His features were Romanesque, with full lips that begged to be lightly bitten and teased. Green eyes that seemed to glow were framed with thick black lashes and they crinkled along the edges when he smiled.

Chance had looked lower, dropping her head to hide her perusal. His body was all man. Powerful, with wide shoulders that dropped to a smaller waistline, thighs that were large and well-defined. All in all he was a perfect male specimen. Raising her head to look into those eyes, she saw something there. Confusion, maybe? Desire, definitely.

But there was something more, something that she couldn't quite put her finger on.

If Sylas was a predator, was she willing to be his prey? Her mind said no, but her body was screaming yes. Chance wasn't sure about the strange feelings suddenly stirring within her body and mind.

* * * *

Chance was walking towards her bike when she heard someone call out her name. She stopped and turned, surprised to find Sylas standing so close. She had to fight the urge to step back.

"You forgot your coat. Here, let me help you with it." He spoke quietly, holding it out for her. She turned to put her arms in. He pulled it up and set the shoulders of her coat down. Gently, he pulled her braid up from under her coat. "Such beautiful hair on an even more beautiful woman."

Chance could barely hear his praise. A rush of heat warmed her. She cleared her throat and asked, "So where are we going to eat?"

"There is a diner on the east end of town that is open all night and they actually have excellent food and a great menu," Jack told her. "You can ride with one of us or follow, it makes no matter to me."

"I'll follow if that's okay. I need to head home after and no reason to come back here since I live on the east side too."

Chance walked towards her bike. She avoided looking at Sylas during the brief exchange with Jack. She was unsure of the feelings he stirred in her. There was no doubt that redness had crawled up her neck and to her cheeks, and she didn't want Sylas to see that. Sylas whistled – almost like a catcall. That was enough to push away the blush. Chance didn't like being objectified.

Sylas' head was cocked slightly and he was smiling when she turned to face him again. That smile instantly brushed away her anger and turned her insides into mush.

"Yes? Something wrong?"

"Is that your ride?" He had a wide grin on his face. The question caught Jack's attention, and he walked over.

"Yes, why?"

"You won't believe me so I guess I better show you." Sylas held out his hand to her. "Come with me?" Chance looked at the hand extended. She wanted to take it and show some trust, but it just wasn't in her. Sylas seemed to understand and motioned for her to follow him.

Jack laughed, a deep low rumble that could make anyone smile. "I don't fucking believe it. Only you, Sy, only you!"

Chance followed Sy, trying to figure out what was so funny. It wasn't until Sy stopped and pointed to the other side of Jack's ride that she figured it out. There, in all its glory sat the twin bike to hers. Only his was mostly all black to her chrome. Opposites, but the same bike. She started laughing with them, lost to Jack's comments about "What were the odds?" and "It must be a sign!"

Riding one after the other through the quiet streets, Chance took advantage of the crisp air and breathed in deeply. Lights from shop windows glistened on wet pavement, making this part of her world beautiful and serene. It wasn't always like this, but when the moments came, who was she to ignore them.

Spring had finally graced this area of the country and the flowers were in full bloom. Fragrant bushes of Roses and Azaleas in every color, Dogwoods in pink and white, Forsythia in yellow, and Wisteria in shades of lavender and purple. Tulips and Irises were in full bloom as well. This was her favorite of all the seasons and she hoped to have all these and more blooming on her property next year.

Too soon they were at the diner and sitting at a four-top. She thanked the Goddess there was one open and available. She didn't want to ruin the camaraderie with having to choose which male to sit beside in a booth. They were having a good time and they'd fought beside her, and still she was wary. She honestly didn't know these guys… yet.

After a short perusal of the menu, they all chose steak and eggs. Hunger gnawed at her insides, grumbling loudly in protest. Jack and Sy found it quite humorous, and Chance could only blush with embarrassment.

They chatted about bars and fights they experienced in the past and she sat listening intently while they talked and ate. Chance thought they sounded older than dirt, with all the tales they regaled her with, but she knew that wasn't possible. Both looked to be her age. *Maybe they were adding in fights they witnessed?* They claimed to have traveled all over the world, and she envied it.

Chance added in a tale or two of her own, not giving away anything personal. She talked about her past to no one, and she wasn't about to start now. That part of her life was over. It wasn't who she was now.

Chance hadn't laughed this much, since when? Never, is what it felt like and it probably was. It felt good and it felt right. She wanted more.

Chapter 6

Craven Doyle paced the floor in the pack's common room. The pack had left straight from the bar and traveled north to their place in the woods. To heal properly the pack knew he needed to shift, and shifting in the city was too dangerous. Even after healing, his voice sounded like gravel, which wasn't present before the bitch tried to kill him. She ruptured his trachea with one of her nails and if they hadn't brought him to the compound in time the injury might have become permanent. Thankfully not all of them had ridden their bikes to the bar.

Craven waited for his Beta to arrive. This bitch was going down and he wanted to be the one to kill her, but he needed to find her first. He put in a call to a west coast pack, which boasted one of the best trackers in the country. His job would be to find her, notify him, and leave. Craven would take over from there, along with plans to take out the owner of the bar. The pack spent a lot of money in his bar since it opened. No one takes his money and kicks him out... *no one.*

The tracker was committed to someone in Canada for the next three weeks so he deployed some of his pack to dig up some dirt on the woman. His Beta, Trey, was one of those. Craven couldn't remember much after the fight, or even during it for that matter, but he couldn't recall hearing her name during the games. They had next to nothing to go on, other than a description. Trey was checking out known biker bars and pool halls in the area, to see if anyone knew who she was.

Craven needed to get this situation under control soon. If he didn't, he would have other problems on his hands. The first and foremost was his pack. They saw their Alpha get taken down twice by a fucking human girl. They would see this as weak, and in a pack full of former rogues, he could count on a challenge from one or several in his pack. He personally selected all of his pack by hand from the worst of the worst. That meant he was precariously hanging on to his Alpha status daily.

Craven heard Trey coming before he saw him. The Beta walked with a distinctive limp, stemming from a fight with a leopard shifter back in the late 1980's. He never went into much detail on it, but the man lived to even the score. Trey was tall and gaunt, haunted by the man who permanently maimed him. He was a man of few words, but the toughest of his pack. If a challenge came from anywhere, he knew Trey would be first in line.

Craven stopped his pacing long enough to bark, "Did you get anything on the bitch?"

"Nothing. Her trail begins and ends at the bar so far. No scent of her anywhere else."

"You heard from any of the others yet?"

"No, too early," Trey said with a frown.

"What is it, Trey?" Craven growled when he saw the change in Trey's posture. "I'm too pissed for games right now. Until that tracker can get here, we have to do everything possible to find her. Move the pack out to a bigger search area. She is mine and she *will* pay!"

"If I'd been there I could have done something. It got too far out of control, Craven. I should have been there."

Craven smirked at his comment. Trey was loyal to a fault, but not to him. The pack held his loyalty. He cared about them far too much. He just wondered when the breaking point towards him would come. "Too late for that now. You were on patrol duty. I need to get this bitch, and show her what pain really is. I'm gonna do her slow, real slow. There is something else I want you to take care of, Trey. I want you to work on plans to set the owner of the bar up. I want him *and* his place to burn, and I want it done after the tracker gets here. No need to bring any more attention to the pack right now. I know I can count on you to do it right."

* * * *

"No problem boss, consider it done," Trey replied through his teeth while watching Craven pace. He was beginning to think this latest fight had loosened another screw in the Alpha's head. The man was right to be pissed about a human kicking his ass, albeit a woman, but he was beginning to think things were getting too far out of control.

He was talking about taking out another shifter and that could be very sticky, especially if the wrong people took offense. Mainly if it got traced back to this pack. Factor in the human and things could go bad for all of them. Craven and the pack were well known from coast to coast. A pack of rogues never happened, but Craven managed it. Too many wanting to be top dog, so to speak, and that was never a good mix. His request for Trey to take out the puma showed Craven still trusted him.

Trey wanted that trust because it served his purpose. He'd always thought Craven was crazy; too crazy to hold this pack together. He watched Craven pace through a Beta's critical eye. Craven was 6'4, lean but broad in the shoulders and chest. Trey was taller, and even though he had a limp, he knew he could take Craven out if he wanted. He would when the time was right. He wanted Craven to lose more face with the pack and then he would make his move. Craven was obsessed with this human, and he could sabotage his hunt for her. *Maybe now is the time to take care of business,* he thought with a grin.

* * * *

Craven stopped pacing again. He had just thought of the other shifter who was in the bar helping the girl. "Trey, there was another shifter with them, but I could not pick up his animal. He's a friend with the puma. Maybe if you find him, you'll find her."

"What did he look like?"

"Tall, black hair, and he was wearing sunglasses."

"What did you say?"

"You fucking heard me, Trey. Not in the mood to repeat it," Craven barked at him. He watched Trey stiffen. He could tell Trey was fighting the urge to shift. He'd never seen him this out of control, since he was literally vibrating with anger. "Spit it out, Trey, before you lose it. I can tell you know him. So who the fuck is he?"

Trey growled long and low before he could speak. "The name Sylas Taiken give you a clue? I'll find you the girl and take out the puma for you, but that fucking asswipe is mine!"

"Fuck! You're telling me the Fate's Enforcer was there? You're sure that's him?"

"Fuckin' positive. He has to hide his eyes because they glow in the dark. He can shift into anything that walks or flies; that's why you couldn't scent his animal. He's mine, Craven. In my time and my way!" Trey growled in warning, his voice raising at the end.

Craven narrowed his eyes and growled his own warning, moving closer and into a fighting stance. "You don't tell me shit, *Beta. I* tell you when to eat, sleep and shit. Don't get me wrong, I get it. He's the one that did this." He motioned to Trey's leg. He waited on acknowledgment from Trey. When he finally got it, he stressed his next words with another loud growl "Don't you *ever* forget your place again and I might consider letting you have him, but not now and not here. There are bigger fish to fry first and we don't need the Fate's watching us any closer than they are. Understood?" Trey automatically tilted his head and bared his neck in supplication. Once he did, Craven eased his stance, but only slightly.

* * * *

It was all Trey could do to keep from challenging for Alpha right then and there. No one was going to take this from him. He'd waited more than a century to get his hands on Sylas. It figured that the time he'd finally decided to show himself, was the same night his Alpha got his ass kicked by a human. Not once, but twice. He was shocked that Sylas let the girl fight. But that tidbit was neither here nor there.

Trey finally had a standing chance now to accomplish a life's vendetta *and* take the pack. Life just got interesting in immortal land and he wasn't going to miss another chance or second of it. Craven's time on earth got a whole lot shorter, and Sylas was going to go right behind him if it was the last thing he did.

Chapter 7

The late dinner with Chance and Jack was exactly what the doctor ordered for Sylas. He finally had a purpose and she was sitting right beside him. The entire conversation was mainly between him and Jack sharing old stories but every chance he got, he pulled Chance in to it. He wanted to know more. Who she was and what made that mind tick. She shared some, but nothing that seemed personal. There was a time or two he kicked Jack under the table to keep him from going too far back in time. It seemed he was pulled into Chance's spell too. His mouth almost got them caught a time or two, but it was good to see the male laugh. It had been way too long.

Jack was older than Sylas by nearly a hundred years. He'd lost two mates in the last two hundred, and the last almost killed him. His mate was shot in the heart while they were in puma form, roaming the mountains of Montana, while carrying Jack's baby. They were so far out in the country that Jack could do nothing but stay at her side, while he watched the love of his life fade away, taking his baby with her.

It took Sylas years to get him back into a normal life. He'd nearly lost him. Jack refused to shift back after the shooting… wanting to lose all human thought and interaction in that form. It happened to others before. Shifters who have been through trauma like this can lose their sense of reality. They forget who they are and live out their lives lost to human civilization. If it hadn't been for his intervention, Jack would be one of those lost immortal souls.

When they finished eating, Chance stood as if to go. Sylas wanted more time with her, but was wary of scaring her away. Luckily, Jack saved his ass again.

"Either of you busy Sunday?" He asked, looking between them.

Sylas waited while Chance thought about her answer. "I have a meeting this morning, but other than that, Sunday is free. Why?"

"I invited my staff up for a barbecue tomorrow, since the bar is closed on Sundays and Mondays. You two are more than welcome to join us. I have a place up on Lanier. It's right on the lake and you've already met most of the staff." Jack replied. "Oh! And there will be plenty of beer!" He added over his shoulder, winking at Sylas when his back was to her, on his way to pay the dinner bill.

Chance looked up at Sylas and he could see the indecision in her eyes. "I'm game if you are, Chance. Jack and his staff are harmless. Could be fun." He said to her quietly, shrugging his shoulders on the last part. "I could meet you somewhere and you can follow me up, or I can drive you up. No pressure, just... fun."

"Okay, I guess. I've nothing else better to do after my meeting. Thank you for inviting me, Jack. I'd love to come," she replied looking at him with those beautiful green eyes, but talking to Jack. They exchanged cell numbers and said she would call sometime after the meeting was done. She would let him know where to meet him when they spoke again.

Sylas followed her out to her bike, wanting to say more to her, but he was tongue-tied for the first time that he could ever remember. She entranced him. She was beautiful and a fierce female. Tough, and yet... vulnerable. He helped her again with her coat, wishing his arms were wrapped around her body, keeping her warm. He never thought he could be jealous of inanimate objects before this evening.

There were two things he wished he could change places with... this coat and her Harley. He wanted to be between her legs, be inside her, be one with her. He shifted his stance as those thoughts made him rock hard. *No need for her to see that yet,* he chastised himself. He knew he couldn't rush this. He needed to gain her trust first. He would have to be content in her presence for now, no matter what his body wanted.

Sylas waved goodbye to Jack as he watched Chance pull away on her Harley. He was enveloped with an overwhelming need to know where she lived. To make sure she was safe. The wolf worried him. He knew the former rogue Alpha would not let this die down and it made him very uncomfortable. He let her get a block away before he followed with his lights off. One of the advantages to being a shifter was night vision. He could see as well at night as he could during the day.

Dropping back a little more to stay out of her sight range, Sylas stayed as close as he could. When she pulled into a housing subdivision, he pulled over and shifted into a husky. His leopard form would frighten anyone who might be out, and he didn't need the hassle of screaming neighbors and police. Tracking her by sound and scent, he located her house at the same time the garage door lowered.

Sylas waited nearby as she entered the house and checked the doors. Hearing the locks clicking was a turning point. He knew leaving her alone was dangerous. Her home was a one level ranch style. Easy in and out if anyone wanted to get to her. He watched lights come on as she moved through and then out when she was finished. He trotted to the back and found where her bedroom should be. He waited until the last light went out, and then moved to the front porch to keep watch.

Now you're a watchdog for a woman you don't even know. You're losing it, Sylas, he thought, trying to relax. *The Fates are definitely fucking with you this time.* Taking a quick sniff of the air, Sylas finally allowed sleep to take over; assured she was safe with his presence.

* * *

"Well, who are you, pretty baby? I don't remember seeing you around here before." Sylas jumped to his feet confused for a few seconds. It was Chance talking to him on the porch. He'd slept longer than he intended. He watched Chance crouch down to his level and reach out her hand to let him sniff it. He did and licked her hand in response. "Are you lost, boy? You sure are beautiful with those striking green eyes."

Sylas moved closer to her as she sat down on the front steps, a glass of water in her hand. "Thirsty boy?" Chance crooned to him and poured some water into her hand, offering it to him. He gratefully drank what she offered. When finished, he sat down on his haunches next to her and leaned in, lowering his head for a scratch.

She obliged until a large white SUV pulled into her driveway. A man got out and raised a hand in greeting and she waved back with a smile. Sylas took this person to be the one she was meeting with and decided it was the perfect time to disappear. He stepped off the porch, looked up at her, and whined once. She walked down, ignoring the man that was waiting on her, and stepped over to where Sylas was standing in her yard.

"Time to go, beautiful boy? You can come back here anytime you want. Maybe next time you can stay longer, okay?"

Chance talked to him as if he was human, as if the dog understood everything she said, and he did. He sat and raised a paw. Chance crouched down to shake his paw, staring into his eyes. "Your eyes. I… I feel like I know you."

Sylas watched as a frown tried to appear while she looked at him, but she erased it with a nervous giggle and the sound made his heart quicken.

"Well, I need to take care of business. Later, beautiful boy," she whispered to him. Then she got up and walked inside her home with the visitor. Sylas smiled inwardly. *I do understand you and I will be back. Later, beautiful girl.*

Sylas shifted to human form behind some trees and walked to his Harley. Thankfully immortals could shift and keep their clothes. He could also magic other clothes if needed, but he was already in his leathers, so there was no need. He rode home in silence, thinking about the woman he left behind. *She is more perceptive than I thought. It may take time, but she will definitely be worth the effort of winning over.*

As he rode, he remembered the fight from the night before, his body responding again to his thoughts of her. She was like a dancer in her comfort level with fighting, and he wanted those warrior legs wrapped tightly around him. He sported another raging hard on thinking about it and no immediate way for relief. He readjusted himself, trying to ease the pain.

Sylas arrived home, shifted to his leopard form, and cat napped the rest of the morning. When he got up, he showered and changed into jeans and a t-shirt. Sylas pulled out his cell and put in a call to Jack to discuss the previous night. They both agreed that she needed protection from the pack.

According to Jack, the entire pack was made up of former rogues and they were considered extremely dangerous. He said the Alpha was the worst of them and would not take the beat down well. They both agreed to talk up a game plan later and Sylas told him that for now he would watch her until they could come up with something better. Since Chance was human they couldn't tell her why she was in danger, and that was the difficulty. Keeping their world secret from humans was priority number one.

Chapter 8

Chance temporarily forgot about the strange dog with those somehow familiar eyes while she talked to Rick, the contractor. She had very solid ideas as to what she wanted built on the property. The requirements were anything over fifty acres, have running stream or pond, and away from any close city. The agent hit the mark with over sixty acres, a stream, and it backed up to a wilderness area. It was pristine land with no previous buildings. Chance wanted a log home, and not prefabricated. The lot was thickly wooded but it did have a clearing on it, situated on the top of a small rise, right in the middle of the property.

Up to this point in her life, nothing excited her more than this. Explaining to Rick in detail what she envisioned, Chance was non-stop with her ideas. Three or four bedroom ranch with a full basement. She would accept a second above ground story, if it could have a loft and lots of windows. She wanted a sub level bomb shelter under the basement. It would be a survivalist's dream.

Each level had to be fire and flood safe. The subbasement would contain a pantry/wine room. The deeper in the earth you go, the more the temperatures level out. It would stay cool year round. She included an emergency generator with ventilation and well water pump system with ventilation. Chance wanted the house to be powered by solar panels and a wind turbine, but if all hell broke out, she could use the generator as a last resort.

Since there wasn't water, septic or power on or near the property, she would need two septic systems dug and placed. She would be going out at some point this week to place orders for any other furniture she might need and appliances for the kitchen. Rick told her she would need to pick the flooring, cabinets, plumbing, and lighting fixtures as well. Her preferences must have pleased him, because he grinned whenever she spoke up about her choices. Roomy and airy, it would be very Feng Shui, and would include the house facing north/south to take full advantage of the tracking sun on the solar panels.

Rounding up the last of the details, they finished up after one in the afternoon and scheduled another meeting in two days. She impressed upon him her time schedule, so he was going to take a design he already had and make it work for her needs. She knew she was pushing the table with wanting this done in weeks and not months. He told her it could not be done in a month, but thought they could complete it in less than two months time. Rick thought most of the time spent would be for the sub levels. He wanted to do that part right and she was glad he was honest about the schedule. Besides, permits and such would take at least a week, if not more.

Chance asked him to go ahead and design her a barn and stable for horses. She would need a garage for her two and four wheeled toys, with a repair area. She asked him to get a permit to install her own gassing station, which would mean more permits and more digging to install underground tanks. *Why not go for the gusto?* She thought as she made those last minute decisions. Self-contained meant exactly how it sounded. She wanted no reason to interact with outsiders any more than was necessary.

Chance giggled as she thought about the locals, and them calling her a recluse some day in the future. She really liked people; she just didn't trust them much. Holding more faith in animals than the two-legged variety. She wanted to trust, she really did. Thinking about the subject, Sylas came to mind. He felt trustworthy to her, like someone she wanted to know more about. He was gentle, thoughtful, and very intuitive when it came to her. It didn't hurt that he sported a rocking hard ass body. Her knees tended to liquefy when he smiled at her. On the one occasion she touched him during the fight, she could tell he was all muscle.

Chance spent the rest of her Saturday packing up the clothes she would never wear again, cleaning house, and getting in a good workout.
When Chance woke up on Sunday morning, she found the husky waiting on her porch again. He followed along when she went out for a long run in the fresh morning air. It was nice to have him there for a change as it took away some of the boredom running tended to bring with it.

Running gave free time to think more about the fight and the two men she met. The more she thought about it, the more unsettled she became. Things had gotten way out of control and fast, much faster than she was prepared for. Chance shook it off and chalked it up to lesson learned. Next time she played, it would be against someone not quite so drunk. She turned her thoughts once again to Sylas. She felt the old soul in him and wanted to learn more about him and hoped to do exactly that today.

Chance really liked his friend, Jack, too. They both made her laugh and it felt good. When she arrived back home, the dog yipped and took off, but she didn't pay it any mind. She was sure he lived in a house nearby. She showered quickly and dressed in low cut skinny jeans and a red tank top. She decided to trust for a change and let Sylas drive her up to Jack's place.

Chance put minimal makeup on and pulled out a black leather jacket that reached her hips. She was still commando under her clothes, preferring it to bothersome underwear. Bras, in her opinion, should be banned. They were uncomfortable in too many ways to count.

It wasn't warm enough yet to go swimming, so she didn't bother with swimwear. Piling her hair into a bun, Chance used a single chopstick to hold it in place. Her mane was heavy, so nothing else was needed. A quick twist and done. All her necessities were in her jacket and boots; weapons, cell phone, and wallet.

Chance called Sylas and gave him directions to her house. While waiting for his arrival, she made them something to eat. She'd skipped breakfast and was starving, and hoped he was too. Brunch was tuna salad, crackers, and some sliced Gouda cheese. She added fresh fruit and chilled some sparkling cider. It wasn't much but it would help ease the hunger pains. She didn't want to drink beer on an empty stomach.

Right as she was pulling down some glasses, she heard his Harley rumbling in her driveway. A minute later the doorbell rang. *Here goes nothing. You can do this, Chance. Time to allow some trust in your life,* she thought as she walked towards the door.

Taking a deep breath, she opened it and stared. Sylas stood in the doorway in jeans and a t-shirt, looking fine and totally GQ centerfold worthy. She started at his boots and drank him in slowly as her eyes roamed up his body. When she finally got to his face, she heard him chuckling and snapped out of the trance.

"Like what you see?" he asked her with an ear to ear grin.

"Um, sorry?" was all she could get out while blushing forty shades of red. "Please come in. I was making us something to eat. I hope you're hungry, because I'm starving. Made enough for both of us."

"Actually, I am hungry and yes, I would love to join you," he replied, but Chance totally heard a completely different meaning in his words. They said, "hungry for her," and she blushed again.

"I made tuna salad. I don't know if you even like the stuff, but I was thinking light and easy"

"I'm not a picky eater and I've yet to turn any kind of food away," he said following her into the kitchen.

Chance smiled at him while handing him his drink and their hands touched for a brief second. Gasping, Chance felt sparks leap between their hands. It traveled all the way from her fingers to her core and it made her instantly wet with desire. Confused and blushing again, she used the food as an excuse to turn away and gather her wits. *What the hell was that? Get a grip, Chance! You don't even know the man and you're ready to jump his bones?* Pulling herself under control, Chance turned back with the plates. She led Sylas over to the kitchen table and set them down.

Sylas asked her what he could do to help and she pointed him to the silverware and napkins. She sat down when he finished and joined her.

"You look beautiful today, Chance. But, you don't look like you're planning on riding a bike today. Change your mind about going?"

"No, actually I hope you don't mind, but I thought maybe we could go in my Jeep. You can drive if you want."

"I'd love to and don't mind at all. Did your meeting go well?"

"Yes, it went really well actually. I can't wait for my plans to be finished," she replied smiling at him.

"Care to tell me about it? I'd really like to get to know you better, Chance. It seems Jack and I did most of the talking the other night and I know less about you, than you know about me." Sylas returned her smile and his posture exuded genuine interest.

Chance relaxed. Sylas didn't feel like a threat to her and it felt right somehow that he was here with her. For the first time in her life she felt like she could share her interests with another person other than Gus, and feel no fear of reprisal. They spent the next hour eating, with Sylas listening as Chance told him about the property and her plans for it. She kept some parts of the plans secret, feeling the need to keep some of it private, by generalizing a lot. She didn't want a friendship centered on her newfound wealth. She needed to know that his interest was real and not materialistic. Sylas chimed in at all the right moments, added his own thoughts and she began to feel a bond of friendship growing.

They cleaned up their lunch and Chance handed him the keys to her Jeep. As they rode, Chance contemplated this enigma called Sylas. The friendship exuded possibilities of much more if she wanted it. The problem was *if* she was ready for more and all that it implied. More meant complete trust in someone else. It meant trusting someone else with her heart, the same heart with years of walls built around it. Trusting someone that much would take a lot of time. She didn't think anyone with any sense about them would stick around long enough for her to heal her soul. Besides, did she really want them to?

Chapter 9

Sylas decided he would have to look into getting a Jeep after the first couple of miles. With the top off and the doors removed it was almost as freeing as riding on his Harley. Keyword… almost. Chance was sitting in the passenger seat being uncomfortably quiet. It concerned him that maybe too many boundaries were pushed, but was pretty sure he hadn't done anything wrong. He kept glancing her way, wondering what kept her so troubled. While stealing those quick glances, her facial expressions changed from a worried frown to a smile. He quietly sighed and relaxed.

Wanting to bring an end to the silence he asked, "You're awfully quiet, Chance. We don't have to go to Jack's if you don't want. There are other places we can be, but only if you wish it."

"No, I really do want to go but thank you, Sylas. I was just thinking about the property again. Rick told me I'll need to do some shopping for the house, and I'm not sure I'm qualified to make the right decisions. I think I'm going to need help with it all." She laughed as she turned to him with an unspoken question in her eyes.

"Well now, are you asking me for help?" He asked, returning her smile.

"Why yes, Sylas, I think I am." Chance turned on her best Scarlett O'Hara southern drawl and he busted out laughing.

"You do that drawl justice, Miss Scarlett," he returned in his best Rhett Butler.

"Oh, Fiddle dee dee, Rhett, you scoundrel!" and that did it. Sylas almost lost control of the Jeep, laughing with her.

Sylas sobered when he realized they were at the entrance to Jack's lake house. "Last chance to change your mind, Miss Scarlett. We've arrived at the ball."

"I do declare, Rhett Butler, you *are* a gentleman. I do love a party!" and with that he pulled in and parked. Sylas gave Chance his arm as they followed the sound of voices mixed with laughter. Jack noticed them when they turned the corner into the backyard, and waved them over. He handed them both an ice-cold beer after giving Chance a quick hug and fist-bumping him.

"Glad to see you made it. Was beginning to think you weren't coming."

"I think I kept Mr. Butler too long talking about my property. Sorry, Jack," Chance replied, blushing a little.

Jack looked at him and raised an eyebrow. Sylas could only shrug and smile. Jack turned to Chance and asked, "You'll have to join me and tell me all about it. Sounds interesting."

They spent the next few hours rehashing to Jack everything they talked about at her house. He asked her where the property was. Sylas knew it was north, but never thought to get specifics. When she told them it butted up against Cohutta National Forest and northeast of Ellijay, they both stiffened a little. "Well now, that's quite a drive from here. You sure that's where the property is, Chance?" Jack asked.

She smiled at him with enthusiasm and nodded. Her excitement was palpable. Theirs… not so much. They knew what she didn't. The property would be just a few short miles from the pack's base, and as Sylas feared, right in the middle of their territory. Things just went from bad to worse. Sylas wasn't going to let anything happen. She might be human, but he still felt a mate calling to him. He wasn't going to lose her, not to anyone, much less to that damned rogue wolf.

While Chance talked more about her plans with Jack, he used the time to study her face. Sylas wanted to reach over and let down her tresses. He had yet to see it loose and knew it must reach almost to her knees. It compelled him to get lost in it and her. Sink his hands in and pull it while he was buried deep within her. He wasn't sure if he said something out loud or if she sensed his thoughts, because right when he thought about it, she reached up and pulled her hairpin loose.

Time slowed as her locks cascaded slowly over her shoulders and down her back. Thick jet-black waves of silken pleasure caressed her skin as it fell. Sylas let out a small groan as he watched it finally touch the ground from where she was sitting. In that single moment, he was lost as never before.

"Excuse me, Sylas, did you say something?" She asked, bringing him out of the fantasy. Jack tried to stifle a laugh, but it didn't work. His immortal ears heard his distinct groan. Sylas chuckled along with him; embarrassed he'd been caught.

"No Dear, I was admiring the view. It's quite spectacular, don't you think so, Jack?" Sylas' double meaning was not lost on him.

"Yes, and the sunsets here are the greatest," Jack said laughing some more.

Chance turned to watch some fluffy white clouds pass in front of the sun, totally oblivious to what they were implying. They took advantage of her distraction to get up for more beer.

"Brother, you seriously got it bad for this woman. I can't remember you ever looking at a female this way. You're thinking she's the one, aren't you?"

"Yes, but even if she isn't, I'm not letting her get away. She does something to me, Jack, that I can't explain."

"It's called soul attraction, Sy. Your eyes never leave her. Even now, you're watching her. I was the same with Becky, bro. It was like she was the air and I couldn't breathe without her. You may not be aware of it, but she watches you too."

"I can't rush this, Jack. Inside that beautiful, but tough exterior is a lot of pain. I can see it in her eyes and taste it in the air when I'm near her. I'm afraid if I do, I'll break us both." Sylas said to him with sadness in his eyes. "First we have to make sure she's safe, so I have time to let her trust me. We only have eight weeks to get all of this in play, or better yet, over with for her protection and my sanity."

"I'm two steps ahead of you, Sy. Since the fight at the bar, I knew something bad might happen. That Alpha will not take his beat down quietly. I've already called my den mates and some bears we can trust in the area. They're waiting on the when and where. I also found out there's been a wolf council meeting called. There is rumbling about this pack, that it should be disbanded and eliminated. They are calling them a danger to all humans and immortals. Maybe it's time you called on Lachesis for guidance, Sylas. If the council meets and places a bounty, it will bring in were-hunters and we don't need this now. It will make it dangerous for all of us and her." He made his point by jerking his chin in Chance's direction.

"I'll call my mother for a meeting, but I need another favor first. Find out when this wolf council has been planned for and where. I may need to be there. If I can calm them down enough, I should be able to avert this catastrophe from happening."

Suddenly, there was a bright light and a shimmering Lachesis was standing before them. "I have heard your plea, my Son. You cannot interfere with the council. You are The Enforcer, not a common mediator. This has to play out for the outcome to be as foreseen." She must have been listening to his thoughts, because as his next question was forming, she spoke again. "I cannot tell you what you want to know. Only we know the outcome. You will have your mate when the time is chosen," and with that said, she faded away saying, "The humans cannot see me and yes, Jack, you will love another."

Sylas and Jack stood in stunned silence. Neither of them able to form words to the thoughts that were running through their minds.

"Well, that was a complete mind blow!" Jack sputtered shaking his head. "Was that who I think it was?"

"Yes, you've just seen and heard Lachesis, my mother. Consider yourself fortunate that she deigned to show herself to you, much less speak," Sylas said while trying to push his irritation and anger aside. Why was it when he thought he had one problem cleared, two more rose up to take its place?

"I'm in awe of you, Sylas, my friend. You have a beautiful woman at your side and a gorgeous mother. I think it's time to let loose a little and party some more, don't you?"

"You've no idea, Jack," was all he was able to get out as he looked at Chance, lost in her beauty once again.

Chapter 10

"We've got a name on the female and it's believed she is not local to the west side." Trey cautiously told his Alpha. "She goes by Chance, but we were unable to get more of her name. They are clueless if it is a first, last, or nickname. She's a hustler from the east side of town, but doesn't show herself often enough to pin her to one area or bar."

Trey watched Craven for any sign of recognition to his news. The Alpha was currently sitting at their dining table eating along with several others of the pack. Trey took an empty seat across from him and filled his plate. He'd been out searching for the last forty eight hours with no break and he was starving.

Craven picked up a beer and took a long pull from it. When he finished he slammed it down on the table, getting everyone's attention. "So, you're fucking telling me that in two days of everyone out looking, all you can tell me is a name? Not good enough!"

Trey watched as most of the pack flinched. They'd all been out searching. Craven was pushing their limits, and he could see the Alpha was losing more of his sanity as time went on. "How many women could have that name? Someone please tell me?" Craven glowered as he scanned the table, waiting on an answer. At least this one Trey could answer.

"Considering we have no idea if it is first or last, or a nickname, there are about forty two people in the area with the last name Chance. About half of those are women. Didn't come up with any that matched it as a first name. The odds against us increase if she is not using her first name, but the letter C." Trey looked down at his plate as if he could hide under it.

"That's why you're my Beta, Trey. At least you came in with something, not like these dogs sitting with us. I want a wolf in every biker bar and pool hall on the east side, starting tomorrow. Get me contacts at the ones not covered; bribe them if you must. She has to go out again at some point and when she does, I want to know immediately!" Craven made his point by slamming his fist into the table.

Trey watched Craven carefully as he shouted orders. While out searching for the woman, he was hatched his own plan to take over the pack. He'd put the word out to certain wolves that the Alpha was a danger. Draw the attention of the council and let them take down Craven. It kept his hands clean, and he could pull the pack together after he was eliminated. He knew the others, with the exception of a few, would not fight him for Alpha. Most of them were on his side these days.

* * * *

Craven sent his pack out to spread the word on the latest news. He wanted them to concentrate their efforts now to one area. He heard from the tracker and it would be two more weeks before he could join the hunt. His only focus now was finding the bitch and making her pay.

Craven knew there was a traitor in his pack. He didn't know who it was but when he found out, they would be eliminated in front of the entire pack of wolves. It was the only way to show them who was Alpha. He heard from a friend that someone was spreading word his pack was dangerous. It was apparently coming from an insider. This would put the council on his back and right now he didn't need the attention. Were hunters would not take kindly to his agenda. If they found out about the human, they would try to take him out before exacting his revenge, and that would not do.

Eyeing his Beta carefully as he ate, Craven watched for any sign of nervousness. He saw the usual hatred, but not anything that would signal more watching than normal. He knew Trey wanted Alpha. He was no fool, but like the rest of his pack, Trey would learn it was not happening. He needed to make sure they all understood, and taking out the traitor would be a lesson they would not soon forget.

The plans for the woman were another matter completely. He was going to bring her here and remind her every second what she did wrong. No one made a fool of him. He would kill her slowly. Craven wanted to strip her naked, use her, and then considered letting the pack have some when he was finished abusing her body. Because he was a master with a whip, he could lash someone and take only one layer of skin at a time. He got hard just thinking about it.

Craven set up a cage for her in the basement of the cabin. It came complete with chains and manacles to spread her wide and keep her helpless. He knew he was a sadistic bastard, but it only made him smile. His evil side was what made him Alpha. He lived and breathed bringing others pain as it brought him pleasure. Satan had nothing on him and his pack was completely in the dark about it. They would find out soon enough and that made him smile more.

* * * *

Trey knew he was being watched, so he exuded the only thing Craven understood and that was anger. He finished his meal and left the room with his plate. It was only when he was out of eyesight that he relaxed. The Alpha was crazed with his agenda against this woman. The sooner he found her, the sooner he could take out Craven.

The years of obeying orders were taking a toll and he was ready to start giving them. *I am an Alpha, not a Beta!*

Maybe he could move the pack to safer territories, north towards Montana. There was plenty of room up there for a pack of rogues. Thoughts filled his mind of making arrangements with other packs for unmated females. This time he wanted a real pack... a real family. Trey was a born shifter. His Alpha parents died in defense of their pack and left Trey alone. The new Alpha threatened to kill him, but an Aunt secreted him away. She left him with an orphanage at five years old, spending another three years there.

Trey left the compound to begin another round of finding this human female. Time was running out. He lied telling Craven there were no people with the first name of Chance. He'd found four. He was on his way to check out the first one on the list and he hoped to get lucky on the first try.

Driving and pulling up the address on his GPS, Trey followed the directions. He found a nice quiet neighborhood at his destination. There was a foreclosure home diagonally across the street from the target address. He went around back and broke a window to get inside. There was a couch left behind and Trey pulled it to the front window. He sat down and began his wait.

Trey had nothing but a description to go on since he was not at the bar when the fight went down. That description was tall, good-looking female with long raven hair and was maybe in her mid twenties and she wore leather. It was all the pack could remember, well, other than the obvious. She was a martial artist, a pool hustler, beautiful, and drank beer. How many of those could there be on the east side?

Chapter 11

Chance turned around from cloud watching and noticed Sylas and Jack talking. It appeared as if she might be the subject of the conversation. Every so often, one of them would turn towards her with a look of worry etched on their face. This tiny bit of information was disconcerting and she was not comfortable being the object of anyone's worry. Besides, the only people to show any concern about her in the past were Gus and Sensei. Right when the thought entered her mind, her phone vibrated.

"Thinking about you.
Hope you're okay and enjoying
your new jobless freedom!
Miss you, Gus"

Chance giggled while reading it.

Sending a quick reply back saying she was great and hoped he was too, Chance returned her attention to the two men talking.

It wouldn't be right or proper to stare at them for too long so she turned to watch some of Jack's staff playing beer pong. Far be it for her to butt into their business. If they wanted her to know, she figured they would say something eventually.

Unable to help herself, Chance turned to look at them again, wondering if Sylas intended on coming back, when the wind picked up. Her hair blew in her face and she heard the staff fussing about the game getting messed up, but what she saw kept her rapt attention. As she brushed the loose strands back, something started to shimmer in front of Sylas and Jack. Chance rubbed her eyes to see if she was hallucinating, but it was still there. It appeared to be a woman but she couldn't make any other distinctions.

As quickly as the shimmer appeared, it was gone. *You've had far too much beer to drink if you're seeing things.* Chance fussed at herself, *Way to impress a man. Getting snockered on your first outing with the hot biker.* Chance shivered, wishing she had dressed a little warmer. The same moment she went to reach for her jacket, she felt a warm solid body next to her. Sylas was back and sitting beside her.

"You looked cold, so I came back to offer you some warmth. I can get your jacket for you if you want it." Sylas looked at her with the question in his eyes. Chance realized he was asking her permission to touch her.

Somehow she trusted this man and that realization shocked her. She'd not allowed physical contact from anyone, other than Gus, since she stopped living in foster care. With Sylas, she felt protected, not fearful, and it was a new, but strange feeling. To answer his question, she reached out for his hand, keeping eye contact with him, and placed his arm over her shoulder. She leaned into him to gather more of his warmth and sighed as it spread through her.

"*I'm not doing this just for the warmth,*" she thought as electric pulses shot through her again. The restless feeling started again, only this time it felt more insistent, as if there was something in her head wanting out. Chance closed her eyes, willing it to stop. "*Not now, please. Lets not lose the nice guy over your craziness!*" Finally it relented and gave her some peace.

The wind died down and the beer pong game restarted after the table was reset with cups. Together, they watched the game until Jack declared the eats were ready. He moved two picnic tables together, making enough room for everyone to sit comfortably. He served steaks cooked to perfection, baked potatoes with all the trimmings, corn on the cob, salad and fresh baked rolls. It didn't take long for all the food to disappear.

When everyone finished and helped clear the mess, Jack led everyone down towards the lake. The sky darkened while they were cleaning, and it was near sunset. Near the waters edge, Jack had a fire pit lined with rock and surrounding it was a round rock bench lined with pillows. Nearby there was a dock with more seats under a gazebo and it was where Sylas led her. Jack lit the fire and pulled out a guitar. Soon everyone was singing along to "The Dock of the Bay".

Chance leaned into Sylas again, as it seemed to be colder there by the lake.

Sylas was singing along with them. Chance closed her eyes and sat back to listen. His voice was deep and clear, with perfect pitch. Chance opened her eyes and blushed, not realizing until that moment he was singing to her. The words caressed over her like a long lost lovers touch.

When the song ended, Sylas whispered in her ear, "But I don't feel like I'm wasting time Chance, not since I met you. I've laughed more with you in these last two days than I have in years. You continue to delight and surprise me. I hope you'll give us both more time to learn more about each other. There is no rush and no demands from me. Will you allow me to spend more time with you?"

Chance looked into his glowing green eyes... deep into the soul of them. She knew then there was nothing to fear from this man and he meant every word. She knew at some point she would have to conquer her fears. Men didn't scare her any more, but giving one her trust was another beast. Looking deep within herself, Chance knew now was the time to let down a few walls. She did like Sylas a lot and did want to know him better. She took a deep breath and replied, "Yes, I think I'd like that too, Sylas. It isn't easy for me to say it, much less do it, so I hope you're a patient person. I don't give my trust lightly."

"I knew that about you from the first night I saw you, Chance. I saw the anger and pain in your eyes when that bastard touched you. I will never do anything without your permission and I need you to know and believe that."

Chance nodded slightly in agreement. "My past has not always been sunshine and roses. I will explain someday, but I'm not ready yet. My demons have been bottled inside for a long time and I'm afraid to let them out. I hope you can understand."

"I can be as patient as you need me to be. Like I said... no rush or demands. You're a special person, Chance, and you have my permission to kick my ass if I get out of line, because I know you can." Sylas chuckled as he said it.

Jack was still playing his guitar but the music and singing were lost to her as she gazed into his green eyes. Chance made up her mind that there was one more thing she needed to know. She grabbed her courage and shyly asked, "Sylas, I… would you kiss me?"

"I thought you would never ask," Sylas stood and reached out to gently pull her up closer. He wanted to feel every inch of her body molded to his. He leaned over and looked deep into her eyes. She could see the question burning there… the "are you sure" plain as day in those emerald eyes. She nodded and closed her eyes as he leaned in the rest of the way to place his soft lips on hers.

Sparks flew between them as he lingered there, waiting for her to take the lead, and she did. She slipped her tongue out to taste him and he gave her access. His hand moved from her shoulder, delving deep into her tresses, cupping the back of her head. With his free hand he caressed her cheek then moved it to her neck, pausing there before he pulled her even closer.

Sylas groaned with pleasure as her hands roamed to his back and cinched themselves around his waist. It was if they both needed the intimate contact of body on body and they were a perfect fit. With her boots on he could look directly into her eyes and it pleased him. Their tongues danced and tangled with each other, heating them both from the inside out.

Chance moaned when Sylas gently pulled her head back with her hair and then delved his tongue deeper, asking silently for more. She was lost to him as he took control. She felt no fear, just hunger for more.

The heat from his kisses went straight to her core and moisture built between her legs. Sylas pulled back and looked into her eyes again. She blushed, suddenly feeling very shy. He smiled and caressed her cheek with his thumb. "You are so beautiful, Chance. Thank you for this. Honey and wine," he whispered as he leaned in to kiss her again. Chance was overwhelmed with the tenderness in his touch. She'd made the right decision. With the emotional release that came with it, a single tear silently coursed its way down her cheek. She'd come for fun and found so much more.

Chapter 12

The party continued into the wee hours of the morning. Chance and Sylas stayed behind after everyone else left. Once again, they volunteered for cleanup duty, since Jack told everyone else he would take care of it. The time spent cleaning gave the three of them more opportunities to talk about Chance's plans with the property without interruptions. Cleaning also gave her time to ponder the kiss. Granted there were many kisses since then, but the only one that mattered at the moment was the first one. Her first kiss… ever.

When all was picked up and put away, they each took one more beer out to the fire pit to watch the last of the logs burn down to embers. Jack reached under a hidden compartment in the bench seats and tossed Sylas a throw blanket. Sylas deftly snatched it from the air and placed it around her, easing closer to add his body warmth.

"It's pretty late. If you aren't up to driving back, I have plenty of room for you both to stay. I don't condone drinking and driving, but it's still up to you," Jack said smiling at them both. "I am really interested in hearing more about your property and building plans, Chance. I've lots of experience in that department. I designed the bar and hired a crew to build it for me." Jack yawned and raised his arms over his head in a long stretch, before looking back at her. "Just offering my help to the prettiest lady I've had the pleasure of meeting in quite a while." He glanced at Sylas as he said it.

Chance wasn't sure what the silent look between them was or what it meant. She guessed it was something to do with the conversation from earlier in the evening. It didn't matter though, since now there were two wonderful and extremely hot men offering their expertise. It would be foolish to turn it down and she was no ones fool. Chance also knew that this would mean telling them the rest of her secrets concerning the house plans. As the thought hit her, she instantly brushed it aside. These two people had her trust and to question it now would be stupid on her part. With the trust issue put aside, she vowed to not bring it up out of the recesses of her mind again.

"I have a confession to make." Chance shifted her position so she could look at both of them. It meant moving away from Sylas and his warmth, but it was a necessary move. Sylas adjusted the blanket for her and gave her a wink. Taking a deep breath, she plunged forward with her admission.

"I am building more than what I told you about. It will contain a complete underground two-level substructure. I have plans on two safe rooms, one on each sub level, a strategically placed emergency exit, and complete martial arts training center. It will be all self-contained. The second level down will also hold my well pump, back up generator, a wine room, and extra food pantry."

Jack gave a long whistle and Sylas just stared at her. She looked at them both shyly and said, "There's more but I think that's enough for right now. From the looks on both of your faces, I'm sure you both have plenty to say."

They both spoke up and quit talking at the same time. Chance just giggled at their shock. Jack was finally the first to speak back up. "Planning on World War III, Chance?"

"No, not exactly. I want a home I can call mine. I want something I've designed and had built from my own imagination. I guess I'm a survivalist at heart, but I want somewhere I can live out the rest of my life and be truly happy. If the hard times come, I want to have no worries about leaving it or losing anyone I care about." Chance whispered the last part more to herself than to them. In her mind, at least someday, there would be people in her life that she would care enough about to keep safe. Shaking her head to wipe the morose thoughts away, she asked them both "So… you still want to help?"

She watched as Sylas and Jack exchanged another of their silent looks. Sylas reached out his hand to rub her shoulder and said, "We're both here for you, babe. Whatever you need, ask and it's yours. When's your builder coming back?"

"Well since it's now a new day, tomorrow at my house, noonish. You both want to come?"

They both replied with an enthusiastic yes. Chance took a deep breath, not realizing until then that she'd been holding it. It felt like for the first time since her Sensei's passing that she was experiencing a family again, and it felt good. They asked more questions and she answered them all as best she could. She wasn't ready yet to tell Sylas her personal secrets, but these questions, for now, were about the property.

They talked until the sun peeked over the horizon. Chance yawned and leaned into Sylas. He must have sensed she was about to fall asleep. Sylas picked her up and moved towards Jack's house. Chance had to fight the need to pull away and protect herself. She hoped he could not feel the tension in her body while he effortlessly carried her inside the house. She felt like a feather in his strong arms.

Jack led the way to one of his spare rooms. Sylas thanked him, closed the door, and set her on her feet. He removed the blanket and her jacket. She looked up and he placed a chaste kiss on her forehead. "No worries, babe. I can sleep in another room. You're safe from unwanted advances."

Chance was seriously conflicted. Her emotions were running rampant and felt she was losing control of them. She wanted to let go of her fears and enjoy the moment. On the other side of the coin, she was scared witless of what could happen if she did. She was not prepared for the different emotions hitting her from all sides. Be alone forever or learn to trust. Chance found herself trembling as she fought the need to run.

"I... I don't want you to go, but," was all she could manage to get out, lost in his glowing gaze again. Sylas seemed to understand and set her on the edge of the bed. "I understand, babe. No worries. I will tuck you in under the covers and sleep on top of them. I promise to behave while you sleep. Scouts honor." Sylas waited while she debated it in her mind. Finally nodding her assent, he pulled her boots off, noticing her weapons as he placed them to the side.

"Always ready for a fight, Chance? Remind me not to piss you off anytime soon." He chuckled. Giving her another chaste kiss, he gently pushed her back onto the pillows and tucked her in under the blankets. She studied him as he removed his boots and jacket. He was the perfect example of the male species; all muscle, strength, and he exuded boundless power, yet he treated her as gently as a newborn. Sylas joined her on the bed, on top of the covers. Reaching under her, he pulled her into him, with her back to his chest and she fell asleep with his arm as her pillow, feeling like she was home.

Chance woke up disoriented and stiffened. There was a man wrapped around her and she started to jump up, when she realized she was still fully dressed and under a blanket. Then she remembered Sylas putting her to bed. "Easy babe. It's just me. Good afternoon, beautiful, sleep well?" he whispered as he placed a kiss on top of her head. Chance turned her body around to look at him. His eyes were half lidded and glowing a dark emerald green. She could stare at those eyes forever if he let her, and it was funny, but the glowing eye thing didn't seem to register as something wrong, just different. It was what made him Sylas to her.

"Yes, did you?" she asked after a moment.

"Better than I have in… a very long time. Thank you for asking me to stay with you last night, but I honestly didn't think you would."

"Why? Because we didn't…" was all she could get out before Sylas stopped the protest with his fingers caressing her lips.

"No, I don't want you to think that, Chance. I know you're not ready for a more intimate relationship. It's far too soon. When you said you didn't want me to leave, I understood exactly what you meant, because I felt the same. You wanted to feel closeness without sexual pressure and I wanted to feel you in my arms for longer than a few minutes. It was selfish of me, but I took advantage of your needs."

"You always seem to know what I'm thinking. I kind of like that," she whispered into his fingers that were still roaming. "I like that you wanted more, Sylas, and you're right, I'm not ready yet. Can I give you one more confession?"

"Only if you want to tell me, Chance." He reached over and replaced his fingers with his lips for a quick kiss.

Chance hesitated; unsure of how to tell him she had never been with a man before, much less kissed one before. "I've never... you know, been with anyone before. Last night, with you, was magical." She blushed and looked him directly in the eyes. "That was my first kiss and I'm glad it was with you."

Sylas smiled at her and pulled her closer. Lightly pulling her hair to expose her neck to him, he whispered between kisses down her chin and onto her neck. "Just the first of many more to come, if you will let me, Chance. Just one of many."

Chance moaned as he tugged her hair. *Who knew that having someone gently tugging on her mane could be so erotic!* Her only experience from the past was yanking it with full intent to harm her. It had been yanked out, used to throw her across the room, and just recently in the bar it was used to try and trap her. As far as she was concerned, after today, Sylas could pull it all he wanted and she secretly hoped that he would want to pull it, a lot.

Sylas gave her one more deep and mind shattering kiss before he got up and pulled her with him. "I'm starving, and I bet you are too. Let's get out of here and find some food."

After she caught her breath back, she smiled and nodded. She was ready to tackle another day and for the first time in a very long while, not alone.

Chapter 13

Trey paced the house, cursing. This was the third subject on his Chance list, and it was another no go. The first one he waited almost a full day for. It turned out to be a male subject who apparently was out of town. The second he waited a few hours for while he waited near the apartment. There were woods on the backside of the building and he was able to shift and watch from some bushes right outside the hall corridor. Again, it was a male.

This third one came home from work and yet again, another male. He confirmed each one by waiting until someone identified them by saying their name. He was tired, hungry, and pissed. If the next one was a washout, he was screwed. There was no possible way he could follow up on thirty eight other people named Chance. He could not go back to Craven and admit lying. Or explain what he was doing for the last two days. His quest for Alpha could be lost if he missed his opportunity on this next, and last, person.

Trey kept his plan simple. Find the girl, allow the pack to see how deranged Craven is, catch his weakness for her, and kill him. He knew there was no way in hell Craven could resist punishing her in front of the pack. Craven wanted to make an example of her, but his mistake and downfall would be the human aspect. If Trey didn't kill him first, the council would call in the Fate's Enforcer. He could lose the pack as well if this wasn't done his way. He didn't want chaos, at least not to the point where he couldn't control the situation. He wanted to kill Sylas, not be hunted by him. This was his row to hoe, and he would finish it.

Letting out a frustrated sigh, Trey started cleaning the house of his prints. He'd found a house empty of the occupants. Early springtime meant a lot of people on vacations. This one was checked for an alarm system and finding it lacking, he picked the back door lock. Some skills came in handier than others did, and in another lifetime his was thief. This was before he found out he was a shifter. He was too young when he lost his parents to know what he was.

A nurse who worked in the orphanage took him in and adopted him. Small town ideals saved him from starving. In the wilds of Washington he wouldn't have lived long. They struggled, but Trey never wanted for anything. He went to school and lived a normal life.

Everything stayed that way until the night of his sixteenth birthday. Growing up without parents to teach him about his gifts caused the greatest harm to the woman he called mother. In his horror of what was suddenly happening to him, he got too close to her, wanting her to fix it like always. She hugged him when it happened. He shifted in her arms and the sudden burst of power in his body crushed her back and neck, killing her instantly. In his world, you didn't care about anyone, because they always ended up dead.

Trey left the house as he found it and returned to his SUV. The Navigator was his home away from home and after the day he just had, it felt good to sink down in the comfortable leather seats. He set the final address into his GPS and left, hoping this last one was his money tree. He stopped at an all night fast food place and purchased several hamburger meals to go. He was starving, again.

Finding the next neighborhood was easy, but there were no empty or vacant homes on the same street. He found one, for sale, on the next one over that was kitty-corner to subject four's backyard. There was one problem he saw right off. The house for number four also had a complete privacy fence. He would deal with that later. Thankfully it was the middle of the night and no dogs were sounding warnings of a stranger being around.

Trey picked the back door lock, hoping he would not have to use this skill again any time in the near future. Never would be too soon, as far as he was concerned. At least this house was set up to sell, complete with furniture. He left the lights off and settled in. Subject four was not home as far as he could tell, so that gave him time to contemplate his life since that fateful night he needlessly killed his adoptive mother. He opened the bag of burgers and ate while he reminisced. Mostly he wondered what he could have done differently. He knew now that he should have never gotten close to her during a shift. Life was full of "if only" and his seemed to have them more than most.

The shock that set in following her death set his feet to running. It seemed that he'd not stopped since. Taking up with a gang of human kids in the streets of Seattle taught him the hard lesson of survival. The gang initiated him in with an attempted beat down, but they were clueless. It ended up being the opposite. By the end of the fight, he was the only one left standing of the baker's dozen that jumped him.

Trey won instant respect and they taught him the fine art of thievery. He ended up being the best of the bunch. He could get in and out a target in less than five minutes, including shutting down the alarm system. In big cities, burglaries were the bottom of the priority list for police intervention. His five minutes snagged them quite a few trinkets before he left the gang to their own devices.

Trey finally discovered he preferred being in the woods. His shift was wolf and that's where they thrive. He met a female wolf while out on one of his forays in the wilds of northern Washington. They stayed together for several years until he caught her with another male. He left her, the state, and never looked back, until now. He was tired of struggling and taking orders, and he was definitely tired of being alone.

Trey contemplated his desire to bring the pack into what it should be, a family. Yes, they were all rogues, but they had the same wants he did. That is how Craven brought them all together. Each and every one of them was tired of being alone. Craven thought he lorded over a pack full of cutthroats. Boy, was he mistaken. Sure, if called upon they would defend the pack to the end, but they really did not want the life of the lone wolf.

This was the difference between him and Craven. He got to know the pack by each individual member. He knew everything about them; all of their individual wants and needs. Craven only wanted to know they were his pack and nothing more. He treated them all like animals; to jump and run when called. To obey without question and to do all his dirty work. As far as Trey was concerned it was about to come to an end. One way or the other, it *would* end.

Trey considered the extra plus to his plan. If the human was attached to the Enforcer, then all the better. He lived and breathed to bring that man to his knees, preferably dead. He did what research he could on the death of his parents. There were several newspaper articles about it, complete with pictures. It seemed the fight and their deaths made the local and statewide news. It had been called a massacre of a local cult. Just because they were different and lived in a commune, they were a cult. It wasn't right, but what could he do. Besides, the real issue behind all the deaths was a rival pack that wanted their land.

Humans didn't understand pack life, but then again, humans didn't know Immortal shifters existed. The common denominator in all the pictures he'd seen was Sylas Taiken. He was shown standing in the background in every picture he saw of the aftermath. This said one thing to Trey… Sylas was part of it somehow, and Trey would make him pay with his life. If not for almost half of the pack getting out when the fight first began, he would not be here today to exact his revenge.

There were enough members of the pack left to reform it, but the new Alpha wanted no part of the old one, they never did. Being born to Alpha's, he was too much of a threat to the new one. He was thankful his Aunt whisked him away that night. It was fine with him. They would get theirs too someday. Karma was a bitch.

Trey smiled as he started to fall asleep in a chair next to a rear window. He was tired and sated, having eaten all but one of the meals. He needed sleep and felt he had time to do so, since subject four was not home yet. His last conscious thoughts were how he couldn't wait to see Craven and Sylas meet their makers.

Trey had nightmares that night about the fight between him and Sylas. He tracked Sylas down after hearing about a shifter who killed a human. He knew the shifter and watched him until Sylas showed up to enforce shifter law. He waited until after the bout with the bear. He wanted Sylas tired. He knew it was his only chance of surviving. He'd barely gotten away with his life. Sylas left him after the fight, thinking he was dead. Hell, he practically was. His leg was broken in several places along with many other bones and a punctured femoral artery. He'd nearly bled out before being found by his Alpha.

Trey remembered the Enforcers words still to this day. "Don't know what this is about wolf. I don't take life without reason, and this fight had no reason to it." That was nearly 30 years ago and still fresh as if it happened yesterday. Craven didn't ask questions and he gave nothing up. This was his battle and he wouldn't lose the next one.

Chapter 14

Jack was up and nursing a cup of coffee by the time they got their shoes on and hit the kitchen. Chance cooked breakfast for the three of them. One of the only things she could cook decent enough to eat was an omelet. She also found some potatoes and grated them into hash browns, adding jalapenos to the mix. She loved spicy food, especially in the mornings. It added the extra wake up one needed after a night of drinking. She topped the omelets off with some salsa and the room stayed silent, with an occasional, "This is good," getting tossed out around mouthfuls, until they were finished.

Chance took her coffee out to the back deck to enjoy some fresh air as the guys cleaned up. She insisted it was only fair; she cooked, they cleaned. She picked a white leather Barcalounger to sit in and it felt like heaven. She made a mental note to get several of these for her cabin. She turned in her chair when she heard a loud bang and then laughter coming from the kitchen. Sylas was loading the dishwasher and had dropped a plate. "OK, sticky fingers Malone, go join your girl. I got this," Jack fussed at him while laughing.

"I had a thought while waiting on you two slowpokes," she said to both of them when Jack finally joined them on the deck.

"Uh oh, she's thinking, Sy. I'll distract her while you run for cover!" Jack laughed, winking at her.

"You can do the running, Jack. I'll stick with my girl, thank-you-very-much!"

"Your girl. Huh. Never been called that before." Chance winked back at Jack then turned to Sylas with a straight face and raised eyebrows.

Chance was surprised when Sylas reached over and gave her a quick peck on the lips. "Yes, my girl. You think I'm gonna let a girl get away that can kick royal ass? I might need you to put Jack in his place one of these days. Since I'm his best friend, it wouldn't be prudent for me to do it, and he doesn't hit women. You'd seriously have one up on him."

"Low blow, brother, low blow." Jack tried to be serious but lost the battle and laughed at him.

"No worries, Jack. I don't hit men either. It's the monsters thinking they are men, the ones who hit women that I have issues with. I can tell neither of you are those kind of men," Chance said quietly. Having turned the conversation towards the serious side unintentionally, she smiled at them both.

"Sorry, didn't mean to get so morose. It's a conversation for another day. What I was trying to say earlier is why don't I ask Rick to meet us at the property tomorrow instead of my house. I'd love for both of you to see it. I've also asked a water dowser if he would dowse the area for underground springs. I think he is available tomorrow as well. Make it a day trip with a picnic? I mean, if you would like to. Since I am happily and permanently unemployed now I have nothing else going. And I'm rambling. Your turn to talk now," she rushed out looking at Sylas and then Jack, blushing furiously.

Nice going, Chance, now they think you're nuts. That must have been the most you've said at one time to either one of them. Scare the hunky men away rambling like an escaped looney. Yea, real smart. Not! She thought to herself as they sat quietly looking at her like she had a third eye or something.

Busting out laughing at the same time, Jack punched Sylas in the arm and said, "I'm game if you are Sy. I can get one of the girls to open and close the bar. Sounds like an adventure to me! I can take care of the eats, if you want to take care of the beverages. Motorcycles or cages?"

Chance piped in before Sylas could reply, "Its very rough terrain up there. I haven't hired out a crew to bulldoze a driveway into the property yet. Cages would be better. Sylas?"

His eyes were glowing bright and beautiful as she looked at him. He was smiling at her with a big grin on his face. "I only have one question. You're happily and permanently unemployed?"

"That was all you got out of the whole conversation, Sylas?" She laughed; totally thrilled that he didn't think she was looney after all. "Yes, I no longer need to work. So… do you want to go see my property?"

"Yes, babe, I'd love to see your property. I got the drinks handled, and I heard every single, lovely word you said," he replied kissing her again. She made all her calls and set the meetings for around noon. It gave them time to sleep in a little and eat before heading out in the morning.

Chance and Sylas agreed to head to their respective homes to shower, change clothes and to meet back at Jack's that evening. He lived closer to the property and it made more sense to leave together from his place. Sylas drove her home and insisted on waiting for her to do what she needed. Chance insisted she was fine. She needed a little space to gather her wits and she couldn't do it when a look from him made her knees weaken. She waved him off from the front door. She could tell he was reluctant to leave, but she promised to lock the door after he left, so he acquiesced.

Chance heard the Jeep round the corner and was about to lock the door, when she heard the neighborhood dogs raising hell. Then she heard scratching at her front door. She cracked the door just enough to peek out. Pretty Boy, the husky, was sitting on her porch. She opened the door enough to let him in and then locked it as she had promised.

"Pretty Boy, I'm so glad to see you're alright! Are you hungry?" The dog wagged his tail with those expressive eyes, so she went into the kitchen and filled a bowl with left over steak and another with fresh water. "I hope you don't mind, but I think I'd like to call you Sy, Pretty Boy. Your eyes remind me of his." He turned a quick circle and reached to lick her hand and she let him. She felt better with him here. It wasn't that she was afraid of anything or anyone hurting her, it just felt better with him there.

"Taking a shower now, Sy, so make yourself at home. Be out in a few minutes." The dog yipped in agreement and she walked into her bathroom to turn the water on. When she came out to decide what to wear, Sy was lying on the end of her bed, curled up watching her. "I see you took that literally, Sy! It's okay, you curl up anywhere you want." She gave him a quick ear scratch. Grabbing a towel, she left him to get clean.

When she finished and turned off the water, Chance grabbed a comb and ran it through her wet locks. She was one the lucky few blessed with thick individual strands of hair that tended not to tangle when wet. Leaving the bathroom wrapped in her towel, she walked into the bedroom to sort through her clothes again, not satisfied with her first choices. Since they were going to spend the day in the woods, she grabbed some comfortable jeans and a tank top with a pull over sweatshirt. She dropped the towel to dress and heard a whine coming from her bed.

"Embarrassing you am I, Sy? Sorry sweets, but I need to get dressed." Chance bent over to pull on her jeans, and the dog jumped from the bed and left the room. She giggled and said aloud, "I can't believe you can't be in the same room with me naked. Too funny!"

Chance finished dressing and picked out another change of clothes should she need them. Sy scratched at the front door, so she quickly let him out. She started to head back to her room to finish when she heard another scratch at the door. "Can't make up your mind, Sy?" she said but stopped short of anything else when he raised his paw to the lock and left again. Shocked, Chance closed the door and locked it. She watched, slack-jawed, out the front window as the dog went on his way, seemingly satisfied the door was locked.

Chapter 15

Sylas was dying. He was in pain. He had to be, because he couldn't breathe. The vision of Chance naked in all her glory was too much. Why he went into that bedroom, knowing... *knowing* she was getting ready for a shower was beyond him. It was all he could do to walk away from her and leave the room.

Chance reminded him of Lady Godiva with all that hair. All he wanted to do the second she dropped her towel was get lost in her. Then she bent over and he was done. He wanted her more than anything he'd ever thought of wanting in his 500 years. He wanted to pull her tresses, be inside her and never come out again. He'd almost shifted, and the pain of needing her right then and there had caused him to whine.

The only reason he came back to the house was her need for a shower. She would be at her most vulnerable then. He had a bad feeling about leaving her there alone, but once out of the shower, he knew she could take care of herself. He took a huge gamble when he didn't hear the lock click shut by pawing at the lock when she opened the door again. He needed to be more careful. If he kept this up, she would learn about the immortal world, and he could not let it happen until he knew she was the one.

Sylas beat a quick path back to her Jeep and raced home. *Speed limits be damned!* He had to get back before she suspected something was up besides his throbbing cock. *Fuck!* He wanted her badly and there was no relief in sight. He arrived home and jumped in the shower. He was never one to play the one-fisted flute, but there was no way he could go back to her in his condition.

Just the image of her bent over, exposing her sweet folds to him did the trick. He almost fell to his knees as the orgasm rocked him to his core. It wasn't what he truly wanted or needed, but he felt he could manage being around her again... for now.

Sylas finished his shower, dressed and raided his pantry for a case of water in record time. The beer he would get on the way back to her house. Picking up everything he needed and shoving it all into the back of the Jeep, he headed back, stopping at the local liquor store for beer and wine.

When he finally arrived, she was waiting for him at the door. She looked good with a loose braid lying over her shoulder, so much so that he had to taste her. "Hey Beautiful. I missed you." He pulled her to him and she went willingly. He pressed a kiss to her forehead as she wrapped her arms around his shoulders. Bending his head down, he dipped his tongue deep within, stroking her with it, as he wanted to do elsewhere.

When they finally came up for air, she was staring into his eyes. He knew they were glowing brightly just like every other time he kissed her. He knew she could see it, and yet she never said anything about it. It was another thing he loved about her. That single, solitary word hit him like a brick wall. He did love her. He hoped that even if she wasn't the one, he could spend a lifetime, her lifetime showing her she was loved. She deserved it. He wanted to wipe all her pain away, remove it from her eyes and replace it with love for him.

"You just left, how could you miss me in so short a time?" She was grinning at him.

Sylas knew she was teasing him and it felt good. It meant she was starting to relax more in his presence, which also meant she was beginning to trust him. Now he needed to keep the wolves at bay. He was not about to lose her, now that he'd found her. Returning her smile was easy.

"Chance, any time away from you is too long. Besides, who else would I want to kiss like this?" and he leaned her back in his arms and starting at the nape of her neck, he ran kisses all the way up until he reached her lips. She giggled just as he was about to dive in for another. "What, don't you trust me?"

She giggled some more and replied "I so have a picture of Edward and Bella in my head right now!"

"Ah, but I'm not a sparkly, cold assed Vampire. Team Jacob here," he threw out, testing the waters while there was an opportunity. Sometimes innocent discussions gave the most informative answers, and he got it with her reply.

"I prefer warmth over cold and besides, Jacob had the better body," she replied pulling him in for another kiss. He pulled them both up out of the dip.. "I think if we continue this, we won't make it back to Jack's," he whispered in her ear. He felt a shudder run its course down her body from the heat of his breath and he smiled, liking the effect he had on her.

"You ready, babe? Point me to your things and let's get this party started. We're losing daylight." She nodded and he finished loading the Jeep, while she locked up the house. Right after they pulled out, Sylas caught sight of a black SUV that had just passed them in the rear view mirror. It was turning into her subdivision and there was a very strong scent of wolf trailing along with it. *"Fuck! How did they find her so fast?"* he thought as he fought to control his anger. It wouldn't do any good for Chance to see him angry for no reason.

Sylas distracted himself by playing a game of movie trivia with Chance, since she was such a fan. They bantered and discussed right up until they pulled into Jack's driveway. He'd gleaned her favorite movies were the Underworld and Twilight series, but the top of the list was Serenity. He'd not seen it and she made him promise to someday sit with her and watch it. Turned out Jack owned the movie and they all watched it while eating dinner. They gathered in the living room and Chance curled up next to him on the couch. He laughed when she would quote her favorite parts word for word.

He was so engrossed in the movie that he didn't notice Chance had fallen asleep and was lightly snoring, until the credits started rolling. He smiled and extricated himself gently away from her, easing her back on the couch and covering her with a throw. She stayed asleep, looking like an angel... his angel. An angel he would die to protect, only she wasn't exactly his yet and she definitely wasn't defenseless. Her face was serene and her lips were turned up in a small smile, one he hoped he'd put there.

Looking at Jack, he jerked his head towards the back door. As soon as they were outside and the door was shut, Sylas let loose. "They've fucking found her, Jack! I saw a wolf pulling into her subdivision as I was leaving. He didn't notice us but I sure as hell smelled his rank ass!"

"Shit Sy, if you go back and try to take him out, you'll be tipping them off that they, in fact, do have her."

Sylas started pacing. "I know and I'm lost as to what to do. This is a first for me, Jack. I can't tell her who we are yet. I still don't know if she's the one. It puts all of us in jeopardy if she's not my mate."

Jack sighed in feigned frustration. Of the two of them, he always seemed cool and collected, and Sylas counted on it to keep straight. "I think you could tell her the human part of it, Sylas. Tell her you heard the bikers from the bar are looking for her. Tell her you saw one of them in her neighborhood, and maybe we can convince her to stay here."

"So many ifs, Jack. I'll try this approach, but I don't like it. I don't like starting a relationship on lies, especially when I just gained a little of her trust. At least it's truth in a white lie. If I lose her over this, I swear the whole pack will go down and they will know the reason when they take their last breaths."

"I never thought I'd see you like this, and it's long overdue, bro. You've given me back my faith. If you can fall this deeply for a woman you've known less than a week, then she has to be the one. There's no other explanation for it, Sy, and I'll be there to make sure it happens."

I've only known her 3 or 4 days? Was she mine forever? Sylas had thousands of questions running through his mind, but he desperately needed some Chance therapy. She'd become his place of Zen in his fucked up world. She made him laugh when he'd forgotten how. He suddenly realized his boredom was gone and he was finally living life, as it should be. She'd completely changed his life for the better in a few short days.

Sylas went back inside, determined to tell Chance the white lie, but it could wait until morning. She was sleeping soundly. He gently picked her up and walked to the same bed they'd used the night before. He managed to pull off her shoes and tuck her back under the covers without waking her. He removed his shoes and joined her, back on top of the covers. Pulling her into his chest, he curled himself around her, breathing in her scent. Honey and wine is what she smelled and tasted like. He closed his eyes and dreamed of showers and lost towels.

Chapter 16

Chance woke up wrapped in security. This time she knew where she was and with whom. She hadn't realized she was tired when they sat down to watch the movie, but she must have fallen asleep. She wanted to spend more quality time with Sylas last night, alone, but it was good. They would have plenty of time for that. Less than a week ago she would never have allowed a man this close and now she couldn't imagine not having him next to her. Now it was a matter of getting through her fears and letting the rest of her walls down.

Chance slipped out of bed and walked to the kitchen. This time she was the first one there. She made a pot of coffee and started some bacon. A simple and quick breakfast of scrambled eggs, bacon, grits and toast sounded good. She started a pot of salted water boiling and cracked the eggs to scramble them. Right when the coffee finished brewing she heard someone padding down the hallway.

"Good morning and what a nice surprise. This old man could get used to waking up this way every morning. I might have to give Sy a run for his money," Jack said as he filled a cup with the steaming black brew.

"Over my dead body, *old* man."

Chance turned to see Sylas in the doorway. He was leaning with his hip against the frame and had his arms crossed over his chest watching her. He gave her one of his special smiles. She returned it and blushed. "You were sleeping so peacefully, I couldn't bear to wake you. Hope your both hungry. Southern style breakfast coming right up."

Jack set the table, while Sylas helped her finish cooking. Every once in a while he would stand behind her and wrap his arms around her waist, pulling her back against him. It felt good to have him so close and she could get very used to having him there. It was the first time she could remember ever feeling this way and it brought her trepidation, mixed with elation. How things had advanced this far was very confusing, but in a good way. Four days ago, if someone had touched her this way, they would have been put swiftly on the ground, before any explanations could be given. Now though? This man made her feel wanted, like she had found a sense of home in his arms.

Chance plated the eggs and bacon, left the grits in the pot and brought it all to the table. She found a tomato in the fridge and sliced it, adding it to the small feast. Sylas finished the toast and brought it with him.

Chance smiled as they gave their approval to her cooking. When they all finished and cleaned up, Sylas called them back to the table. Chance grew concerned when she saw his face. He wasn't smiling anymore and seemed a bit on edge. The muscle in his cheek was ticking and his lips were pressed into a thin line. She wasn't sure she wanted to know what was wrong. She was starting to get comfortable with him, and this was definitely scaring her. She edged into her seat, ready to run if she needed to. Self-preservation was trying to kick into first gear.

Jack reached over and patted her on the arm, trying to reassure her, but she only had eyes for Sylas.

"I have something to tell you babe, and I'm not sure how to begin. It concerns you and your safety."

Chance relaxed a little. She was sure this was going in a totally different direction. The thought he was married or seeing someone else had been at the forefront of her mind. "Okay, but I don't understand. Why wouldn't I be safe?"

"You remember the fight in the bar with the bikers?"

"Yes, but…"

Sylas raised his hand. It was a polite, but silent request to let him finish. "I have it through the grapevine, and Jack has confirmed it. The man who attacked you in the bar was a gang leader and he wants revenge. When we left your house last night, I saw one of the bikers entering your subdivision. He wasn't on a motorcycle but in a SUV."

Jack piped in when she turned to look at him in shock. "These guys are known to be very hostile towards women, Chance, and you took down the head guy. Now they know where you live. I don't know how they found you, but Sy and I would feel more comfortable if you stayed here for a little while."

"Is this what you two were talking about the other night at the party? And why didn't you say something to me then?"

Sylas answered the questions, his face etched with worry. "That is my fault, Chance. I was sure they wouldn't be able to find you so quickly. Please forgive me, but when it comes to you I am a bit over protective. Please try to understand that I know you can handle yourself, but this is an entire gang after you, not just one or two people. I was serious when I said we were here for you. We won't let you face them alone, Chance. I wouldn't even if you left right now and told me you never wanted to see me again. I would still be there for you."

Chance looked down at her hands and thought about what he said. She wouldn't be alone and that was key. Sylas got up, nervously pacing while she contemplated. She wasn't used to having someone else to think about, or worry about before. She felt she could handle this fine, but it was Sylas and Jack she was concerned over. They were there too, and if she wasn't safe, neither were they.

Chance's life had completely turned some major corners in the last week. Did she want this? She wasn't sure. Was she ready for it? No. She only knew that the thought of not having Sylas in her life any longer was the real tragedy and that thought she could not bear. Did she like him? Yes. Did she love him? No, but there was a real chance she could in time. She still had her demons to deal with and dragging an unsuspecting person into her hell did not seem right.

Quietly she said, "I couldn't do that, Sylas."

She looked up to see alarm written all over his face. That fact alone spoke volumes about the man standing in front of her. Shaking her head slightly, she continued, "What I mean is I wouldn't ask you to leave. I have to admit, I like this thing we seem to be sharing, but it is confusing me. I know this will sound corny, but these past few days with you have been the best days I can ever remember. I'm not ready to walk away from this and I'm not really sure why. You both feel like family, each in your own way."

Her answer must have quieted some of Sylas' nerves, because she heard him sigh, but he was still pacing. "What about my house and things. I worked hard for them. I know it sounds selfish, but growing up without has made them all the more precious to me."

Jack patted her hand again. "I can take care of that for you, Chance, no worries. We want you to be safe and you are safer here with us, than you'd be there alone. It doesn't have to be a long time. We both feel the need to protect you until we know the threat is gone. Will you let us do that and stay here until then?"

"I'm not worried about my safety, so much as I am yours. You both were there and that worries me too. But yes, if it makes you both feel better, I will stay… for a while. I want a promise from both of you though, no more secrets after today. Okay?"

Jack looked at Sylas and he came over to sit down next to her. "Chance there are some things that I want desperately to tell you, but I can't right now. Can you accept that I will tell them to you when the time is right? And for the record, as far as we know now, Jack and I are not on their radar, just you."

"Are you married or seeing someone else?" she blurted out before she could put a zipper on her mouth, ignoring the rest of his statement.

Sylas laughed for the first time since they started this conversation. "No babe, you are the only woman in my life and the only one I care to know. I swear to you, I will tell you everything later. I think this is enough for now, if you are okay with this and us. I told you before, no pressure, but I needed to know you would be safe."

"You and I are going to have a long talk later, Sylas, and you both are going to get lessons in the martial arts. Like I said, I'm not worried about me, but I am about you. You both are good fighters, but you both lack some finesse. I can give you the edge you are lacking. You both have strength, but power alone will not always win in the end. Since you are taking care of me, it is only fair that I take care of you." She smiled at them both with a "don't-fight-me-on-this" look on her face.

"Now we need to go. We have meetings and we'll be late if we don't leave in the next thirty minutes. Round it up boys, we have things to do." Sylas stood up and she joined him. She grabbed his arm before he could walk away, pulling him into her. Reaching up to wrap her arms around his neck, she pulled his lips to hers. This time she was the one letting him know how she felt. She kissed him for all she was worth, then stepped back and away, leaving him both stunned and breathless.

Chapter 17

The scenic route to the property was breathtaking to say the least. Chance drove this time and Jack followed in his Rover. The drive gave Sylas plenty of time to think, since Chance was unusually quiet. It bothered him that her beautiful smile disappeared with his news this morning. It seemed he had taken four giant steps back in his progress with her. Then he remembered the kiss. She had taken his breath away in one simple act. It seemed desperate and yet very passionate, like she was trying to say everything inside her head with one mind-blowing kiss. She was tough, but kept that shyness that was so contradictory. He loved it when she blushed, which was often.

Chance was definitely still worried about his news and he tried to reassure her by taking and holding her free hand while she drove. She stayed silent, but passed him a smile that didn't seem to reach her eyes. He gave her hand a squeeze and said, "I'm so sorry babe. I know I dropped a major bomb on you this morning. I hate this more than you know."

Chance didn't reply and Sylas didn't know how to fix it. He noticed Chance's demeanor this morning. He could tell right away that she was ready to bolt. She calmed down quickly enough, but now he was worried about telling her the rest. She was definitely a runner and Sylas wasn't sure how to handle it. Would she run when or if this situation went bad, or would she stand and fight?

Sylas wasn't sure what exactly triggered her flight response, but he made a silent vow to watch Chance more closely. He wanted to learn all the special nuances of this human woman he was falling for. *How do you tell someone you barely know that you live to make her smile?* Then, to take that beautiful smile away with mere words? It was nothing short of hell on earth.

Chance reached the edge of her property and pulled to the side of the main road. Everyone took advantage and got out to stretch their legs. From here on out they would be four wheeling into the center of the property. "If you need to make any calls, do it now. No cell coverage once we get over the first rise," she told them while calling the dowser. Sylas took the time to talk with Jack out of earshot.

"I think I've taken us back to square one, Jack. I may have broken any shot I had for us as a couple and it honestly worries me."

"Then you aren't looking close enough, Sy. She still looks at you like she did before the news. You worry too much over nothing."

"I'm new at this, Jack. Right when I think I have it figured out, I'm at a loss again."

Jack laughed and put his arm over his shoulder in a quick bump man hug. "That, my friend, is called a woman. They'll always leave you guessing!"

Chance walked back and said the dowser was just down the road. They would wait on him and then head into the property. She told them Rick was already here and waiting, pointing to a white rock with an arrow pointed away from the road. "That is the signal we came up with that lets us know someone is here. Last person out, turns it around to point at the road."

"Ingenious idea, Chance! I'll have to remember that one next time I get an urge to build again." Jack laughed and shook his head as if there was a bad memory to clear away.

A Jeep that looked like it had been through several wars pulled up in front of them. The man who stepped out was tall and lanky with long silver hair, worn loose and it framed his tanned and weathered face. First glance told you he was American Indian. He smiled a gapped-toothed grin and waved as he walked up. He reached out to shake hands with Chance first. "John Littlecreek, and you must be Chance." He pulled her hand up and gave her a quick peck on the knuckles, before turning to shake hands with him and Jack.

The handshake was firmer than Sylas was expecting and he held it longer than necessary. John looked at them both dead in the eyes, and his expression spoke volumes. He seemed to know what they were and it shocked Sylas. Chance introduced them and then explained there were no roads into where they were headed. John smiled and turned to his Jeep. "That's no problem. My Usdi will get me there just fine."

Everyone piled back in to their respective rides and followed Chance in. Sylas was impressed with her choice to buy this property. It was raw and beautiful. Nothing was cut down and it was loaded with older hardwoods, a rarity this far north. It appeared some of the oaks were quite ancient. Her choice to build in the center was smart. No one from the main road would be able to see her home since it was very hilly and hidden from the main thoroughfare. Chance drove through several small gullies and over several hills before he spotted the build site.

Rick was leaning against his SUV with what looked like sketches in his hands. He finally looked up and waved as they drew closer. Chance pulled to a stop at the top of the rise and Sylas immediately knew why she'd chosen it. It provided a three hundred and sixty degree view of the entire property and you could see the rise of the Smoky Mountains off in the distance to the northeast.

Chance again made introductions once everyone gathered together. She explained to Rick that he and Jack were there to add input. John had already wandered off; his dowsing sticks ready in his hands. Sylas glanced at Jack and could tell he was concerned about the Indian too, but now was not the time to discuss it.

They spent the next three hours pouring over and discussing Rick's plans. They changed a few things but needed to wait until John came back before they could complete them. He finally came back about 30 minutes later. He was wearing a huge smile for Chance and she took it as a good sign.

"You have lots of natural springs and underground systems here, Uweji Agehya, which means beautiful daughter in my language. The Mother favors you and your land. It stands unchanged and unbroken, like you." He glanced with a quick frown at Sylas when he said the last sentence. "I have marked your springs and underground waterways with markers you will recognize. I also have a gift for you. Please excuse me, I'll return in a moment."

Sylas glanced again at Jack and he just shrugged at him. This was starting to concern him but he didn't show any outward discomfort with Chance standing next to him. John returned, holding a necklace in his hand. It was made of turquoise and silver, with a pendant in the shape of a wolf. He placed it around her neck and explained its meaning to her, but he was clearly speaking to all of them.

"This is a powerful amulet that will protect you from anyone meaning you harm, Uweji Agehya. You are one of us, of the Nation. Your ancestors walked here many years ago. I have seen animal sign here. There are many tracks in this forest and they are not all friendly. There are predators here, Uweji Agehya, and it would be wrong to not warn you."

Chance thanked him and he said his good byes. Sylas noticed right away that Chance was trembling and stepped closer to lend her warmth and support. She glanced up and smiled. This time it reached her eyes and it melted his heart to see it. She stepped in closer and wrapped an arm about his waist. He could tell John was unhappy with their little show of affection, but didn't say anything.

John explained he would come back and teach Chance the ways of her people after she settled in. "Wait, how do you know I am of the Nation, John? I don't know my parents."

Sylas held back and bit his tongue to keep quiet. He wanted to know more as well, but this was not his time to pry. Chance had more to tell, but he could wait.

"All will be explained to you in due course, little one. When you get as old as I am, you just know these things. I will be seeing you soon, Uweji Agehya."

John turned to Sylas and gave him a warning look. He motioned for Sylas to follow so he would not be overheard. "I will be watching you, immortal one. Make no mistakes with this one. She is a precious star of my people and I will not see her harmed in any way. Understood?" Not waiting for a reply, John walked to his Jeep and left, leaving Sylas standing there shocked and stunned.

Jack walked up behind him, placing one hand on his shoulder. "You okay, Bro? You look like you just saw the grim reaper."

"He called her the star of his people and he knows who we are, Jack. I don't know how, but he knows."

"Shit, Sy, he knows who we are? I'm speechless."

Sylas rolled his eyes at his last comment. "You're never speechless, Jack. I think this could be a good thing. Now we have more than the two of us watching out for her. I have a feeling he will not be far away, ever."

They walked back and discussed the rest of the plans that included the water lines. Jack suggested she add a mill to the stream that was beyond the next hill, since it was always good to have another power source. Chance remembered the area was considered tornado alley and made last minute changes to the plans to include steel reinforcement beams to the buildings above ground.

Rick left shortly thereafter. Everyone was starving by this time, so Chance led the way to a small meadow full of spring flowers over the next rise. Sylas went back and drove the Jeep in so they would not have to make multiple trips. Sylas shook out a large blanket, while Chance made herself busy setting out the food and drinks. "This didn't take as long as we thought it would, but it will still be dark by the time we are ready to leave. Anyone want to over night it?" Jack mentioned between bites of his sandwich.

Chance passed on a sandwich and was picking at some cheese and crackers, not really eating. She glanced up and nodded, still quiet. They ate in silence for about five minutes before she looked up and asked, "Did I hear John right? He called me one of his people. What did he mean by that?"

"We were wondering the same thing, Chance. I think we are as confused as you are, but I think he was referring to your looks, since you have such strong American Indian features. I hate to ask, but where are your parents, babe?" Sylas asked her as gently as he could. He didn't want to broach a subject that she wasn't ready to talk about yet.

She looked at him; her eyes glittering with unshed tears. "I don't know. They gave me up before I ever knew them."

He reached for her and pulled her into his lap and she went willingly. She curled into him and he heard a small sniffle. His heart was breaking for her. Now he knew part of her pain and he was determined to repair the damage done, no matter how long it took or how much she resisted it. He loved her, all of her, so how could he not?

Chapter 18

Jack always seemed to plan ahead. He'd brought tents along, and he was right on the money. By the time they were finished eating, it was too dark to navigate out. The terrain here was too rough to chance a breakdown. They set up camp below the rise, between the vehicles, using them and the hill as a windbreak. Chance was mentally exhausted, and apparently on information overload. They built a small fire and sat around it drinking beer and enjoying the peace from the woods surrounding them. No one really had much to say and that was okay. Chance stared at the night sky, lost in the beauty the naked eye could not see from where she lived. The city lights dimmed out the stars, but here you could see all that were visible.

She was sitting between Sylas' well-defined legs with her back against his chest. He kept one arm wrapped around her waist and it felt good, like she belonged with him. He drew one knee up and she rested an arm there, unconsciously running her fingers around and under it. She felt Sylas' breath hitch and his heart rate increase. She stilled her roaming fingers; not wanting to encourage more. She wasn't ready yet. His arm pulled her in tighter and he leaned down and kissed the top of her head. Moving lower to kiss her neck, he whispered in her ear; his breath sending shivers throughout her body. "No pressure, babe. Touching me is not going to make me forget my promise. Exploration is a natural response, Chance. Try to relax and let your fear go. I will never go farther than you want me to, never without your permission."

Hearing those words repeated that she had said only days before calmed her anxiety. Sylas understood her more than she gave him credit for. She felt safe when she was with him, but it was more than that. She felt like she was home with him, and it meant more than all the rest. She looked over and noticed Jack asleep. "Should we wake him so he can get inside his tent?"

"I think he is fine where he is, babe, but you on the other hand, need to rest. Shall we?"

Chance stood up and pulled Sylas up when he gave her his hand. She knew he didn't need her help, the man was all muscle, but it was another excuse to touch him. Contact with him still sent sparks running through her body at the slightest touch. He pulled her back into him and planted a soft kiss to her lips. She wrapped her arms around his waist and leaned her head to his chest, listening to his heart beating steady and strong. She wondered how fast his heart would beat when they finally made love. She wanted him, but didn't trust herself to let go of her fears enough to let it happen. His touch caused her heart to race and his scent made her senses reel.

They broke contact and he bent to check the tent first. She heard him rustling around inside and then he poked his head out to reach for her hand. Pulling her inside, she noticed that he had taken two sleeping bags and attached them together, making one large one. He pulled the top cover aside and after removing his boots; he lay down and patted the spot next to him. She repeated his actions and laid down facing him. Using his arm as a pillow, she curled around him, throwing one leg over his. He leaned over and kissed her forehead. "We okay, babe? You seem so quiet and it bothers me that you seem to have lost your smile. Knowing I took it away is killing me."

"I still trust you, Sylas. It really isn't you. It's all of this. I fear for you and Jack, because you were with me. The gang doesn't scare me, but possibly losing you does. I know you can handle them, but it's not your responsibility to protect me."

Sylas leaned over her, placing his fingers on her lips to stop her talking. "Chance, I know that we have only known each other a few days, but to me it feels like I've known you for years. I waited a very long time for you, babe. There's been no other before you and there will never be another. I know this sounds crazy, but I've already fallen deeply in love with you. You are the light to my darkness. There is more to me than you know. I'm fully capable of taking care of you, and I intend to do so. I am also aware you can protect yourself, but this time allow me to take care of you and this situation. I won't fail you, Chance. I can't fail you, because if I do then I fail myself."

"But…" she tried to get out before he stopped her again with a deep kiss.

When they finally broke apart to catch a breath, he told her "In the morning, Jack and I will show you what I am trying to tell you, Chance. We'll have a training lesson, but I think it'll be you doing the learning. Now, sleep love. It will be a busy morning." He laid back and pulled her in close. His strong heart beat lulling her to sleep.

The next morning, she woke up to the smell of sausage, eggs, and brewed coffee. Jack was already up and cooked them all breakfast. Once they finished and cleaned up the mess, Sylas explained to Jack that it was time for a training lesson… hers. Chance went to her tent and pulled out some comfortable sweats and put them on, along with some tennis shoes. She braided her hair as she went out to get her lesson. Sylas and Jack were waiting for her on top of the rise. "Jack will be the bad guy for this first scenario, Chance. He will come up behind and grab you and I want you to break free, okay?"

She nodded, already in a fighting stance. "Relax, babe. Pretend he catches you unaware. Let him get a hold on you before you try to break free." She relaxed her stance and allowed Jack to wrap his arms about hers. This time it was Jack that spoke. "Now, Chance, break free." She suddenly relaxed completely in his arms and folded her shoulders in towards each other. Her unexpected loose body weight allowed her to drop out of his grip. As soon as her hands touched the ground, she spun and wrapped her legs up in his, causing him to fall backwards. Chance spun free again, rounded on him and dropped her elbow into his solar plexus with all her weight behind it, taking his breath away.

Chance stood up, bouncing on the pads of her feet. "You let me do that to you, Jack. Now get up and stop holding back. I won't break that easy." She beckoned to him with her palm up, wiggling her fingers in the classic come and get it movement. "Give me all you got, Jack. If you hold back, I will go after you twice as hard." She watched him glance at Sylas and he responded with a shrug. "Shrug all you want, Sylas, you're next." She taunted him with a smile that this time reached her eyes.

Jack gave her a good match, but he only managed to take her down twice in what would have been a killing blow if they weren't sparring. It was a full hour before she called Sylas in. She needed this. She was carrying a lot of pent up emotion with no release outlet and she gave as well as she got. Sylas got the better of her in every bout, but she learned quickly from it. Each time they fought, she improved. Finally after three hours of one or the other and sometimes both of them, she relented and called it quits. She was out of shape more than she thought and was breathing heavily. Collapsing to the ground, she lay on her back and grinned from ear to ear. *I may be out of shape, but I think I just showed them a thing or two*, she thought to herself.

"That's a shit eating grin if I ever saw one!" Jack said to her as he dropped down beside her. He was breathing harder than she was. "Remind me to never, ever piss you off, Chance. Although, I do love a woman that has some spunk to her," Jack started laughing when he heard a loud growl coming from Sylas' direction. Sylas tossed them both a towel to dry some of the sweat off, but Chance stopped Jack and then bounced up to her feet. "Come on boys, I have a better idea. Follow me." She led them on a short half-mile trek to the westside of the rise. She got to her destination and only stopped long enough to take off her shoes.

Chance led them to her favorite spot on the whole property. It was a small waterfall with a large clear pool under it. She knew the water would be cold, but not so cold that it would be intolerable. She'd already been in it once since buying the property and it was heavenly. She dove in without looking back and swam up under the falls. She heard two more splashes and knew they both joined her. Sylas came up behind her. She felt him pulling her braid loose from the band. He pulled her back into him and she turned in his arms, wrapping hers around his neck. Moving her hands up into his hair, she pulled his lips to hers. She licked at his bottom lip and then bit it lightly, tugging at it with her teeth. He responded by dipping his tongue deep, stroking at her until she grabbed hold and sucked on it. She heard him groan and the sound set her core on fire. Chance pulled back before she got too carried away.

Sylas reached down and picked her up, cradling her against his chest. She felt the same; it was if they could not get close enough. "This place is breathtaking Chance, but it pales to your beauty. Thank you for bringing me here." She looked up into his glowing eyes and saw the love he held for her and it warmed her all the way to her soul. Sylas let her down and they rinsed off under the falls. When they finished, they noticed that Jack was asleep in the sun on top of a large flat rock. Chance giggled. "He looks like a cat sunning himself. So peaceful and warm."

Sylas chuckled and said mysteriously, "You have no idea how close you are, Chance. Shall we join him?" Sylas picked her back up and carried her out of the pond, sitting with her still wrapped in his arms. He slowly reclined his body, taking her with him. They were wrapped around each other, neither wanting to let go, and they fell asleep listening to the sounds of the forest surrounding them.

The workout and subsequent swim and nap had done wonders for her mind and body. She almost hated leaving, but knew she would be back in a few days. She wanted to map out the drive for the bulldozers, so she could minimize tree and habitat destruction. She also needed to check in with Gus. She was sure he was frantic by now, not knowing what was happening with her. They packed up and left around 3pm that afternoon.

An hour later and they were back at Jack's and the real world came rushing back at her. She needed to go home and get some things. She knew that Sylas would never let her go alone, but this was something that she needed to do for herself. She grabbed a beer and walked out to the gazebo on Jack's dock. She needed some time on her own; they seemed to sense it, and left her alone. She glanced once at the house feeling Sylas' gaze, but he didn't approach her and she was grateful.

Chance pulled out her cell and dialed Gus. He was the one person that she really needed to hear right now. He picked up on the first ring. "Chance! Damn it, woman! Where have you been? Do you not check your phone? I've left you at least 5 messages!"

She stifled a giggle. "Whoa! Miss me that much, Gus? I'm fine, but I did warn you I would be out of cell range a lot. I really don't pay that much attention to my phone. Forgive me?"

"Forgiveness only comes when you explain to me what is going on, my sister from another mother. You gave me a butt load of cash, a list and nothing else. Now 'fess up or you shall feel my nerdy wrath!"

This time she could not hold the giggle in. "Shit, I've missed you something awful, Gus. There is much to tell and I can't spill all the beans yet. The long story short version is I won a recent and really large lottery. I haven't told anyone how much I won and no one at work knew about it. I have someone, well, make it two someone's I want you to meet *and* I want to show you something special. You down for a small adventure?"

"You know I am, Chance. By the way, I looked up pricing for everything on your list. The money you gave me is almost enough and I can cover the rest until I see you. Just so you know, you will need someone other than my awesome self to install some of this stuff."

"Find someone you trust and have them on standby, Gus. I won't be ready for installations for another month or so. You'll know why in a few days. Love you, brother-not-mine." They ended the call and she felt much better for having made it.

Chapter 19

Sylas paced the kitchen, watching Chance through the patio door. She knew he was watching her, but he didn't care. He needed to find a way to fix this. Sometimes it seemed everything he touched broke and he refused to let it happen this time. She appeared to be okay with him, but it was times like these, when she went silent, that frustrated him. If only he could hear her thoughts… but decided that maybe it was not such a good idea either, at least right now. He longed to feel her passion and her love should it happen. He constantly had to remind himself that she was human.

She exhibited some signs of being his mate, like now when she looked up, feeling his gaze. She always seemed to know when he was near and recently stopped turning to see him approach. Then there was the training. She showed more than enough ability to protect herself. She was able to get the better of Jack in almost every bout against each other. He was still reeling over the 3 solid hours she spent battling them. No normal human being could have gone the distance she did. Sylas made sure she was tested on her endurance and she passed with flying colors. Yes, he beat her in every match, but she didn't know that was how it should be. Yet, she learned and improved to the point that she could maybe best him with more training.

Sylas knew instinctively that he needed to give her more space. He could feel it radiating from her. It was all too new and raw for her and he could feel it. She may not agree to it, but there were some things he needed to take care of and maybe some time away from him would help her cope. Having made up his mind, he walked into Jack's study. "Jack, how are you set for your work schedule this week?"

Jack looked up from his laptop. He appeared to be bothered by something. "I've promoted Sandy, my bartender, to manager. She's a den mate and a puma. I trust her to handle things. I've no need to be anywhere now. Why?"

"I have a few things I need to take care of. Mother has called on me to take care of a situation in Tennessee. There's a bear there she fears will impregnate a human. Not often I get the chance to take care of things before the fact. Plus, I think Chance needs a break from me, even if it is a short one. Should be gone no more than a day, at most. It's an hour there if I fly and I can be back at a moments call."

"You're over analyzing again, Bro. It's not you causing the turmoil, it's the wolves. Her life has been turned upside down and it's eating at her. You didn't see the frustration in her this morning during training? She used it and us to cleanse her mind. She was a new person when we finished. It did her some good to have an outlet for her pent up emotions."

Sylas shook his head. *Women. Would he ever understand?* He still felt the need to give her space. He wasn't sure it was the right thing to do, but he was his parent's child. There was a job to do and he couldn't shirk it for anyone, least of all for himself. "I still need to go take care of the bear. It's not a kill order, just a major warning. I'll tell her I have some legal matters and I will be back by tomorrow afternoon. Watch her for me, Jack. I need her safe."

Sylas walked out to the gazebo, feeling like shit. He didn't want to leave her side for more than a second, much less a day. He watched her carefully for any sign that his presence was unwanted, and saw none. "Chance… baby." His words came out sounding like a plea. She looked up into his eyes and he stopped short. Hers were glistening with more unshed tears. Sylas went straight to her. He pulled her up to his chest and stroked her hair. "Shhh, love. It's okay. Don't cry. Tell me what's bothering you."

"If I knew, Sylas, I swear I'd tell you," she hitched between sobs. "I never cry, I just don't. Now it's all I seem to do lately. I was fine after talking to my best friend and then I suddenly felt an overwhelming sense of panic. You're leaving, aren't you? It's the dream all over again."

Sylas was floored. *How could she know he was leaving? And what dream?* Fuck, there was so much he didn't know about her and he wanted to know everything, like… yesterday. "Baby, I am not sure how you knew I need to leave, but I swear to you now I will be gone less than a day. I'm coming back to you, baby girl. I have a few legal matters to attend to, and I'll be back as soon as I'm done. I could never leave you, Chance. I know you don't believe or understand this, but you are the other half of me. I couldn't walk away from you, even if I wanted to and I don't."

She reached up and pulled him in for a life-affirming kiss. God, he wanted her. He wanted to lay down with her right now and make love to her for hours. She always tasted of honey and wine and he knew she tasted that way everywhere. Sylas wrapped his hand in her tresses and pulled her head back with it, exposing her neck. He skimmed her sensitive skin there with his teeth. Moving down to her shoulder, he latched on, suckling the muscle he knew would send shivers down her. He was careful to keep control. Now was not the time for his fangs to extend, even though he wanted to more than life itself. He wanted to mark her as his, but until he knew this for certain she was his mate, he couldn't. The leopard within growled with frustration.

Chance moaned as he lingered there, warring with the beast. Finally his inner-cat relented, but he didn't. He gave her small nip, unable to resist the temptation. There would not be a permanent mark, just a small reminder to her that she was his. The bite seemed to fuel something inside her. She grabbed his hair and pulled him back down to her shoulder, almost as if she wanted him to mark her. He resisted and instead placed a kiss over the bite. He hadn't drawn blood. It would be a huge mistake on his part. He and the beast may not be able to resist her demands if he broke the skin.

Sylas moved his lips back up to her mouth, invading her with his tongue. He wasn't sure how long they stood there, as time seemed to stand still. His hands roamed down her back to her beautiful heart shaped ass. Cupping each cheek, he pulled her into him; his desire for her was obvious. His right hand roamed lower to pull her leg up and she didn't resist. He was throbbing for her, but he would not take this farther than she was willing to go. It felt way too good to rub his cock against her mound. He moaned into her mouth and stopped before he was unable.

Sylas closed his eyes and just held her. She had to be his mate. He could not imagine ever loving another. Chance owned him, heart and soul. Her head was pressed against his chest as if she was listening to his heart beating, and it was racing just for her. Finally he dropped her leg and pulled back to look into her eyes again. He could almost swear her eyes were starting to glow, but he put that off to his overactive and undersexed imagination.

"You okay now, love? I won't leave until we've eaten and you've gone to sleep. Will that make it easier for you?" Chance nodded and he took her hand, kissing it. They turned to watch the sunset, still holding each other and then walked back in the house to cook dinner. Sylas poured all three of them a large glass of Merlot, since Jack was cooking steaks on his indoor grill. Sylas made Chance sit and watch, insisting that they could handle dinner. He made them a quick salad, to go along with some baked potatoes and began to sauté some baby Portabella mushrooms in butter and onions on the stove.

After eating their late dinner and quick clean up, they all moved into the living room to watch a movie. Sylas wasn't paying attention to it; he only had eyes for Chance. He watched as she relaxed into him and he sighed. It felt good to have her there with him. She was leaning into him; her head on his shoulder and her free hand was resting on his chest, over his heart. It was almost like she was checking to make sure his heart still beat. It warmed him to know she cared that much.

Too soon the movie was over. Sylas noticed Chance started to yawn and took his cue. He pulled her up and walked with her to their room. This time he insisted that she change for bed. He would not be there for her to feel uncomfortable. She went into the bathroom to shower and change. When she came back out, Sylas took her brush and sat her on a chair he moved to the end of the bed. Gently he pulled the wet strands loose from the towel it was wrapped in and brushed it out for her until it was nearly dry. "A girl could get used to this, Sylas Taiken. Better watch out or you might be in for more than you bargained for." He chuckled after she said it, relieved that her sense of humor was back.

"I could do this for hours on end, Chance Cadens. Maybe I'm not the one that needs warning."

He chuckled when she turned to give him a light slap on the arm. He stood up and pulled her with him. She was wearing an old t-shirt and some shorts that looked like boxers. When he looked closer he realized she *was* wearing a pair of boxers... his. "You look quite sexy in those, babe. Remind me to buy *us* some more." He winked at her and she wrapped her arms around his waist. "It's debatable, since I have yet to see you in yours. I also prefer commando under my clothes, so I borrowed these to cover up." She reached up on her tiptoes and planted a kiss to his cheek. "Tuck me in, Sylas, and promise me I will see you by tomorrow afternoon or I'll not let you go."

"I promise, love. There is nothing in this world that can keep me away, I swear it." Sylas sealed his promise with a kiss and then led her to bed, tucking her in under the covers. He rounded the bed to the other side, took off his boots and joined her. He already promised not to leave until she was asleep and he was keeping it. Pulling her into his chest, he spooned her body with his and waited for her to sleep. Once her breathing evened into a steady rhythm, he eased out of the bed, picked up his boots and left the room. He glanced back one more time to make sure she was still out. She looked like an angel lying there. She wore a slight smile on her lips and her hair was fanned out around her like wings. He took that memory with him when he left; he would need it to get him through this day.

Chapter 20

She watched him from under her lashes when he turned back to look at her. It made her heart flutter to see the love for her in his eyes. She was starting to fall for him too and it surprised her. She never thought she could feel this strongly for a man, but she did and she actually found that she liked it.

Chance waited until she heard the Harley start and move off into the distance. Once she knew Sylas was gone, she dressed readied herself quickly. This time she dressed in leathers. Her special boots and duster finished off the look. She quickly braided her mane, took one last glance in the mirror and pulled open the door to her bedroom. She didn't see Jack anywhere so she quietly left the house. She waited to start the Jeep by letting it roll down the incline as far as she could before cranking it. She needed to go home alone and with Sylas gone, this would be her only time to do so.

An hour later and she was unlocking her front door. Chance walked out to her mailbox and grabbed her mail, checking it as she flipped on the lights. She remembered what Sylas said and made sure the front door was locked behind her. This needed to be a quickie and she wanted to get back before Jack woke up. After checking all the rooms, she sat down for a few minutes to pay bills and check her balances. When she found all in order, she moved to her bedroom and pulled out her suitcases. She filled them with everything she might need in the next few weeks, and filled an overnight backpack with her toiletries. When finished she moved all her bags to the front door.

Chance decided last minute that she should check the basement. She also wondered about Pretty Boy Sy; hoping he was being taken care of by a good family. She would miss that overly smart dog. All of this nonsense was making her miserable. One stupid pool game and her life changed. The only good part of that whole night was Sylas and Jack. *Well, fuck them and the tricycles they rode in on!* She walked downstairs and took out her frustrations on Bill, the robot. Chance was just about to throw a roundhouse kick at Bill's head when she heard what sounded like a crash, then a quiet curse, and footsteps upstairs near her kitchen.

Chance ran to her light switch and turned it off. She had excellent night vision and could see almost as good in the dark as she could in the daylight. She didn't know where it came from but she was grateful now. She shook her head at herself. *You should have listened to Sylas, dumb-ass. Now look at the mess you're in.* Her heart was racing, not from fear, but from the excitement of a potential fight. *She would show them!*

Chance slowly hugged the wall as she walked up the stairs. She knew every creak and avoided them all. She listened at the door and then bent down to look under it to see if she could tell where they were in the house. It sounded like they were looking in the front of the house and moving her way. She heard him curse again. He found her suitcases. Chance crouched, waiting for feet to appear near the door. When they did, she saw the handle turning and she quickened her breathing. Her adrenaline was at full peak.

As soon as the door opened, Chance shot up and punched him as hard as she could in the nads. He folded over when the unexpected punch registered. She used his forward momentum to pull him over her and down the stairs. He fell ungracefully to the bottom and she followed. The man was still doubled over, but she didn't care. She pulled him up and squared him one right in the jaw with her fist. He fell back but not before throwing a punch back at her. Chance saw it coming and blocked it. The stranger seemed to come back to life and it was all out war. She was suddenly fighting for more than just anger over someone in her home; it was now her life on the line.

Before it was over, they had somehow moved the fight back up the stairs. Furniture was broken and glass went flying in her kitchen and living room. She finally got the upper hand and knocked him out cold. She was bruised everywhere and she was sporting several cuts. One nasty slice did worry her, since it was on the inside of her thigh, but she dismissed it. He was worse. She'd cut his cheek, arms and thighs with her boot knife. Chance was exhausted.

Chance looked over the man out cold on her kitchen floor. None of his wounds seemed to be life threatening, and she didn't recognize him from the bar. She looked at his face, memorizing it. It was almost familiar. In another place and time, she might have found him handsome. Now though, all men paled to Sylas. He had a limp that was pronounced and it was the limp that gave her the upper edge. She'd concentrated most of her kicks to that gimpy leg and it took a toll.

Chance took all of her suitcases and bags out to her Jeep and left, making a quick decision to leave him lying on the floor. Yes, she should have killed the bastard, but today was not the day. It wasn't in her to take a life. She was sure that Sensei was disappointed in her, but she was gone now, and Chance was the one who would have to live with it. She made it about halfway back to Jack's before she could drive no more. She found a motel and checked in, ignoring the stares from the desk clerk. Then she sent out text messages to Jack and Sylas. They were short and to the point.

> "I'm okay. Went home. Biker broke in.
> Big fight. I won. Can't drive anymore.
> Crashed at hotel off 400 in Alpharetta.
> Don't worry. Be home later. Chance."

Chance stepped into her room, dropped her bags and headed for the shower to wash away all the blood. Most of it was his thankfully. At one point he pulled a knife and struck her twice with it. The cuts would have been to the bone if not for her leathers. One was on her inner thigh and the other across her abdomen, with the latter being more a scratch than anything else. It was the one on her thigh that worried her. It had not stopped bleeding yet. The rest of her cuts and scrapes were from punches and flying glass. She got out of the shower and tied a towel around her leg. She didn't have a belt, so this would have to do for now.

Chance avoided looking in a mirror. She didn't want to see what she could feel. Cut and bruised cheekbone and her right eye swelling shut.

It seemed she was asleep only a few minutes when a loud banging started at her door. Chance frowned in her sleep. "Damn it, Chance, open this door right now before I break it down!" Sylas suddenly registered in her head, but she was too dizzy to get up.

"Sylas…can't get up. Get manager, please," she managed to croak out. Chance didn't remember passing out again, but must have since she woke up much later under a different blanket. She cracked open her good eye and saw Sylas sitting next to her and Jack pacing the floor.

"What… what are you doing here, Sylas? How did you get back so fast?"

They both suddenly turned to her and she flinched- hard. Jack had both a look of worry and relief written all over his face and Sylas' was pure anger. Sylas must have seen the flinch because his gaze softened but only a little.

"Baby, you scared the fuck out of me. What the hell were you thinking?"

"I wanted to go home and get my things, Sylas. I needed to do this on my own. And you didn't answer my question." Chance winced as she sat up.

"Jack saw you leave and tried to follow you, but he didn't know exactly where you were going. He sent me a text and I told him where your house was. By the time he got there, you were gone and so was the biker. I think you owe Jack some of his years back, because when he saw your house, he lost a couple. We were lucky to get to you on time, Chance. You've lost quite a bit of blood.

"I'm so sorry, Jack. I really thought I would be okay. Forgive me?"

Jack walked over and sat down on the other side of the bed. He took her hand and pressed it gently to his lips, avoiding her wounds. "Chance, I've come to think of you as a sister. When you took off without saying anything, it hurt to my core. All you needed to do was ask and I would've gone with you. Not as a protector, but as a friend who cares, understand?"

Chance felt hot tears run down her cheeks. She hadn't meant to hurt him or Sylas. She whispered between the hitches in her breath. "Please, I never meant to hurt either of you. This is all so new to me. I've never had anyone other than my Sensei and my friend from work, Gus, give two shits about me. I grew up without a family and no real home. I was moved constantly from place to place and the families I lived with treated me like shit. I was beaten all the time by different people who tried to take advantage of me."

Chance was sobbing now and it was hard to speak. Sylas started to say something, but she stopped him with a look. "I have to get this out or I'll never be able to. I have been on my own since I was sixteen. I emancipated myself from the system and never looked back. I finished high school, worked and paid my own way from then on. I don't know what it is to have friends. I've never had anyone love me or who cared other than Gus and Sensei."

Chance looked back and forth between them. Finally finished she croaked out, "Please don't hate me, but I will understand if you do." She closed her eyes and started to curl in on herself; afraid they would leave her.

Sylas pulled her gently up into his arms. "No one hates you, Chance and neither of us are leaving you. You will never be alone again. You have our word on it."

Chance heard an affirmation from Jack. Sylas talked low into her ear "I love you, Chance Cadens. I knew there was pain in your eyes, but I had no idea it was this bad for you. I wish you felt enough trust to talk to me about it. I can understand needing your independence. Please indulge my compulsion to keep you safe until these bikers have been taken care of. Will you let me do that?" She answered him with a nod. It hurt too much to hug him right now.

Jack spoke up finally. "From the looks of things at your house, the biker got the worst end of the deal. When you've had time to rest and recover, can you describe him to us?" She nodded and started to speak, but he cut her off.

"Not now, Chance. We have plenty of time. We need to get you home so I can stitch up that leg wound. It's been a while since I got to play doctor, and this time Sylas will have to put up with it." Jack smiled at her and winked.

Sylas picked her up and carried her out to the Jeep. He gently put her down in the front seat and then let the seat back a little. He drove her back to Jack's place holding her hand the entire way, with Jack following on his Harley. It never occurred to her to ask Sylas where his bike was... she was just happy to have him back.

Chapter 21

Trey was hanging on by a thread and he knew it. For the second time in his life, he was afraid of dying. There were more than enough reasons to know this woman was the Chance he was looking for. The second it registered that he was under attack, all sanity left him. She fought like a demon possessed and he understood it. When he broke in, he was hoping to catch the person unaware, but it backfired when no one was upstairs. He hadn't expected to be attacked before getting the basement door all the way open and that was his first mistake.

He saw her arrive from an upstairs window when she pulled into the driveway. He left the house and observed her from outside as she moved through her house. Her beauty floored him and found himself lost to it.

The Alpha inside him insisted that he claim her for his own. If he weren't so distracted by the pain of wanting to take her, he would have been more on guard. He still wanted her; the hellcat in her be damned, he would have her and she almost killed him. He was positive when he collapsed she would kill him. He saw her beautiful face through his glazed eyes and she didn't look at him with fear or anger, no; it was curiosity and maybe a bit of guilt.

He hadn't intended to harm her, but she would have killed him if he didn't fight back. The instinct to protect his body took over and she gave him the fight of a lifetime. That solitary fact made him want her even more. She was Alpha material all rolled into one sexy female. How she was human was beyond him. He noticed she was able to fight him in the dark and only immortals could do that. He was betting even the bastard Sylas was unaware of it. Craven could go to hell if he thought he was going to touch this woman, much less get near her.

The thought of Craven pulled him out of his reverie. He sent a short text; one that would keep him at a distance while Trey figured this out. "Have a lead. Following up. Will contact soon with details.

Trey." Having done that, Trey shifted. It was the only way he could heal enough to get to the female, before he lost his opportunity.

* * * *

Craven snorted when the text from Trey came in. He was already aware of what happened. He couldn't stay Alpha by trusting anyone. He put a tracking device on Treys phone and when it showed him stationary for several days, he sent another of the pack to watch him. So the bitch bested him. Craven laughed. She definitely showed promise. He looked forward to breaking the bitch and now he would make sure Trey watched while he did it. Trey was not aware he'd given himself away. In his delirium, he professed his love for her; it was loud enough to be overheard. In fact, this other pack member heard more… a lot more.

So his Beta had his own agenda. Craven was not surprised. He would have been shocked if he hadn't wanted to take over the pack. They were a pack of rogues, it was a given. Constant infighting was another. He was always looking over his shoulder for the next attack from one of his own. Lately there hadn't been any and now he knew why. His pack was expecting Trey to do it and they were waiting on him to make the next move. There was a surprise in store for all of them. When Trey came home, with or without the bitch, he would take him down. He had no intentions of killing him yet, though. He planned on making sure he lived to watch the female die first… then it would be Trey's turn. He would kill them both in front of the entire pack.

Craven was no longer worried about finding the female now. The tracker contacted him. He finished with his job in Canada and was, at this very minute, on a flight here. He would get her first and then call his Beta home. Two birds, one stone. Craven rubbed his hands together at the thought he would soon have the bitch and his betrayer back here where he would take care of them both. *Yes, this day just got a whole lot better.*

* * * *

Sylas paced the floor while Jack stitched up Chance's leg wound. *Damn her!* He'd asked her for one thing and she went behind his back to do it anyway. Fuck, he and Jack both asked her to stay here at the house. She needed her independence and he accepted it. She wasn't his prisoner by any means. It was the sneaky way she went around him that bothered him. He would forgive her though; hell, he already had. He loved her too much to let this come between them. Besides, he was sure she learned a lesson and was sure she wouldn't do it again.

Sylas thought back to her revelation. Now it was all out in the open and his heart ached for her. No wonder she flinched on occasion. She only knew pain from the previous men around her. Love was a foreign concept to her mind. She wasn't even aware of doing it half the time. A raised voice or hand and she would unconsciously cringe. Sylas groaned with the pain he knew was in her heart. He needed to prove to her that love was all she needed in her heart and mind.

"Sylas, if you keep pacing like that I'll never get this finished. She can't stay still because you can't," Jack growled at him while trying to place another stitch.

Sylas looked over at her and saw the blush creep up her beautiful, but wounded face. He stopped his pacing and moved to the bed. He took her hand and held it and felt her squeeze it every time Jack broke the skin with his needle. She still amazed him. She'd not made a single sound through this whole repair job on her leg. How many people could stay silent without complaint? Not very many, he was sure of it. He kept her focused with his unerring gaze.

"Done, and I expect you to stay put and not rip these out, Chance. Let me wrap this and then I will go fix dinner. I'm sure you're starving, hell, I know I am." Jack ran his fingers through his hair in a gesture of pent up frustration.
"No more sneaking around, Chance. If you do, I won't stop Sy from taking you over a much deserved knee!" After he got her reassurance that she would behave and her leg was properly dressed, Jack left them alone.

Sylas was too emotionally drained to talk. He just held her gaze and she let him, not up to talking either. Gently he sat her up and smoothed out her pillows and then helped her to lie down again. He joined her and she curled into him, still staring up into his eyes. She reached out and ran her fingers through his hair and it suddenly felt like mountains had fallen off his shoulders. Sylas watched as she yawned and felt the familiarity of her hand over his heart. She fell asleep and he was once again grateful that Chance was still in his life.

It was so close, too close. If they hadn't arrived when they did, she might have bled out. An artery in her thigh had been almost severed. It was a small prick, but enough to cause a near bleed out. Jack quickly set up a triage and pulled a Macgyver out of his ass and gave her some of Sylas' blood. Being immortal, their blood could mix with any human type. He still was not sure what the side effects would be. This was a first for both of them, but at least Jack knew what to do. They might both be experienced medics, but Sylas was too distraught to be of any assistance. Sylas would be forever in Jack's debt. He had saved Chance's life with his quick thinking and it was done while she was passed out, none the wiser.

Sylas didn't want any more secrets with her. He wanted desperately to tell Chance everything, but vows and his purpose kept him silent. Only when absolutely sure, could he explain things. He never wanted to know this feeling again. To see the woman he loved on the edge of death, well, it gave him a blow he was not prepared for.

Jack finally came back in with some chicken broth in a cup. Sylas gently woke Chance up and she managed to swallow most of it before passing out again. Jack waited to see if she would take more before leaving again. Before he got away, Sylas thanked him again. "I owe you one, Bro. She's everything to me."

"No, Sy, I still owe you. You've saved my ass more than once. Besides, this one's on me. I let her get away before I knew what she was doing. I promised you and I failed you both. Besides, I'd have done it any way. She's brought you a peace I thought I would never see in you. She really is like the sister I lost all those years ago; she means all that and more. Be good to her Sylas, or I might have to kick your ass. She deserves much better than she's gotten."

Jack left the room to finish cooking their dinner. He came back later with plate of food, knowing that until Sylas knew for sure Chance was going to be okay, he was not leaving her side again.

Chapter 22

Chance was hot… more like on fire and she didn't know why. She kept fading in and out; lost between dream and reality. The dream kept coming back, starting out the same but she could never finish it. No matter what she did, she never saw his face. He would disappear into a mist, right after he changed from the big cat. She wanted him, no, she wanted to love him and she didn't know who he was. All she ever saw in the mists were his haunting green eyes, and they burned her soul with desire.

Being a leopard in the dream doesn't concern her. Dreams are never as one would expect anyway. She just wants her man… her leopard man. The dreams at first faded out before they made love, but now since her fight at the house, they are making love before it is gone. They are running and he stops and drops to the ground. She approaches him and runs her head down his body, licking and washing as she goes, marking him with her scent and he does the same. They shift and the new dream sequence begins.

Now he is standing behind her. She can feel his thick shaft poised at the ready, waiting at her wet entrance and she pushes into him, the need throwing away all thought processes. At the exact moment he finally thrusts into her, he bites her shoulder, right over that sensitive muscle with his hands wrapped over her breasts, kneading and pinching her nipples. He stays latched to her, bringing her closer and closer to release with each suckle and thrust. She wakes up moaning and wet because their time runs out before they can finish. She tries to return, only to see him fading away again.

Chance was feverish. She had to be sick to be tormented over a dream that keeps repeating. She kept waking up with her clothes soaking wet, semi-conscious. She barely registered Sylas was there, but knew she wasn't alone. He bathed her from head to toe frequently with a cool cloth. She also knew he changed her clothes several times and didn't care. Chance had lost all sense of time, but the only thing that mattered to her was finishing the dream. Chance was so completely lost in it that the torment of no release was going to kill her, she was sure of it. Being in a constant erotic state was worse than being in hell as far as she was concerned.

Chance didn't know how many days she was out of it. It could have been one or several. The only thing she knew for certain was the pain and it felt like the fire in her blood was boiling her alive. Sylas managed to wake her up to take water or soup a few times, but she didn't want that kind of nourishment. It kept getting worse and she couldn't lie still any longer. Moaning from her discomfort once again, she felt Sylas pick her up and cradle her in his arms. It hurt to open her eyes. Light, if any kind shot arrows right into her brain. "Sylas, please help me. I'm so hot and the pain is too much. Please!" She felt him stand up and carry her into the bathroom.

"Chance baby, can you stand for just a minute, or do I need to call Jack to help?"

Chance nodded, unable to speak or open her eyes. He carefully set her feet on the ground and the cool tiles felt like heaven. He kept one arm on her, while he started the water running in the shower. He carefully removed her clothes, trying not to bring her more anguish. Picking her up again, he stepped into the shower with her in his arms, holding her to his chest. The water was cool and she felt like she was back under the waterfall. Chance sighed as the water helped to cool her blood down. If she was hallucinating, she sure as hell didn't want to wake up now. She wasn't sure when Sylas put her back to bed, but knew the dream was starting again.

* * * *

Sylas knew something had gone terribly wrong. Chance was in a constant aroused state and he could smell it. His inner beast was in an uproar for his chosen mate and he was fighting with it and the panic over her condition. She was running a major fever but there was no sign of infection anywhere on her. This was different and it was scaring him. It had to be the blood he gave her. There was no other explanation for it. She was talking in her sleep about a dream and it sounded suspiciously like his. *Was this the sign he was looking for?* Even if it was, he couldn't take her like this. He needed to be absolutely sure and he wasn't. Besides, he promised he would never do anything without permission.

Able to do nothing but watch was killing him. He kept her as comfortable as he could. She woke several times soaking wet and he would change her and the sheets as carefully as he could trying not to cause more pain. Her state of mind kept his self-control in the right place, even if the beast wanted something else. Chance came first and always would. The shower with her naked had almost done him in, but it was only a brief respite for her. Almost as soon as he put her back in bed, it started again. Unable to stand it any longer, he called Jack. Something needed to be done.

"I was wondering how long it would take you to call me, Bro. I can smell her arousal from here and it is all I can do to control my cat, Sy. You have to give her release or it's going to kill her. If you don't, I can't promise I won't."

"I just need to know if that will help her, Jack, and then you can leave. Scratch that. I *need* you to leave. I don't want to fight you over her, okay?"

Sylas ran his fingers through his hair in frustration. How he was going to handle this and the possible repercussions was beyond him. He would not, could not take her without her being in her right mind, but if he could stop this… whatever it was, then he would do so. He needed to keep his sanity and her virginity intact. Silently he cursed his mother for this one. There was nothing like pushing his limits to the edge.

"From what I've been able to read about this in the last few hours, yes. Giving her a release from the aroused state she is in will stop the process… for a while. It can be days or weeks before it comes back, but it will come back, Sy. I have to warn you. This in no way means that she is or will turn immortal. There are too many variables to count on anything changing outside of what she is now. She's still human, Sy. Just keep that in mind while you are doing whatever you need to do for her. I don't want to lose both of you over my mistake."

Right when the last word left Jack's mouth, Chance started moaning and tossing in her sleep. Her hips were undulating under the sheets and her scent filled the room, stronger than before.

"Leave now! I got this." He growled out his warning to the other male.

Jack wasted no time leaving the house. He heard his Harley crank and roar down the driveway less than a minute after. Turning to Chance, he touched her cheek.

"Chance baby, I need you to wake up for me. Come on love; wake up now. I'm going to help you, but you have to be awake."

Sylas shook her gently as he spoke to her. She responded by nodding, but she couldn't open her eyes. Sylas quickly went to the windows and pulled the shades and curtains. He closed all the doors and turned off all the lights, except the one in the bathroom and he pulled the door shut, so the light was diffused under it.

"The lights are almost all off now. Please, try to open your eyes and look at me Chance."

He watched as she carefully opened her eyes. She was still moaning, and the pain showed in them.

"Chance, I need to know that you understand everything I'm saying to you. Please tell me you are awake and able to comprehend what I've told you."

She managed a whisper between the moans, "You're trying to help me. Please, Sylas, do something. This is… unbearable."

He looked at her pain-racked face and made up his mind. "Chance love, I'm going help you, but I need to know you understand me and I need your permission. I promise I won't do anything other than give you relief. I need you to let me do this, Chance. I can't lose you. May I do this for you?"

"Just make it stop, Sylas. You have my permission…" Chance was silenced by another wave of need. She couldn't contain the pain and the moan was almost a wail.

Sylas wasted no time pulling down the sheets that were covering his precious female. The beast inside was roaring his approval. Sylas took no chances with the beast nearly out of his control and left his clothes on. He kissed her as he moved to lie beside her on the bed. Her hands found their way to his hair and she was pulling on him, desperately trying to pull him closer to her. He reached up and grasped both of her wrists and moved them over her head. Moving down her body he captured a nipple and suckled it. Chance arched her back into him, wanting more and he gave it to her. He finished with one and moved to the other. Her breasts were perfect twin mounds with her hardened nipples poking up, begging for more. As he suckled he felt his fangs extend and he did nothing to stop it.

Sylas almost came when he gently bit down and then licked the tiny drop of blood that rose to the surface. His cat growled in satisfaction, knowing he had gotten away with marking her in some way. Sylas kept his grip on her wrists by pulling her arms down to her sides. With both hands occupied keeping her still, he let his mouth do the rest. He moved slowly down her body, grazing his teeth and licking her, relishing her taste. Reaching her bellybutton, he ringed it with his tongue and pushed in and out, sending her wriggling all the more.

Moving his body lower to the triangle above her mound, Sylas scraped his beard and fangs over the sensitive skin between her thighs, raising goose bumps where he touched her. The closer he got to the honey pot, the more her scent aroused him. His cock strained painfully against his zipper and he used the pain to keep his lust for her in check. She opened her legs to him and wrapped them over his shoulders. He let go of her wrists, knowing that he was already where she needed him. Her hands found his hair again, but this time she was pushing him to her core. He took one hand and slid it up under her to lift her hips up and with the other he parted her inner lips that were soaked with desire. She was hot, wet and ready; he could not hold back any longer. His inner cat was purring loudly and the deep constant rumble just added to her need.

Sylas licked her up and down, lapping up the juices that were already flowing. Honey and wine filled his mouth and senses. He pushed his tongue between those luscious lapped up her flowing juices. Chance raised her hips to meet every stroke. He felt her quiver but she was not close enough. He moved his tongue in and around, staying shallow to keep her hymen intact.

Chance was directing this dance with every moan and hip thrust. Moving up to her nub, he nibbled and suckled it. Sylas felt her legs start to tremble and her breathing quickened. She was so close and he was aching with need. He was trembling nearly as much as she was. He suckled harder and then bit her nub, unable to resist. Chance exploded around him and he with her, but he didn't stop until taking her over the edge several times more. Sylas greedily lapped up all her juices, not wanting to miss a drop of her sweetness. Her taste was like a drug and he was definitely addicted. Chance collapsed and passed out, and he barely made it back up the bed to cover her and lie down next to her before he was out too.

Chapter 23

Chance stayed passed out for another two days before waking and didn't remember much of it. Sylas explained what happened and Jack confirmed it. She felt like there was something they were keeping from her, but for once she didn't ask. She was embarrassed enough as it was. She didn't know what to think. Sylas saw her naked, took a shower with her, and apparently helped her through the transition with her permission. So why could she not pull any of the details out? She was just thankful Sylas was the one who kept her alive by not leaving her side during the whole ordeal.

Chance noticed Sylas was on edge, obviously nervous about something. He would look deep into her eyes, as if looking for something and then turn away, seemingly disappointed. She ached to be able to tell him she remembered it all, but she couldn't and didn't. At least her injuries were almost healed. There were only yellowed marks on her skin from the bruises. Jack had even taken out her stitches already. Was she out that long?

Chance couldn't recall ever feeling this good before or healing this fast. There were some things she kept to herself, afraid it would upset Sylas if she said anything. Like the fact that her hearing and eyesight had improved. Her complexion was amazingly clear, as if her skin was glowing with health. She felt like she was carrying around enough energy for 10 people and it was freaking her out.

Sylas and Jack took shifts watching her while she was passed out and they took turns going to her house to pack her things. The movers were there now with Jack supervising the loading of the moving pod. They salvaged what they could from the fight and cleaned up or trashed the rest. She wanted to be there but Sylas insisted she stay at Jacks for now. Jack was going to store her pod in his garage until she was ready to move it out to the property. Today Chance had called her realtor and explained after she did a few minor repairs, her house would be going on the market for sale. Then she called Rick to do the damage repairs and give her a status update on the build. He told her he moved some equipment in but he was in limbo waiting on permits and her bulldozers.

Chance asked Sylas if he could take her back up to the property to show Rick where to have the road put in. He said they could go in the morning, so she called Rick back to work out a time. She called Gus and asked him if he wanted to come to meet everyone. Gus agreed with enthusiasm, saying he was anxious to see her again. With everything under control now, there was nothing else to do and she was starting to get antsy. She wasn't sure she could take any more of his looks of disappointment and decided to do something about it. Chance took a deep breath and sat down with him so they could talk. She turned to look him straight in his beautiful green eyes.

"Sylas, I know there is something you're not telling me."

Chance held up her hand to stop his protests. "But, I think we have a good understanding of each other now. I know there is something that you want to tell me, but can't. I get that. But since I woke up, you seem to have this disappointed look that is tearing me up inside. I want to remember everything that happened, but it hasn't come back to me yet. I do know this though; I felt safe knowing you were there with me. I knew you were there and it felt right. No matter what else happens, or what I do or do not remember, I felt your love and concern and that truly matters to me."

Chance reached up and held her hand to his cheek and he leaned into it. "I know someday we will have no more secrets. Can we move forward so we can reach that day sooner? I... I care about you, Sylas. I want more from this, but it will take me some time to knock down the last walls guarding my heart."

Sylas pulled her onto his lap, and she heard him sigh. Curling her body into his, she laid her head over his heart. It was her new comfort zone and the sound of his heart beating gave her a complete feeling of serenity. She knew he was struggling with his emotions. She could feel it in the way his arms were wrapped protectively around her.

Sylas leaned down, burying his face in her hair, and whispered, "I love you enough for the both of us, Chance. It wasn't disappointment you've seen, love; it was my need for you to remember. I'll tell you this though… You're mine, Chance Cadens, and I'm yours. I'll never let anyone change it or take it away."

Chance felt electricity course through her body with his declaration. She wondered about the last part, but pushed it aside. It warmed her to him like nothing before. She liked belonging to him and being declared his. She could feel his heart racing and she knew he meant every word. She felt him pull her hair to bend her head back and she let him. Reaching for his, she repeated his action and pulled his head down to hers. Sylas kissed her and then gently bit her bottom lip. It sent fire coursing through her. The kiss deepened, affirming his love for her and it was all she needed for now. They were going to survive this and once again, they were okay.

When Jack arrived back and the pod put away, they talked about going back to the property. Jack said he would spend the day at the bar while they were gone. He had been away a week now and needed to make sure all was kosher there. Chance was disappointed Jack wouldn't be around to meet Gus, but she knew there would be more times when he could. Sylas suggested food at one point and Chance's stomach took that exact moment to growl quite loudly. She had yet to eat a major meal and was starving. They found it quite amusing, that is, until she declared they would be joining her for training after. They both grumbled but didn't fight her on the issue. She suddenly found herself to be the number one priority in this house of roosters and she liked it.

Jack cooked them a hobo dinner out on the fire pit. She'd never heard of this dish before and found it quite satisfying. Who knew that hamburger, potatoes, carrots and onions with just salt and pepper wrapped in tin foil could taste so good. Chance added it to her list of dinners to cook at her new home when it was finished. She kept a whole list of mental recipes filed away in her brain now thanks to Jack and Sylas. Spending time with them was a definite learning experience she loved getting. To imagine how close she came to not meeting or knowing them gave her chills.

Chance finally cajoled them into training mode and she warned them she was feeling just fine and they were not to take it easy on her. This time there were no tests of her skills. She warmed up by taking on Jack first. Krav Maga is total defense against attack and with her mixed martial arts training, she already felt like she was one up on them. She had defense and offense on her side. Now with this new strength and energy, Chance felt she was easing through the attacks, as if in slow motion. Every time Jack went to grab her in different attacks, she was already ahead of him. This new strength baffled her and so she called Sylas in to simulate two attackers.

Her kicks were now deadly accurate and so fast they seemed a blur. There was no dead space between hits now and before she couldn't always control it. Spin kicks felt like she was taking two turns in the air, instead of one. Once she even miscalculated and instead of striking Jack with a spin kick, she actually spun right over his head and caught him on the opposite side. During a break just to see what would happen, she tried to walk a wall, which had evaded her in the past. She not only walked up it, but did a complete back flip out of it, landing in a perfect crouch position to continue fighting. She could not stop grinning or fighting… it was like a breath of fresh air.

The only one who managed to take her down into submission was Sylas. She would make an error in judgment or timing and he would have her beat. They went for a couple of hours this way and she was enjoying it. Jack finally called a time out and went to bring them some water after he got his breath back.

Sylas turned to her with a question in his eyes, his head cocked slightly to one side. "Babe, something is different with you tonight. Are you aware of how long we've been sparring?"

Jack came back at the same moment and handed them both a bottle of cold water. She guzzled a few swallows before shaking her head. "No, why? Is something wrong? Were you both holding out on me? You know that makes me angry."

Sylas laughed and Jack just shook his head. "Chance, we've been out here sparring for well over 5 hours. You didn't see the sun setting?"

Chance felt her jaw drop and clamped it shut. "No way! I knew it was dark but I've never worked out that long, even at the house in my basement. I'm not even winded. You sure?"

"Yes, love, I'm sure. It's been over 5 hours," he said it to her with the biggest grin she'd ever seen. Next thing she knew, she was in his arms and he was kissing the confusion right out of her and she melted, forgetting all the rest.

Chapter 24

Sylas was as close to cloud nine as any one person could be. He was almost positive Chance was his mate; at least as close to positive one could be without confirmation from his mother. The changes since the fight at her house were obvious to him, so much so, he was surprised no one else mentioned it. Granted, he hadn't talked to Jack because they were on swing shifts with guard duty, and Chance wouldn't understand the reasons. He wasn't going to let the little things get to him, like the fact her eyes were still not glowing and she showed precursor signs of shifting. The latter wouldn't happen until they mated.

They spent the night in their usual fashion. Chance under the covers and he on top, holding each other as they slept. His purpose now was to make sure she felt safe and secure with him. To dissolve her mistrust of men was his main focus. Secondary was her memory. He would help her remember… he had to. She needed to know that sex was nothing to fear. He was starving for more, more of her, but he refused to push before she was ready.

After a quick breakfast, they headed up to the property. He would've loved to take her up on his Harley, but the terrain up there was too rough for it. Rick was waiting on them at the entrance to the property when they arrived. They parked alongside the road and conducted the meeting there, instead driving in to the work site. Rick took down her ideas as to where she wanted the driveway to start and end.

Sylas was impressed with her choices when he saw the route would only take down about five of the older trees. They would have to build a bridge over a small creek and ravine, but all in all, she made the right choice. Rick promised they would start in the morning, since he was due to receive all permits by end of day. Sylas wasn't sure how the permits had been rushed through, but the smile on Chance's face was enough to wipe the question from his mind.

Rick's phone rang and he walked away to answer it. While they waited for Rick to finish his conversation, Sylas wrapped his arms around Chance, taking advantage of their alone time. Hearing a car approach, he glanced down the road. A small sports car slowed and pulled up behind Rick's truck. Sylas watched a man step out and suddenly Chance pulled out of his embrace, grinning from ear to ear. *This must be Gus.* Chance quickly walked over and gave him a hug and peck on the cheek. Sylas was surprised to find himself jealous of their friendship and bristled at their familiarity.

When they walked back arm in arm, Sylas tried his best to not show what he was feeling, and was quite sure he was failing to do so. Chance introduced Gus to everyone and by the look on Chance's face, he could tell this was someone she cared for. Even though Sylas was jealous, he didn't feel threatened by him, and that fact set him at ease. He could tell Chance's feelings for Gus were purely sisterly in nature. Gus on the other hand was like a puppy dog around her. He never took his eyes off Chance and that might be a problem down the road.

Walking the property with everyone in tow, Chance showed Rick where she wanted her wind turbines set. The turbines were far enough away from the buildings, that in case of trouble, the towers might avoid becoming a target. The cost to run the power lines underground would be high, but worth it. She also let Rick know she wanted a satellite tower or cell tower, which was Gus' area of expertise.

Rick assured her, and Gus agreed that a satellite tower was not beyond getting done on time and they could possibly place the tower inline with the turbines, so the cables could be buried together. When they got back to the construction site, Gus begged off, saying he needed to go do a repair on a system. He exchanged numbers with Rick and promised to help out once they were ready with the sat tower. He told Rick he already had a crew on standby for it. Chance hugged him and they said their good byes.

Construction would start in less than forty eight hours and Sylas drank in the excitement on Chance's face. More than once she had turned to kiss him, her excitement overflowing. He was happy to see her alive and enjoying this. This was his version of heaven on earth and he would not have it any other way. Chance gave him a small tour of the property, covering the areas they hadn't gone to during the last time they were there. They hiked most of the outer edge and it gave him a better idea about the wolves and if they were in this area much. There didn't appear to be any recent activity since he saw only older tracks.

Sylas secretly hoped the construction crews would keep the wolves at bay. While hiking, they came across two caves that held potential. One was close to her home site and it could be used for the escape route she spoke of. They discussed it as while exploring it. The cave went deep enough and was well enough hidden to serve the purpose. The other one turned out not quite as deep in but would be a perfect hiding place should the need ever arise.

The second cave was well hidden behind a large granite boulder that looked as if it abutted the ravine wall behind it. If you didn't know it was there, you would never see it. He only happened to find it by following an old game trail and his nose told him there was water nearby. He followed the scent and stumbled on the entrance. The inside opened into a large cavern with a deep natural pool of spring water on one side. There was a smaller cave in the back that could serve as storage or for sleeping. If nothing else, he could use it for when he shifted and needed a place to crash when he was watching out for Chance.

"It'll be dark in another hour or so, Sy. Maybe we should head back?"

Chance broke his thoughts into tiny slivers when she slipped up behind him and placed her arms around his waist, pulling him into a tight hug. He turned to gaze upon her face. She looked at him with emerald green eyes he could easily get lost in. Sylas couldn't help but kiss each one in turn, then kissed her lips that were slightly parted in a shy smile.

"I wish there was more time, but you're right, we should head back. I know trying to walk out of here in the dark is not your cup of tea.

Mine either, for that matter. Anything you would like to do, once we get on the road?"

"Not thought about it. Got something in mind?"

They started walking as he spoke, "How about a real date? Maybe dinner and a movie at the cinema… you know, popcorn, candy, drinks, holding hands, and making out in the back?"

Sylas grinned at her and waggled his eyebrows. She giggled, and the sound was like music to his ears.

"It sounds like a great idea. Never been on a date with someone before, I usually go alone when I want to see a movie. I'm glad you asked." Chance blushed as she said it.

For the life of him, Sylas could not imagine how his beautiful girl led such a life. She was beautiful, intelligent, and funny. A great catch and no one before him managed to steal her heart. Was it no one ever tried, or she never let anyone close enough to give it a shot? He could only thank his mother for saving her just for him. The Fate's may have put him on the right path, but the rest was all up to him. He smiled at the challenge set before him.

They managed to traverse the ravine and make their way out. Sylas remembered the rock and turned it in the right direction. Rick had left a few hours before to get his permits. Right as he was standing up to get back in the Jeep, the hairs on the back of his neck stood on end. He didn't see who was watching but he could feel their eyes on him. Sylas growled and scanned the woods across the road. He eased into the Jeep not taking his eyes off the woods in front of him. He hit the bright lights and saw a gray form flash off in the other direction. It was a wolf that ran with a limp.

Sylas pushed his unease away. It wouldn't do to let Chance see him worried. He put a smile back on his face and they drove back towards town. They stopped at a small Italian restaurant Jack told him about once. The pizza was New York style and was as good as he said it would be. From there they went to the theater and watched the new Fast & Furious movie. Sylas was determined to give her the whole teenage experience she'd missed.

Sylas led Chance to the back row and they snacked on popcorn and candy. They shared a drink and held hands. Before the movie reached the halfway point they were kissing. Only his kisses were not awkward and sloppy. They were hot and he was hard as a rock before they were done. Sylas learned her triggers and took advantage whenever he could. One moan from her would send fire racing through his veins. In the dark he could see her face after he pulled back from one rather tantalizing session. Her eyes were half-lidded and they had darkened in her passion. She was chewing her bottom lip and he quickly stopped her by leaning in and giving it a quick nip.

Sylas heard Chance gasp and pulled back to study her face. He saw her eyes spark. It was a tiny spark that faded quickly away, but he saw it. He thought back to the other times he had bitten her, suddenly realizing that she acted the same way each time. Was this what she needed to change? Was it the mix of his blood and the love bites? He couldn't exactly find out the normal way, and as he thought about it more, it could backfire on him. He didn't really have her permission to change her. It was already happening, but she wasn't aware of it. This could either bring her to him forever or send her running in fear.

Sylas would have to take this even slower than he thought. He could not and would not lose her. He took a deep breath to settle his heart and mind. The beast inside was warring with him again. He already knew what Sylas didn't. This was his mate and he wanted her, all of her. Sylas coughed to cover a small growl that escaped his lips. The beast would have her right here in the theater if he let him loose, and that was not happening.

Distracted, Sylas didn't feel his cell vibrating in his pocket at first. When it persisted, it finally caught his attention. He passed the popcorn over to Chance to look at his phone. There were several text messages from Jack. The first had been sent over two hours before. The last was the one he looked at first and his heart stopped.

"Need you"

Sylas grabbed Chance and pulled her out of the theater as fast as he could without raising eyebrows. When they got outside, he rushed faster to the Jeep. Chance must have sensed his urgency because she didn't protest, but followed behind without question. They jumped in the Jeep and he was on the road before he told her Jack was in trouble.

"Got your weapons, Chance?"

Chance nodded and pointed to her boots.

"Good, because I think we're going to need them."

Sylas stopped at the house first since it was on the way, but Jack wasn't there. That meant only one thing. Something was wrong at the bar and it worried him. Sylas scanned the other messages from Jack but they didn't give him any clue to what was wrong. One said "trouble" and the other read "now". Sylas tossed Chance his cell and asked her to send Jack a text asking where he was. She did and they waited for a response that never came.

Chapter 25

Chance kept her eyes on Sylas as he drove. Jack didn't send them a reply and she could see the worry in the deep furrow between his brows. He wasn't talking about it, but she knew it was something to do with the biker gang.

Did they hurt him and was it why he wasn't responding? Jack was like a brother to her and if anything happened to him she would make sure they paid, in blood if necessary. She may not have been able to kill the one in her house, but Jack was family, and that was a completely different issue. She realized she would kill to save either one of them, without second thought. Sylas and Jack were closer to her than anyone, including Sensei. She spent time with her growing up, but never felt the kind of kinship she did with these two men. Gus was another story.

Chance kept glancing down at the cell phone in her hand. She almost had a death grip on it, willing it to sound off with a reply. Sylas was driving like a man possessed, weaving in and out of traffic. She was glad she asked the dealership to install extra stabilizers and wider track tires in the Jeep. They took some corners fast enough to turn over a regular one. Once or twice she felt tires come off the ground, but he would slow enough to let it right itself and she could feel it settle to all 4 tires again. It was extra money well spent in her book.

Sylas turned off the lights about a block from the bar. He slowed down and pulled off into an unlit and deserted parking lot nearby. They got out and she set Sylas' cell to vibrate only and handed it back. She was glad now she had dressed in dark skinny jeans and tank top for the trip to her property. She pulled one of her knives she kept in her pocket, a switchblade with brass knuckles she'd ordered special for her smaller hand. They didn't speak as they moved along the shadows, hugging what buildings were available. Finally, after inching their way forward one building at a time, they were able to see Jack's bar.

Sylas whispered he was headed to the backside of the bar and to stay where she was until he gave her the signal to move. A nightingale call would tell her it was time to go in. Chance watched him move away, not making a sound. She worried her bottom lip after he was out of sight. She could not bear to see him go alone, but knew it was necessary.

Chance glanced at her watch. The bar should still have patrons, but she didn't see any vehicles in the parking area. It wasn't a good sign. She wouldn't be able to move much closer without losing cover. She drew on her instincts and looked for a puddle nearby from the recent rains in this area. Moving to it, she sloshed the water and took a handful of mud and smeared it over her exposed skin. Luckily the puddle was not all red Georgia clay.

Chance heard Sylas whistle and she crept closer. She heard music coming from the jukebox inside the bar, but no voices. She went as close as she could without breaking cover and had just stepped out when the explosion hit. The concussion from the blast threw her back about ten feet into the wall she was standing by. Her momentum slammed her head into the concrete wall and she started to pass out, sliding to the ground. Her adrenaline kicked in and she scrambled up running towards the bar. She screamed for Sylas and Jack as she ran.

* * * *

Craven watched as Chance ran with full intentions of running into the bar, but the bastard Sylas caught her before she could get in the door. She was screaming for the owner Jack, but they wouldn't be able to search for him with the fire still raging. What a luscious little thing she was and he could see why Trey wanted her so badly. The night she sharked him, he was too drunk to notice anything but her curves. When the time was right, he would have her tied up and they could all watch as he tortured and used her.

Tonight was not the night though. He needed to catch them each alone, as these two were too dangerous together. He would need to have the whole pack with him to even stand a chance in hell of taking Sylas down. Sylas Taiken was the most powerful shifter on the planet, and Craven knew better than to go it alone.

Now he had his revenge on the bar owner, and it was one down, with two to go. They'd caught Jack unaware as he was shutting down the bar. It was a slow night and the pack busted the front door in, right after he turned away from locking it. As half of his men set the explosives, the others took Jack to the back office. The orders were to take all the cash and leave him tied up. Craven had taken Jack's cell and sent the text messages, knowing it would bring the Enforcer to him. He just hadn't counted on the bitch being with him.

Craven laughed almost maniacally at the thought of what he planned for Chance. He left them to their fears and drove off, grinning at the thought of fucking that bitch in front of her lover and his former Beta. Trey didn't know he was now an outcast, but he would find out soon enough. The Tracker's flight was due to land any minute, and Craven had already told him he would meet him outside and what car to look for. When the bitch hit the wall, she'd left a blood trail behind. That was better than the scent of her clothes and he knew he would have her before the week was out.

* * * *

"Chance! Chance, baby! It's too late! We can't go in there now."

Chance was fighting him for everything she was worth and he was struggling to keep her away from the bar. She couldn't hear him over her own screaming and the noise from the fire. Something else exploded and it sent them both flying to the ground. Sylas kept his arms around her, trying to shield her from flying glass and wood. He rolled with her to put his back to the danger and felt something pierce his skin. He grunted from the pain and the sound brought Chance out of her hysterics.

Chance quickly scrambled out from under him to see what caused his pain. He heard her gasp, then it seemed she went into survival mode, all business.

"Sy, you have several large pieces of glass sticking out of your back. I can't tell how deep they are. Please hold still while I check them."

Chance found a piece of leather from one of the barstools and
handed it to him to bite down on. None were deep enough to worry
over and Sylas waited while Chance gently removed them. She held
her hand down on the worst cut in an attempt to stem the blood
flow. Sylas heard sirens way off in the distance and worried they
would be found and detained if they didn't leave.

"We need to go now, Chance. We don't need to be found here."

Sylas rushed to his feet and grabbed her hand. Together they ran
back to the Jeep and he pulled out, turning to head north toward
Jack's. Hearing the siren's grow closer, he pulled into a side alley,
leaving the lights off. Several police and fire trucks flew by as they
waited. Sylas listened for more sirens and when none came, he pulled
out and drove away. The only place he could think to go at the
moment was Jack's. He had keys to the house and he needed time to
process everything.

Chance was quiet the entire drive; too quiet. He glanced in her
direction several times. She was white as a ghost and he could see
her chin quivering with unshed tears. He reached over and took her
hand, but she made no indication that she knew he was there. Things
were fucked royally and he knew it was time to end this pack issue
now. *How* was the question of the day, and he needed Chance's help.
She was his chosen and there were no doubts about it now. First
thing to do when they got to Jack's was to settle her nerves and then
contact his mother. He could not take out an entire pack at once
without her permission. Not if there were any innocents involved.
He needed to know who his targets were and only she would know.
He would also drill her about Chance. He needed answers and he
needed them now.

* * * *

Trey followed Sylas and Chance from a distance to a property in
north Georgia, and had actually been tailing Sylas and the other man
since recovering from the fight. He got lucky when they came back

for Chance's things at the house. It made it too easy. He now knew where they were living.

He parked about a mile away and shifted to follow them into the woods. He stayed well back from them and down wind so the Enforcer wouldn't catch his scent. *So his female bought property here... just miles from pack central. Wasn't this just peachy!* His thoughts were loaded with sarcasm. It seemed she went no where without his nemesis. He kept telling himself this would make things easier. Take her and remove him. He only needed to figure out how.

There was a moment when he was watching them from the forest line when he was sure Sylas had seen him. There was no way Sylas would know who he was in wolf form, but now the Enforcer would be watching Chance more carefully.

Trey trailed them again all night. It was boring but necessary. When he saw them leave the movies in a rush, he perked up fast. Staying discretely behind them, he observed the two of them go back to the new house and then leave. Once he realized where they were going, Trey went a faster way there and parked.

Shifting to his wolf, he moved towards the bar and saw Craven issuing orders. Staying hidden he noticed some of the pack members moving explosives inside. Hearing Craven barking orders at the pack, he realized he had already been replaced. He was fine with it. There was his own agenda to meet and this would help him further it along. He heard Craven order them to take the bar owner to the back and leave him there. He could also see the man was unconscious.

Just about then he caught Chance's scent on the slight breeze. They arrived nearly 15 minutes after he did and he noticed they were edging closer to the bar. He couldn't get to her with Craven watching everything. He heard him laughing quietly with the new Beta about something, and he bristled again. It figured Craven chose Ryder as the new Beta. *He's nearly as crazy as his boss is.* He would have to wait to take his former Alpha out, but at least he was on to him now. Chance and Sylas were still too far away to see what was happening inside the bar. As soon as Craven pulled his men out of the bar, Trey went into instant action. He shifted and broke in the back door.

Chapter 26

Sylas pulled into the garage at Jack's house and killed the motor. He rushed to pull the door down and lock it. Thankfully the garage was attached to the house. Walking around to the passenger side, he picked Chance up and walked with her inside to their room. He didn't stop until he got them both into the bathroom. She was mostly catatonic at this point. She hadn't spoken a word and her eyes held a blank stare. He set her down on the edge of the tub while he started the shower. He got it as hot as he dared before he knelt down to talk to her.

He pulled off her boots as he spoke, "Chance, I need you to look at me. I went inside, baby. Jack wasn't there. I didn't find him." She finally looked up at him and the nerve dam broke. She was shaking, not from fear but from the adrenaline rush she went through. Chance didn't let a single tear fall and he was worried she would shut completely down. The changes to her body were almost too much for her human side to handle.

Sylas reached up and tucked a strand of hair behind her ear and leaned in to give her a quick nip to her bottom lip. His canines were needle sharp and nearly painless, and he could extend and retract them so fast the human eye couldn't follow. He covered the bite with a gentle kiss and lick. He leaned back and watched as a tiny spark showed in her eyes and then it slowly faded. It lasted longer this time. The nudge seemed to work as she finally focused on him. "Did you hear me, love? Jack wasn't there."

"You're sure?" she croaked out. Her voice sounded horrible and it was no wonder. She screamed for them both and then later for Jack for quite a while.

"I'm positive, love. I looked everywhere I could. When I saw the explosives, I got out. The whole place went up just seconds after I got out the door. Then I heard you scream and I came to get you."

"I thought the explosion killed you, Sylas. I... I thought I lost you both." She reached out and pulled him in for a breath-stealing hug and buried her head in his chest.

"I promised I wouldn't leave you and I meant it, Chance. Now let me help you into the shower. I need to check you for wounds. May I help you, love?"

Chance didn't give it a second thought and nodded. Then she looked up, her eyes wide. "You were hurt! The glass!"

"I'm okay, Chance. The cuts were not that deep. It's you I'm worried about." Sylas helped her undress and then checked her for injuries. He noticed blood in her hair and parted it, only to find the cut already healed. He nudged her into the shower and promised he would be right back.

Sylas went into the kitchen and poured them both a large glass of wine. He downed his in one long thirst quenching pull. He poured another glass full and then with both glasses and bottle in hand he walked back to the bedroom. His nerves were on edge. He needed to talk to his mother, but was too angry right now. He needed to calm down more for that conversation. He looked up when Chance came out of the bathroom and couldn't help but sigh at the sight of her in nothing but a towel. He flashed back to the last time he saw her this way. He needed to bury himself in her, but this was not the time. She had to trust him enough to let him into her heart, and to want him with her always. He still wasn't sure if he could win her heart in time.

"I left the water running for you and I want to see your back, please." Sylas was stunned. How was he to explain away the healed skin on his back? She didn't give him any more time to think it over. Chance walked over to the bed, climbed up behind him and pulled his shirt up. She didn't say anything with words. Her fingers did all the talking. Sylas felt her fingers roaming the pink skin where the cuts were already healed. Then they roamed over other marks on his back, and he heard her sigh. She put her hands on his waist and turned him around to face her. Sylas watched her face as she examined his chest and arms.

"Sylas, I need to know what is happening here. You've told me there was a secret you couldn't tell me, but after tonight I think I have a right to know what it is. I trust you and Jack with my life, but there is something here not quite right. No one heals this fast." Chance pointed to her exposed leg and motioned to the scorch marks on his arms, where he was burned by the explosion.

"I'm falling in love with you, Sylas, but..."

Sylas didn't need to hear another word. He stopped her by pulling her into his chest. "I'm going to tell you everything, baby. I promise. I need to talk to someone first. Give me enough time to do that, please? It won't take long and then you will know everything."

"Wait, Sylas. Please hear me out?"

Reluctantly he pulled back, but she didn't let him get far. She had a grip on his waist that said he wasn't going anywhere. "I'm all yours, love. Go ahead and say what you need to, but it won't change how I feel about you."

"You're reading me wrong, Sy. When that building exploded tonight and I thought I lost you, it changed me. I couldn't imagine my life without you in it, or Jack, for that matter. That defining moment is when the last of the walls around my heart gave way. I knew it in that single moment of time, Sylas. I care more for you than anyone before in my lifetime. I felt love and it shocked and scared me. I don't know your secret, but I will tell you this: My heart and trust are yours. You could be an alien from another planet and I could care less. I will follow you to the ends of the earth and back, Sylas Taiken. All I ask for is time to let that love blossom into something more than it is now, okay?"

"Chance Cadens, you already know my feelings for you. I'll do my best to give you the time you need, but time may not be on our side anymore. Let me take care of you for now. I need to talk to someone and I need to do it before morning." Sylas could tell his words confused her, but she stayed quiet, content to be held by him. Sylas picked her up and sat down with her in his lap, his back against the headboard. He reached over to the nightstand and handed her one of the glasses of wine.

Just as he had done, she downed it in one long drink. Sylas chuckled and refilled it for her. He sat with her until she yawned. He stood up again with her in his arms and pulled back the covers. He laid her down, took her glass, kissed her forehead, and tucked her in.

"I'm taking my shower now. Sleep love. We're safe for the moment. After I make my call, I'll join you, okay?" Chance was asleep before she finished nodding.

Sylas took his shower with the door standing open. He wasn't comfortable enough to close it and not be able to see Chance. Her safety was still his top priority. As he washed away the blood and grime, he racked his brain trying to figure out where Jack might be. His scent was in the bar, but Sylas was only able to track him to his office. There were too many other shifter scents mixed with his to track him after that point. Once he saw the explosives in the kitchen, he bailed. His only thought in that moment was to get to Chance. Even now, he couldn't get over how close he came to losing her. She would've run headlong into the fire without a second thought if he hadn't reached her first.

She loved him. He ran her words over and over again. It was the sign he longed for and now he needed to make absolutely sure she was the one. He felt confident his mother would confirm her as his mate. Once she did and gave her permission, he would tell Chance everything. He wanted no more secrets with her. He knew her secrets and he hated not sharing all of his.

Sylas stepped out of the shower and wrapped a towel around his waist. He yearned for the time when he could slip into bed with her and feel her naked skin sliding against his. Sylas pulled out some old sweat pants and slipped them on. Taking another quick glance at Chance, he went to Jack's office to call his mother. He rounded the office door and found her already there. She was beautiful, with long golden hair draped over her back and shoulders. Dressed all in white in a Grecian styled dress and sandals, his mother stood as tall as he did. She had a regal air that made her seem taller. This time she didn't bother with hiding her presence, but she still glowed golden in the light.

"I have heard your pain, my son. I am here for you." She reached out a hand and brushed back an unruly lock of wet hair from his face. Sylas felt her love radiating through her touch and all at once he felt calm and peaceful.

Sylas lingered in her touch, pulling her hand to his cheek; kissing it before letting go. "Mother, I need to know for sure. I love this woman with everything I am. She is already changing into an immortal. Please tell me she is my mate."

"Yes, Sylas, she is the one. I could no longer bear your pain and loneliness. I chose her for you when she was a baby and have nurtured and followed her throughout her life. I could not interfere with what was already her fate when she was younger. She has been through much more than she has told you, but those trials are what made her your equal. She *will* be your equal, son. She was not made to follow you, but to walk beside you. I need to warn you, Sylas. You can not mate with her now. Her changes are not complete. If you do, it could kill her. Her human body would not be able to withstand a complete change all at once."

"Tell me what I must do. Things here have gotten out of my control. This rogue pack and their leader are hell bent on killing her. I can't let that happen. I need to know whom I can target and who are the innocents."

"Craven is your primary target, son, and his new Beta. The rest are innocent in all this. Craven thinks they are his pack and they are not. His old Beta has a different fate and must not be touched."

She looked up, her face going blank for a moment. "I must go soon; your father is calling me. Chance must be turned slowly, son. You already know the trigger to her change. When she is ready, you will know it without question. She will dream tonight and it will help you explain all of this to her. She will wake with questions of what you are, so be prepared. The rest is up to you. Chance is my gift to you, Sylas. Love her always, as I love you."

His mother reached out to touch his face one more time as she faded away.

Sylas walked back into the bedroom to look upon his mate. She was everything a man could hope for. Strong, willful, stubborn, loving, caring, and last but certainly not least, beautiful. Her attributes were perfect for him. They would have forever together and he knew the years to come would never again be boring with her at his side. He crawled on top of the covers next to her and pulled her to him. He wrapped his arms around her in a possessive gesture and smiled as she sighed contentedly in her sleep.

Chapter 27

The dream starts again. Chance is standing in a dark green forest in leopard form waiting on her mate to join her. He pads up behind her purring and bumps his head into her shoulder, rubbing along her. She can feel the rumble coming from his chest all through her body. It stirs her to purr back in contentment. She wraps her tail over his back in a loving gesture. He nudges her and takes off running into the misty forest. She follows him and they run and play along the forest floor. He swats at her, claws retracted, and she dodges him. Sometimes she runs ahead and hides, pouncing on him as he flies by. He always finds her though and she him. His scent is strong in the air. He smells like spice and fresh air full of forest pines and it is intoxicating.

Chance knows this dream and doesn't want to dream it again. It always ends the same. She never sees his face and she dreads the pain of him leaving her alone. But the dream has changed, she suddenly realizes. The wolf joins them, but only stays briefly, then fades away and they don't hunt. She is slightly confused and more than a bit lost. Why didn't the wolf stay this time?

Chance pads over to a small break in the trees. The clearing is covered with wild flowers and the scent is wondrous. This is new, she thinks to herself. She looks around for her mate and he isn't anywhere she can see. Chance wanders into the center of the clearing with her nose down, letting the flowers and grass tickle her whiskers. She lies down and rolls in them, enjoying the smell of the petals as they are crushed against her fur.

She hears him before she sees him. He pads up to her purring again. He bumps his head into hers and then sits down on his haunches to look at her. His purring increases in volume and its mesmerizing. Chance watches as his green cat eyes, those eyes that she loves, change. They change into the eyes of the human she loves. As she watches, her mate morphs into Sylas. He stays still watching her reaction. Chance gets up and walks to him, unafraid. She bumps her head into his chest in greeting, purring as she lies down on his lap.

He reaches down and scratches under her chin and she knows she is home.

* * * *

Sunlight poured in from a part in the curtains and the brightness and warmth wake her. Sylas is at her back, curled around her. Chance can't help but move closer so she can feel all of him against her body. She feels protected by the arms that are closed around her, one as her pillow and the other wrapped possessively around her waist. Closing her eyes to enjoy the moment, Chance wishes for this moment not to end. The real world would be crashing in too soon as it was. She hadn't felt this content in far too long.

Chance remembers snatches of the dream. It changed, but it all wasn't quite there in her head. She hated when she would dream and then have it start to fade almost as soon as she woke. She must have stirred in her frustration trying to remember, because Sylas pulled her tighter into his chest.

"Morning, beautiful. Sleep well?" His breath tickles her neck as he plants butterfly kisses down it.

"Yes, for a change, I did. I feel wonderful." She turned her body to look at him and when she saw his eyes, she remembered the dream. She must have had a shocked look on her face, because Sylas was looking at her strangely.

"What are you thinking about, Chance?" Sylas started to pull away, but she stopped him with a hand on his arm.

Chance thought about the dream. She wasn't sure if it was real or just an overactive imagination. She thought about all of the things happening over the past couple of weeks. It just didn't add up in her mind. Her body was changing. She healed in hours; she had more stamina and strength. Sylas' eyes glowed and he was able to beat her in their training sessions, and she was a fourth degree black belt. Then there was the leopard in her dreams and Pretty Boy Sy, both with his eyes.

"Chance?" She looked back at those eyes and recalled what she told him the night before. She didn't care if he was from another planet, but she knew she loved him and wasn't going to lose him. There was a definite need to know and now.

"Sylas, did you make your call last night? I think there is something going on here you need to tell me about."

Sylas sighed. He leaned his body into hers and kissed her as if his life depended on it. Whispering over her lips, he said, "Chance, I need you to remember first and foremost I love you with all that I am. I need you to keep an open mind and promise me you will let me finish before you say anything. Can you do that for me, baby?"

Chance looked at the sincerity in his eyes. She sat up and moved to the edge of the bed away from him, suddenly afraid. "Am I going to need a drink for this Sylas? Right now, to be honest, my mind is stuck in overdrive. I want no more secrets and I meant what I said, I love you no matter what you tell me. I can't help feeling scared, but I trust you."

Chance felt the bed shift as he got up. He walked around and knelt in front of her. The dream flashed in her mind. This is exactly what he did when he changed from cat to man. She felt her pulse rising and she was definitely breathing faster.

"Chance, before I start, how well do you know your Greek mythology?"

"I remember what I learned in school. It was one of my favorite subjects. Why?"

"Then you understand who Zeus and the Fates are?" She nodded at him but kept quiet as she promised. Her heart rate was still up and she felt a shiver run down her spine.
He took her hands in his, pleading with his eyes for understanding. "I'm not sure how to even begin this, but I'm going to do the best I can so you'll understand. As you know, Zeus fathered children with

many human females. He also had affairs with other Gods, creating Demigods. Zeus also had the ability to create some of his children as full-grown adults. Chance, I am one of those children. Zeus is my father and Lachesis, one of the Fates, is my mother."

Chance could feel her body trembling now and she felt the blood drain from her face. She couldn't stand it any longer. "What do you mean Zeus is your father? He's nothing but a myth, right?"

Chance's voice rose almost to hysteria level. She felt like she was hyperventilating, because she could see he was telling her what he believed to be the truth. Chance grabbed the almost empty bottle of wine off the nightstand from the night before. She turned it up and drained it, hoping it would bolster her courage.

"Chance. Baby, please. I'm not lying to you. I'm a Demigod and I cannot die. I am immortal and I was made in the year 1500AD. I am the absolute Alpha of my kind. There is a whole world out there kept secret from humans. There are many of us here amongst you. We are called were-shifters. We can morph or shift into a companion animal form."

Chance gasped with the realization her dream was about to become reality. She stopped him, stood up, and moved around him. She started pacing, worrying her bottom lip while she thought about the implications she was being presented with. Suddenly she turned to him. He stood up and turned, watching her.

"So what you're telling me is a repeating dream I've had since I was a child is real? The dream came last night, but it changed. You were in it. We both were. For the first time since the dreams started I saw you change from a black leopard to a man. I'd never seen your face until last night. In the dream I was your mate and I was just like you. Sylas, I'm human, so explain please!"

"Chance, yes, you're intended to be my mate and will be my equal. You haven't completed the change yet. I know you've seen the differences in your body. Increased strength and stamina. You can heal almost as fast as I do. My mother has been with you since you were a child. She sent you the dreams, Chance. She was preparing you for this day. You were changing before we met, am I correct?"

Chance reluctantly nodded. "I started seeing things a normal person can't. I can also see just as clear in the dark as I can in the light. My hearing increased too. Is that what you mean?"

"That's some of it, yes. You should also have the ability to see what's happening before it occurs, like time slowing down. That's probably why you learned your martial arts to such a high degree, yes?" Again she nodded.

"There is one difference between myself and other shifters. I can be any animal or bird. I am the Alpha over every shifter alive. My purpose, *and yours*, is to keep the balance between the human world and the shifter population. Since you're still human, the change has to take place slowly for you. For one, you're not ready to accept me yet and secondly, if you change too quickly it might kill you."

Sylas pleaded with her now; worried he was losing her. "Chance, I love you. I have since the night I saw you in Jack's bar. I knew you as soon as I saw you. My animal recognized you before I did. I couldn't keep this secret from you any longer and so I begged my mother last night to allow me to tell you now."

Chance felt her eyes get big. "The shimmering woman you and Jack talked to the night of his party here. That was your mother, right?"

"You saw her? She should've been invisible to you. This is more proof you're my mate, love." Chance nodded but her mind was racing, not really comprehending what Sylas was telling her. Another thought hit her. "Jack? Is he like you?"

"Yes, Jack is a puma, but our primary animal is a black leopard. You said you've dreamt of us. Were we running in the forest and playing?" When she nodded affirmation, he continued. "Chance, I've had the same dream for the last 20 or so years. They were my mothers gift to us both."

"The bikers, they're not a gang, are they?"

Sylas shook his head. "No love, they are rogue wolves and extremely dangerous. The man you took down in the bar is their Alpha male and he is an evil and deranged man. He is out for blood… yours. He will have to go through me first, because I will never let him get to you, Chance. I would lay down my life to keep you safe. This is my vow to you."

She stood still, listening to him pour his heart out to her and she loved him more every moment she was with him. Immortal or human, she really didn't care. She knew him and his heart. Somehow she'd known him all her life. Chance walked over to him and placed her head on his chest to listen to the heart she loved. "I've so many questions, Sylas, but I know I couldn't live a single day without you in it."

She felt him sigh; his chest rising and falling with her still leaning into him, it felt deep and cleansing. He relaxed and pulled her closer as if now realizing he wasn't going to lose her. Hell, she didn't know until this very moment either. She put up a decent poker face, but inside she'd been scared shitless. She still didn't understand it all, but for him, she could do anything and she would. She knew she still had issues, but now felt like there was hope for her after all. It was time to open Pandora's box and ask the one question she didn't want to voice.

"Okay, so I am changing. What exactly does that entail, Sylas? I feel like I can handle most everything you throw at me, but to be honest, I still have issues to work out in my head."

"I know love and I hope there is time for us to do so. I know you're not ready for complete intimacy and we can work together to get to that point. The changes have been sped up and pushed forward by a blood transfusion. You received it from me when you were hurt in the fight at your house."

Sylas must have felt her stiffen, because he stroked her back in an effort to calm her. "You were dying, Chance. We didn't have a choice. You lost too much blood. I refused to let you die and Jack did the only thing he could to save you. You were passed out when the transfusion took place. We couldn't tell you for obvious reasons."

"There is one other trigger to your change, love. I wasn't sure until I saw it, but it seems to occur when I nip or bite you. The best way I can explain it is like this… think of your bike. When you hit the kick-start, your motorcycle cranks up the engine. My bites are like a kick-start to your metabolism."

Chance frowned. He had bitten her? She felt him nibble at her lip and once on her shoulder, but she didn't remember him actually biting her. Sylas put his finger under her chin and pulled her face up to meet his eyes. "Close your eyes, Chance, and feel the changes in your body as I kiss you. Focus inward and not on me."

Chance closed her eyes and felt him brush his lips over hers. He pulled at her bottom lip and she felt the tiniest of stings. Suddenly it felt like molten lava was running through her veins. Her body was warm all over and she felt her adrenaline spike. She gasped and opened her eyes. Everything became sharper and then slowly diminished.

"The more I bite you, the longer the change lasts. You will not become my mate until the change from the bite does not leave you. There is one more thing I have to tell you, love. For you to become my mate, my equal, I must be the one who takes your virginity. If anyone else gets to you before I do, then I lose you to that person and their animal. You'll never be able to be with me should this happen. Now you know why I've been so protective, Chance. I can't lose you. I waited over 500 years for you and there will never be another for me, other than you. Understand, baby, I love you. It isn't just about being my mate. It's so much more. You are the other half of my soul. If I can't have you with me… I…"

Chance stopped him with a finger to his lips. "I understand, Sylas, more than you know. You are the air I breathe. Without you, I feel I am nothing." She gazed up at him, willing him to see her heart. She smiled at him and saw his eyes glow darker with passion. They kissed as if there was nothing else in the world but them.

Chance finally came up for air. Grinning like a fool, she said the one thing that had been irking at her since he confessed. "So Pretty Boy, are you thirsty?" Sylas chuckled and panted. "I know we have urgent things pressing in on us, but I need to see it. Show me, Sylas?"

Chance backed away and sat on the bed. She watched the man she loved shift in one smooth progression to a gorgeous black leopard. He leapt onto the bed beside her, sinking it with his weight. He bumped his head into her arm in a show of affection and started to purr. The rumble coming from him was the same as in her dreams. She leaned back against the headboard. He sank down beside her and put his head in her lap. She ran her hands down his back and then scratched him under his chin. "I love you, Sylas, all of you." He licked her hand with his rough tongue as an answer.

Sylas shifted into Pretty Boy for a quick second, which brought a fit of giggles before shifting back to his human form. He laughed with her as he pulled her down into a hug. Chance sobered almost as fast. They didn't have much time and there were a lot of things they needed to figure out from here. If the wolves/bikers had Jack, then they probably knew where he lived. They needed to move quickly and find a safer place. Chance didn't want to think anymore on the bad stuff right now though. She was with Sylas and she felt they could take a little more time to savor this moment, and they did. They kissed and forgot the world for just a little while longer.

Chapter 28

Sylas watched Chance as she packed up her few belongings now that they'd finally come down to earth from the morning's revelations. It felt good to finally offload his secrets to her, but now they had other worries. What to do and where to go was the main topic of conversation. The pack knew where her house was and now, more than likely, knew where Jack lived as well.

Chance finally offered up the only thing that made sense. They needed to be constantly on the move. Until he could take care of the Alpha and find Jack, she suggested purchasing a motor home. She considered getting one anyway so she could live on the property during the build. They would need to move her pod and their motorcycles into storage for now. The Jeep could be used to make short errands and hitch it to the home when on the move.

Chance got on the phone and called in a moving truck to pick up the pod and bikes. While she was doing that, he worked on finding storage nearby and priced it out. She told him they might as well get a large unit and put all of it into one. She also thought that using a climate controlled indoor unit would be best to put off any attempts to get to their things.

The next project was hiring out a security unit to patrol Jack's house and property on a 24/7 basis. He already lost the bar and she wasn't taking any chances with his home. She told the security team to bring a trailer with them for living quarters and gave them an advance to cover all costs.

Sylas insisted he had more than enough money to cover all of their expenses, but Chance was adamant. This was her doing, or so she thought, and she was paying for it. They waited for the head of security to arrive so they could show him the hookups already in place and hand him a key to the house. He was a shifter, so he understood what was at stake. They both stressed the importance of watching out for anyone suspicious and any animals that didn't belong. If it wasn't Jack in human or in puma form, their orders were to shoot first and ask questions later. They gave him a picture of Jack they found in the house and their numbers, should he happen to show up. He had already heard of the bombing in town and was aware Jack was still missing.

Once all was done, they went shopping for supplies and the motor home. The motor home came first. Chance chose one that was road ready and contained all the requirements that she was looking for. She wanted solar, washer & dryer, large refrigerator, and she wanted a regular bathroom with a large shower. Sylas gave her credit; she didn't skimp. She ordered a hitch installed and they drove it off the lot with the Jeep in tow.

Next, they stopped a local club store and bought enough food to keep them both for weeks. She also bought things he didn't think about needing. She took care of the entire kitchen, bed and bath supplies. She even went so far to purchase them spare clothing. Chance used the storage area and the extra bed to keep it all. They would not have to stop again for quite sometime. He shook his head when he thought back to her asking for his help purchasing things needed for her new house. He was definitely outclassed, but he was proud of her.

They found several RV campsites in the surrounding area and chose the nearest one to park for the time being. They spent most of the day organizing and putting things most needed within easy reach. The rest was stored under the camper in the storage areas.

When they finished, Sylas cooked barbecue chicken on the attached storage grill. They dined while talking about what needed to be done first. He took his time filling her in on all the details he was aware of concerning the pack. Sylas stressed to her again how dangerous the pack Alpha was. He gave her a bit of the background on them, which included that they were considered rogues until they hooked up with Craven.

Chance asked if anyone else could be in danger from the pack. He knew where her mind was instantly. She was worried about the construction crew and Rick, since the build was so close to their base of operation. He promptly assured her they didn't want her crew and they would most likely not want to call any more attention to themselves than they already had.

"I can't let anyone else be hurt by this, Sylas. This is my doing and I can't have anyone's death hanging over me. I'd never be able to forgive myself something happened."

"Baby, they might try to stop construction, but they're not stupid. I'm positive they have no idea my mother and I already know they are behind the bombing. All immortals know who and what I am, Chance. They really don't want me on their backs. Little do they know, it's too late to hide what they've done."

"So how do we draw them out? If it's me they want, then I think it's time to set a little trap. Me as bait should do it."

Sylas took a sharp intake of breath at her words. "NO! That is not acceptable, Chance, ever!"

Chance flinched. He regretted yelling within a heartbeat of seeing her cringe. "Baby, I'm sorry I yelled. The thought of him even laying a finger on you makes my blood boil. I couldn't take it if you were hurt again."

Chance stood up, suddenly angry. "Sylas, I may be human now but there is more to me than what you seem to see. I *will* be the bait and you *will* allow it. There is no other way. Until we are ready for this to happen, we will train and you will continue to help the change. I won't take no for an answer. I want to live without fear again. I have no desire to hide forever from this asshole. I took him down twice and I could've easily killed him, but I held back. I won't do it again. You forgot that perhaps?"

"Chance, I can't help my instincts to protect you…"

She cut him off with a huff of frustration and shoved the palm of her hand towards his face. *What the fuck? She just gave me the hand?* It was all Sylas could do to stifle the urge to laugh, but he knew it would only make things worse. *I'm learning Jack, you'd be proud,* Sylas thought while still trying to control the grin trying to creep across his face. He watched Chance pace the floor. He could see the wheels turning in her beautiful head but she was wound-up tighter than a drum. She was gorgeous even when angry.

Sylas did the only thing he knew to do to calm her down. He shifted. He started purring as he moved towards her. He watched as she turned around in surprise. She promptly fell to the floor on her rump when he head bumped her. He'd caught her totally off guard and loved it. He straddled her legs and walked up her body, pushing her completely down. He licked her exposed neck and gave her a small nip before shifting back. She was wriggling under him, trying to escape the now perfect hold he had on her.

She was still miffed but he was about to change that. His mouth descended upon hers, demanding she open for him. Her hands were pressed to his chest in a futile attempt to push him away. As soon as his tongue gained entrance, she moaned and stopped struggling. Her hands snaked up his chest to his shoulders and one continued up to his hair. She pulled him into her as she kissed him back. Next thing he knew, he was on the floor beside her curled up into a fetal position cupping his now aching balls.

Chance stood over him with her hands on her hips. "First mistake you made was exposing yourself by straddling me. Second was assuming you were in control in the first place." Through blurry eyes he watched as she left the room still huffing and throwing her hands up in the air.

When Sylas was finally able to stand up, he walked to the back looking for her. She had taken a shower and was now lying down on top of the comforter, curled up and wrapped only in a towel. Her eyes looked as if she had been crying. They were red and puffy. She was breathing steadily but he was sure she wasn't asleep. Sylas kicked off his boots and lay down behind her. He didn't try to touch her, as he now understood where the attack came from. He had tried to force her to do something without her permission. She didn't move away and took it as a positive sign.

He sighed, and whispered to her, "Sorry baby. I never meant to make you feel threatened. I thought it would calm you, not scare you. I'm here if you want to talk about it." She didn't respond, but he was willing to wait for as long as it took. Sylas closed his eyes to replay the fight. She had caught him unaware and taken him out. She was truly going to be an equal. He knew then and there that he needed to rethink his stance on using her as bait. She was right. There was more to Chance than being human. She was fully capable of handling any threats that may or may not come her way.

A few minutes later she turned around and curled into him. Sylas pulled her with him as he rolled to his back. She rested her head in the crook of his arm, with her hand lying across his chest. He waited for her to calm herself. Chance was shaking from head to toe. Knowing her as well as he did, he knew she was sorting out what she needed to say. When he felt her breathe deep and relax, he braced himself. He knew this was going to help her, but what was it going to do to him?

"When I was in foster care, I was moved to a lot of different homes. Never the same family for very long because of the bruises the social workers or my teachers would find. When I was younger, they hit me for stupid reasons. Sometimes it was because they thought I sassed them, or I didn't do something right or fast enough."

"The unwanted advances didn't start until I was older. By then I was already experiencing a change in my body. I was stronger than a girl should be at those ages. The men... they used to mostly come in the night, drunk or high on something. I would wake up with hands on me in places they shouldn't. I always managed to fight them off. I would scream, bite, hit, and scratch until they would leave. I refused to give in."

"The men never beat me unconscious, but it came close a few times. They would punch or slap me in the face or stomach. I honestly don't know how many broken bones there are in my medical records. One visit to the doctor or hospital with a broken bone would get me moved again."

"It didn't matter though, it was always the same. There was always an abuser in the new house. If they weren't trying to get in my pants, they were making me clean their filth. If the house wasn't just so, I was beaten for that too. Women can be just as cruel as men can when it comes right down to it. I don't know if it was me they hated or life itself. I knew I was different, but why hate me so much?"

"I was just a scared little girl who needed someone to love her. I kept hoping the new house would be different, that someone there could love me. It never happened though and it broke me, Sylas. I guess now I know why I was different and where my strength to fight them off came from."

Chance paused and whispered, "I'm just sorry that you're stuck with such a fucked up and broken mate."

Sylas suffered for her silently as he listened to her pour out her hurt. He wanted to track down each and every person that ever laid a hand on her. He could kill them all without a second thought. When she said the last line, he sucked air in through his teeth.

"You are not broken, Chance. Stop thinking that right now!" He sat up, taking her with him and turned her so she could see his eyes.

"You are smart, talented, beautiful, and street wise, Chance. You are who you are because of them. I wouldn't change anything about you. If I could go back in time, I would so I could stop the tortures, but then I wouldn't have the woman I fell in love with. Never think you are broken, baby. Cautious, maybe, but never broken."

A tear formed and fell, tracing down her cheek. Sylas reached up with his finger and wiped it away gently. "No more tears for something you can't change, love. Those people were wrong, not you. They were the broken ones. I love you, Chance, and we will have forever. I will show you every second of our time together what real love is. Karma always comes back to those who abuse the trust of a child and they will get theirs in the end. In the true scale of time, those assholes are just a blip, nothing more."

Sylas pulled her in for another embrace. He would never tire of holding her. He gently picked her up and pulled down the comforter and placed her back down, pulling it back up and over her.

"Rest baby. I'm going to shower and change. I can sleep in the other room on the sofa tonight if you want to be alone."

"No, Sylas. I'm done sleeping alone. This is our bed, not just mine. Okay?"

Sylas could see the threat of more tears shining in her eyes and it broke his heart to see it. "I'll be back in a few minutes, love. Go to sleep. I will be here with you, always."

Sylas turned and walked back to the front of the motor home. He pulled his phone out to check for any messages from Jack. There were none. He checked in with the security detail and no change there either. He locked everything down and walked to the back stripping his clothes off as he went. In the morning he would have to take another look at the situation with a fresh mind. Right now though, he wanted a shower and to spend the night with the only woman that made him whole.

Chapter 29

Craven sat waiting for the tracker at the airport. The flight was
slightly delayed, and he was waiting for a text saying he was outside
waiting in the pick up lane. This guy boasted the best reputation in
the business. He never failed to find anyone he was asked to find,
and this was what he was counting on. He wanted the bitch chained
up in his basement yesterday. It was all he could do to contain
himself as he thought of all the little delicacies he had in mind for
her. After all, who didn't get off on a little S&M every so often?
Caligula was a pussy when it came to delivering pain in his book. His
little torture devices made the old Roman Emperor look like an
amateur.

He fantasized while he waited. He pictured Chance naked with a
spreader stretched wide between her ankles and her arms chained
apart on the ceiling. He had her gagged, but not blindfolded. He
wanted, no, needed to see her fear. His cat-o-nine selection was one
of the best. He would start with a regular whip to bring her tears and
muffled screams before he moved on to the wired one that could cut
the flesh a layer at a time. He wanted her to stay alive long enough to
have a decent amount of fun, so he would only mar one spot at a
time. He planned on fucking the bitch in front of the Enforcer and
Trey. He would get pleasure while they suffered the pain of being
forced to watch.

Cravens cell finally buzzed with a text. "Out front waiting." He
started his SUV and pulled forward into the pick up lane. He saw a
tall male with silver gray eyes and long black hair pulled into a
ponytail at the nape of his neck. He looked like he was bronzed from
the sun. He seemed muscular, but then he would be. He was a wolf
and they tended to have little to no body fat. He was wearing a black
Stetson, jeans, t-shirt, and western styled boots. He carried no
luggage, just a backpack. He pulled up beside him and rolled down
the passenger window. "You Dakota?" The man looked him over
before nodding. "Get in then, I'm Craven. I've got you a place to
crash and can take you to the spots I spoke to you about when
you're ready."

Dakota slid into the seat and shut the door. "You can take me now.
I'm ready to start. Take me to all the places you know she's been."

Craven grinned. "Just what I was hoping for. I like your no nonsense
attitude. The sooner you bring me the girl, the more money for you.
A bonus if you bring her to me within the week."

Dakota nodded but stayed quiet. Craven wasn't put off by his
silence. It was fine with him. He wasn't much of a talker either. He
preferred the quiet. It gave him more time for his fantasies.

* * * *

Dakota always got the job done. It was his reputation on the line and
it served him well. The fucker who picked him up was clearly a nut
job, but money talked and he was here for that reason alone. He was
ready to get this over with and get home to his wife. She was
carrying his pup and due to give birth in the next three weeks. The
last job was a breeze. The guy he'd hunted owed a casino boss a lot
of money. Needless to say, they took the money owed out of his
hide.

As they rode, he contemplated how much this area had changed
over the years. He was Alpha of a pack here a long time ago in the
foothills of the Smokey Mountains, near where the Appalachian
Trail started. The memories almost brought him pain, but he fought
it back. That pack and those days were long gone and he'd moved
on with his life.

Moving out to California and then into Oregon was the best move
he ever made. He met his new wife in Cali, and she changed his life
for the better. She removed the pain of losing his previous family by
simply loving him. Now he had a new family, new pack, and a baby
on the way. Life could only be better if he was home, and he
intended to get there by week's end.

Craven pulled up to a small quaint house that had a for-sale sign in
the front yard. He explained they were here on the pretense of
looking at it as a potential purchase. He'd called earlier and set up an

appointment with the realtor. She was all bubbly and smiles when she met them at the door. Craven distracted her as Dakota walked through the house. He caught faint hints of the scent, but someone very smart had scrubbed the place down with bleach and repainted both the interior and exterior. He hoped this guy had something better to go on than this. He shook his head at Craven, signaling this was a washout and it was time to go.

They loaded back into the SUV and about 30 minutes later pulled up to a burned out shell of a building. Dakota turned to Craven with disbelief. "I can track most anything, but you've got to be kidding me! All I can smell here is burned wood and wire. Take me back to the airport, I'm done here."

Craven held up his hand, stopping him. "Hold on, Dakota. I have something here that will take you right to her. Follow me."

He followed Craven to another building nearby and he pointed to the wall. He walked closer and saw what looked like a rust streak running down part of it. He moved closer and then the scent hit him. Blood. He caught the scent of copper and then a light scent of honey and what smelled like dark sweet wine. Dakota narrowed his eyes. *What is going on? Who is this woman?* The scent was familiar but he couldn't put his finger on it. Shaking his head, he turned and forgot it. It was time to go do his thing. There was enough to go on now. Pulling his backpack from Craven's SUV, he turned and told him he would see him within the week. The sick bastard just smiled like Lucifer himself. He had a sick feeling in the pit of his stomach he was going to regret taking this job.

* * * *

Trey paced his apartment for what felt like the gazillionth time. He rented it before the bombing and now he was glad he did. He'd bought a second car; one the pack knew nothing about. Trey was sure they put a hidden tracker in it and by now picked up the fact it hadn't moved in a while. He'd dumped his cell along with it. He put nothing past Craven now. He was officially off their radar and he intended on staying off. He'd seen Craven with the strange man, having tracked him from a distance. He put the pieces together when he noticed the man lift his head scenting the air near that building.

Since the night of the fight, Trey had gone back to her house after healing and followed the moving truck to the lake house. From there he had followed them out to her property. They never left her alone long enough to do a snatch and run.

Trey needed to do something to find her before the tracker did. Chance dropped off the face of the earth after the bombing. He'd gone to the house on the lake the next day and found them gone. A security detail had taken over, so Trey left to retrace his steps. He figured the only way to find her now was to track Craven or head out to her property again.

The only consolation to all of this was if he couldn't find her, then neither could the tracker. Trey struggled with his attraction to her and the fact she was with the one man he hated above all others. At least she was safe with him, but it didn't mollify him. He would still kill the man the first chance open to him.

His insurance package was all he had right now to keep things from going wrong. He needed more, but the how was bothering him. He prayed she would go back to the property so he could snatch her there. Decided on his plan of action, Trey packed a duffel bag with spare clothes and food. He locked the house, got in his car and headed out.

* * * *

Sylas did his best to not wake Chance when he finally went to bed. He'd stayed up for a few more hours, unable to reconcile everything she told him. He never understood how humans could be so cruel to children. In the animal world, babies were top priority. They were cared for even if it meant the parent going without. He knew not all humans were like this, but what were the odds on every home she lived in had abusers? Unable to stand it any longer, he called his mother for an explanation.

She came to him dressed in normal human clothing this time, a break from the norm. She was wearing jeans and an electric blue silk blouse that accentuated her eyes and hair. He gave her a small smile and hug. It was all he could manage at the moment.

"I know your questions, son. It needed to be this way as I explained before. If she had not gone through life this way, she would not be fit to be your mate. Now she will be as strong as you will, in mind and spirit. Once the string of life has been cast, there is nothing that can be done to change it. Only my sister, Atropos, can end a life when she chooses. I can foresee where the life will go and this is how I chose her for you. It was written in the strings. My sisters told me Chance was the one for you and you both would live out your lives forever, together. Clotho made her for you, and I guided her path to you. My sisters and I have only your best interest at heart, Sylas. Try to understand this, son. She needed to go through it to truly be yours."

His mother left him alone to sort it out in his mind. She confirmed what he told Chance earlier. It was fate for her to go through the pain, but it still didn't change the fact he wanted to ease it.

Sylas pulled back the comforter and slid in behind Chance. She'd gotten up at some point and dressed in an old t-shirt and a pair of his boxers. He was dressed the same and for once he could feel more of her skin on his. Chance turned as his body weight shifted the mattress. He pulled her into him and breathed in her unique scent of honey and wine. Sylas wound his arm under her and rolled her even closer. He closed his eyes as he listened to her heartbeat and placed a kiss to her forehead. The sound of the steady beat soothed him and he fell asleep with his mind finally at ease.

Chapter 30

Dakota lifted his nose to the air, sniffing to catch the faint scent of
the woman he was tracking. His special skills came in handy. If the
scent wasn't more than a week or two old, give or take a few days, he
could find them, no matter how far they went. As soon as Craven
left he shifted. He was grateful that when he shifted everything he
kept with him as a human stayed with him. It was why he traveled
light. His backpack was always with him when he needed it, not that
he knew where it went, but he didn't care as long as it came back
with his clothes.

He was fast tracking now. Her scent grew stronger the farther north
he went. He could run like this for days at a time. His wolf never
seemed to tire of the chase. His inner beast thought it was a game of
hide-and-seek. For Dakota it was a job; one that paid very well. The
scent brought him to a house on Lake Lanier. She was long gone,
but her strangely familiar scent was very strong here. Unfortunately,
he couldn't get close enough to the house to go inside to investigate.
There were shifters guarding the place and they were toting high-
powered weapons. He didn't want the pay enough to get his ass shot
or killed.

There were two trails leading away from here. Dakota debated on
which one to follow. They were both pretty strong, but a recent rain
messed them up as to which was more recent. He picked one and
went with it. It took a northerly track. He was starting to feel tired
but he wanted to go home more than sleep. A few hours later he was
on a track of land being developed or seemed to be. Her scent was
very strong here; in fact it was everywhere on the property. There
were two sets of prints in the outlying area, along with some wolf
tracks. He caught scent of her and the wolf, but not the third person.

He found a cave they had been in and decided he would use it to
crash. There was a water supply inside and dry earth to sleep on. He
shifted and bathed in the spring. He ate sparingly and settled in for
the night. The next morning, Dakota explored more of the property.
He saw a construction crew working on a build up on a rise in the
middle of the acreage. He stayed as far as he could from the crew,

but he picked up on a very familiar scent and followed it. *What the hell was he doing here?* Dakota bristled and let out a small growl. What he didn't need was old ghosts showing up in the middle of a job. Dakota trotted back to the cave, shifted, and pulled out his SAT phone. He needed answers and he needed them now.

* * * *

Trey walked up to the lead man on the site asking if they were hiring. He figured the best way to watch for Chance was to be here, out in the open. The builder's name was Rick and it just so happened he was short handed. His time limitations had him in a crunch. He was asked the usual – experience, ID's and such. He was hired on the spot and set to helping on the dig site for the underground levels. Trey thanked his stars he had experience with backhoes. He paused for a split second while digging when he caught a whiff of wolf on the air. It was unfamiliar. *Must be the tracker sniffing around.* He got back to work right away. There was no reason for concern since she wasn't here. If he came here, then he must have lost her trail. That gave him a small bit of comfort. He still had time on his side, at least for now.

While Trey worked, he marveled at the magnitude of the project. To him, she was tough but more feminine somehow. She showed him compassion and that is something you don't see in survivalists. She could have killed him and she didn't. That made her different and unique in his book. He also wondered at how much money Chance actually kept in her bank account. There was several million being spent on the build and he was sure he was under guessing it.
.

Trey used his breaks exploring the other areas of the property where there was even more construction. He was surprised again at her ingenuity. Power supplies from four different sources. Rick showed him the site plans when they started the digs for the septic and well. He knew now she was going solar. This site would be 99% green, with the exception of her gas tank. If she handled her own stock and grew her own vegetables, Chance would never have to go off property. Trey had to admit he was impressed with it all.

Now all he needed was the patience to wait for her to come back here. He hoped it was sooner than later. He needed to get to her before the tracker did. He really didn't relish the idea of having to go in and get her from Craven. He understood his chances of it happening were slim to none. Craven wanted him too and probably had teams looking for him as well. Trey was using the old adage, "Hidden within plain sight," and hoped the pack would not venture out here with all the construction going on. He was playing with a lot of ifs these days and he knew he was on thin ice with it all. One slip up and all his work would flush down the proverbial crapper.

* * * *

Chance woke up with Sylas wrapped around her and she felt his warm skin against hers. She smiled. He was under the comforter for the first time and she liked the feeling. She wanted to stay this way and not move, but the urge to relieve her full bladder was too great. She slipped out from his arms and walked over to the bathroom. A wolf whistle followed her in. It brought on a fit of giggles. "Hey! I thought you were a cat, not a wolf!"

She took care of business and came out wondering why he hadn't replied. What greeted her at the door caught her off guard and she stepped back before thinking about it. Sylas had shifted into a rather large black wolf with green eyes. He gave her a version of what sounded like a laugh, but it came out in quick huffs. Chance lowered to her knees and moved over to him, throwing her arms around him. She buried her head into the fur at his neck. Laughing, she said "You are beautiful to me, no matter what form you are in, Sylas Taiken."

Sylas shifted back and she noticed he was dressed only in his boxers. "I still can't decide if I like those better on me or you, sexy Sylas." Chance blushed when he grinned at her and waggled his brows. He pulled her to him and lowered her to the floor. "I much prefer them on you, Chance Cadens. May I kiss you or do I need to go looking for a sports cup first?"

"Oooo, I don't know. Hmmm. Can you kiss me? Should I let you off the hook yet?" Chance put a finger on her chin, pretending to be deep in thought. Sylas raised an eyebrow at her and she lost control in another fit of giggles. Matters worsened when he started tickling her. She was gasping for air when she finally called Uncle.

Sylas bent over her slowly, asking her with his eyes for permission. She reached up and pulled him to her waiting lips. She was reminded again why he was her future mate. His kisses made her body tingle from head to toe. Her core melted into a fire pit of molten need. She pulled back gasping again, but this time it was for another reason. She wanted him and could feel his need for her pressing into her thigh.

Sylas shushed her before she could say anything with his finger pressed to her lower lip. "It's okay, baby. Your body and scent do this to me every time I'm around you. It isn't time for that yet and I'm ready to wait."

He kissed her again and then moved to her ear with his kisses. Whispering hotly into her neck, he said, "It is time, however, for a little nibble to help your change. Do you want it, Chance? I can smell your desire, baby. I can ease it, but I will need to touch you." Chance felt her heart rate increase with every word he said. She could only nod, silenced with desire.

"Close your eyes, Chance. Just let the feelings flow through and around you." She felt his hands at her waist. Sylas turned her so her back was against his chest. They were sitting up with her between his legs. Sylas began by running his hands up and down her arms lightly, and then he used one to pull her hair to one side, exposing her neck. She was wearing an oversized t-shirt and he pulled it to the side as well. He tasted her skin with his tongue and breathed against her now damp skin. With her eyes closed it seemed to increase what she was feeling ten fold. One of his hands moved under her arm and caressed the skin just under her breast. She took hold of his hand and moved it up, arching into it, wanting more.

Sylas took her signal and moved his other free hand to caress both at
the same time. He pulled and pinched her now hardened nipples.
His movements were causing her to tingle with need; her core
dripping with it. She felt him tug her hair, pulling her head back,
giving him access to her mouth. He drove his tongue in deep and
she sucked on it, causing his inner beast to purr. She felt his canines
extend and it only seemed to excite her more. She released his
tongue, moaning at what his hands were doing to her. One was at a
nipple and the other was snaking down her belly. She didn't stop
him, lost in his touch, she wanted him there to ease her need.

Sylas moved his hand under the waistband of the boxers she had on
and the other moved under her t-shirt to play with her bare breast.
He nibbled at her shoulder with light kisses and nips that weren't
breaking the skin. She felt his fingers reach her core and she arched
into his chest needing more. Her body was nearly vibrating now.

"Keep your eyes closed baby, feel me touching you. Feel the
pleasure I'm giving you with my hands." She answered him with a
needy moan as a finger parted her folds and ran around the exterior,
spreading her juices. His thumb circled her nub, and her hips were
grinding into his hand, matching the rhythm of his thumb. Sylas
moved his hand and thumb faster, building friction where she
wanted it most. She was close to losing control when she felt him
sink his teeth into her shoulder. All at once she exploded, screaming
his name. Chance collapsed back into his chest, but he wasn't done
yet. He brought her to orgasmic heaven three more times before he
picked her up and moved them both to the bed. He pulled her shirt
and boxers off, wanting to see her body as he made her scream
several times more, this time with his very talented tongue and
mouth.

While they were relaxing in each other's arms Chance realized she
would have no hesitations when the time came. The very last fear
vanished with his loving touch. Over the last few weeks Sylas had
done nothing but show her what real love was and she wanted it
with every fiber of her being. Nothing else mattered, the pain of
abuse, losing her Sensei, and all the trials of her young life melted
away. While she thought about it more, she realized that even the

involuntary flinching was gone. She could not imagine how she became so lucky as to have this man in her life. He became her everything and she was determined to keep him, forever and a day.

Chapter 31

Craven stared at the unfortunate pack member lying dead on the floor in front of him. He smiled. The dead shifter was the one who'd brought him the news they lost track of Trey. His temper was at the boiling point, with no outlet for it. He'd rushed him and pulled his throat apart with his teeth before the fellow knew what hit him. He looked up at the rest of the pack. They were all in shock and shifting on their feet nervously. One actually shifted into wolf form and was now on the floor in a submissive pose.

"Now you see what will happen if I don't get what I want!" Lowering his voice, he continued, "I want Trey found and I want him here before the tracker gets back with the bitch." He started pacing and stopped, glaring at the lot of them. "You're still here? Take care of this mess and get the hell out!"

He watched them scramble to do his bidding and laughed to himself. *That should put some respect into their worthless hides.* Soon they were all gone and it gave him a chance to walk down to the basement. He surveyed his handiwork. He'd added another set of manacles to the wall. One set for Trey and the other for her lover, the Enforcer.

Once he captured her, they would follow right behind her. He'd designed the room into a trap. He placed cameras in the walls, stairs and the hall leading to the basement. The door was set with a remote. There were cages hidden in the recesses of the ceiling that would drop with the push of a button. With her as bait, he carried no doubts he would have them too. He had several tranquilizer guns on standby. Not even the Enforcer could withstand these drugs.

As soon as they were captured and drugged it would be nothing to move them to the manacles imbedded in the cement walls. He could keep them drugged enough to keep them from shifting and still be awake to watch as he tortured the female.

Only his new Beta was in on the plan. He'd known the man was crazy and it was all he needed. In a drunken discussion, he discovered the man had a pension for pain. Giving and receiving it.

He took great pleasure in giving it to him in more ways than one. With whips, chains, and then fucking the Beta's virginal ass made the man his personal slave for life. He was not gentle or caring, and the man begged for more. Craven promised him more, but not until he brought Trey back… alive.

* * * *

Sylas helped get the motor home ready to be moved again. They decided to move it every other day. Any longer in one place increased the chances of them being found before she was ready. This time they were moving across the state lines into Alabama. They would move around there for a week and then move back closer. If Chance wasn't ready in another week, he would call his mother down again to see if she could give them a better time line. He still needed to take the Alpha and his Beta out, but Chance's needs came first. She would have to change before anything else could happen.

Sylas was hopeful. Chances eyes started to actually glow after their lovemaking this morning. It lasted nearly an hour before fading away. He didn't want to over do it or push her more than she was ready for, but he was having a harder time controlling himself with her now. His beast wanted to take her as his mate now, not later. It also didn't help he had a major case of blue balls. No relief from his needs felt like it was going to kill him. He was distracted and that was never a good thing.

As if she was reading his mind, Chance walked back to where he was sitting on the bed. "You look like you're a million miles away, Sylas. What's wrong?" He pulled her into him and placed his head against her stomach with his arms wrapped tightly around her waist. She was dressed in her leathers and the combination of her smell mixed with the leather was making him heady with desire. It didn't help knowing she was commando under those tight pants. "Mmmm, do you know how good you smell right now?" he asked her while avoiding her question. She was having none of his avoidance.

Chance ran her fingers through his hair and she pulled his head back with it. "I asked you a question, Sylas. Please answer me."

Sylas opened his eyes and met hers with his frustration obvious on his face. Her eyes grew bigger with understanding. "Oh... Oh! I got so lost in what you were doing to me, that I forgot what this is doing to you. I'm sorry, Sylas. I want to make you as happy as you have made me... but I've never..."

Sylas knew Chance had never been with a man this way, and didn't want her to do anything she was uncomfortable with.

"Chance, I can deal because I know the end result will be worth the sacrifice. You are more important, besides, I don't think you will be comfortable with this just yet."

"Denying yourself and your needs for me is not right, Sylas. I want to be everything to you and for you. I want to know I can be what you need. If I do something wrong, then show me what is right, okay?"

Not waiting for an answer, Chance knelt down in front of him and pushed him down on the bed.

Chance ran her hands up his thighs, lingering a second over his hard shaft. Then she moved higher up to his chest. She climbed up on the bed, straddling him. Chance kissed him deeply, taking and keeping control of him and he let her. She slid back to the floor, kneeling between his legs. Sylas thought he heard her say she was curious, but her hand rubbing again against his hard cock shut his mind down.

He felt her popping his jean buttons one at a time and then tugged them and his boxers down after he rose his hips up into the hand that was still caressing him. His cock was standing free and proud with her hands making him harder. Then he felt her lick the tip to taste the pre-cum that had pearled there. He could tell she was experimenting and it aroused him further.

Chance whispered to him, "I am not sure how to do this, Sylas, I hope I'm doing it right."

Sylas let out a long moan when he felt her lips descend down and around his shaft, wetting it with her tongue as she went. Chance was exploring him everywhere. She had one hand on his sac, gently squeezing and he felt a fingernail run down his tender flesh. Sylas thought he was going to come right at that moment and she must have felt it, because she moved her hand away. Sylas grabbed the comforter in both fists, nearly ripping it to help control his need to take her. He rose up and leaned back on his elbows so he could watch her.

With each movement down his shaft with her warm mouth and lips, she took him deeper. She was pushing her tongue against the soft ridges and veins while her hands pumped him. Sylas reached down and showed her how to move her hands. She learned fast.

Chance watched him for his reactions, making sure he liked what she was doing to him. Sylas buried a hand in her hair and encouraged her with another moan. "I'm ready baby, you can stop. You might not like the taste." She ignored him and increased her pace.

Sylas felt the rush coming all the way from his toes. He cried out her name and stiffened, shooting his seed deep into her mouth. Chance swallowed every last drop, smiling up at him with her eyes. Sylas stared at her with amazement. She had taken him deep within her throat and she didn't gag. With one last suck that popped as she pulled away, Chance licked her lips and smiled.

"Did I do that right, Sylas? I've never…" He didn't give her time to say any more. He pulled her up and kissed her, tasting himself as he drove his tongue into her mouth. His hand pulled her closer and held her there. His other hand dove down into her pants finding her soaking wet with desire.

"Oh baby, you have no idea how much I've wanted to be inside you. You were perfect and you can do that to me any time you want." He felt her shudder when his finger slightly dipped inside her wet, hot core.

"This is where I want to be, Chance." Sylas pressed the heel of his hand against her nub, rubbing it as he stroked her. Unable to resist, Sylas bit her shoulder again, claiming her in the only way he could for now. Chance came as soon as his teeth sunk into her soft flesh and he could feel her muscles clench with her release. He gently sucked the muscle with his teeth still imbedded as she rode out the orgasm. She was his mate and he was not the only one who had staked a claim, she had staked hers permanently on his heart.

An hour later they were on the road with Sylas driving. Chance set the GPS with the address of their destination and was now sitting in the passenger seat smiling at him. He glanced over and saw her eyes were still glowing. He grinned and pointed to the visor vanity mirror, telling her to take a look. He heard her gasp and then laugh. He loved the sound of it. Her laughter came from deep inside and was never faked. If he had his way he would have her laughing all the time. Soon he hoped they could relax enough for him to make it happen. If time was on their side for a change.

* * * *

Jack woke with a pounding headache. His head hurt so badly he didn't dare open his eyes. He could feel the sun on his skin, but nothing smelled familiar. He scented water was somewhere close and tried to reach for it. Suddenly he realized he was not in human form. Something was clamped around his neck and was pressing into his flesh. He opened one eye but everything was fuzzy and the light pierced his brain with lightning hot flashes of pain. He passed out, welcoming the dark void.

It was sometime later when he woke again. It was cooler and he could tell it was dark now. He opened his eyes to find himself in a cage. There was food and water in the corner, but he didn't trust the smell coming from the food. It was tainted with something and he was not going there. He carefully sniffed and then lapped a quick taste of the water. It seemed okay and he drank his fill. The container of water was fed from a hose into a gravity bowl. At least he would have enough to drink until he could figure this out.

Jack didn't recognize his surroundings. It seemed to be a bedroom and had no furniture, other than the cage. The walls wore no decorations and were a dingy yellow. He tested the air and smelled shifter… a wolf. The last thing he could remember was locking the door at the bar. Everything beyond that was a blank.

The collar on his neck had spikes buried deep in his skin. He was pretty sure if he tried to completely shift, the spikes would shred his human neck. His captor obviously didn't know Jack had a special talent and he was about to use it. He could shift a single area of his body at a time. It took years to perfect, but when you were over 600 years old, one had plenty of time to practice.

Lying on his back, Jack shifted his front appendages into arms and hands. He reached up and felt around the collar for a latch. Once he found it and released the collar, it fell to the floor. Inspecting his body for more traps and finding none, he shifted completely into his human form. His clothes were nearly rags and smelled burnt, but they at least covered the important parts.

His captor must have hinged all this on the collar, because there wasn't a keyed lock on the cage. He opened it and carefully moved from room to room, finding the place empty. He found the drugs that were used to put him to sleep. Jack seethed with anger when he discovered the bottle and house smelled like the Beta from the wolf pack. He'd locked his scent down in his brain at Chance's house the night she was attacked. The man would pay, but first he had to get to Sylas.

Wasting no more time, Jack left the house. Once he was far enough away from civilization he shifted back to his puma form and ran towards his house.

Jack arrived at his property and shifted when a man holding a high-powered rifle aimed directly at his chest confronted him. His confusion doubled when he saw more guards headed his way. He could tell from their scent that they were all shifters. Jack kept his arms in the air as he asked for the person in charge.

Jack heard the man before he saw him. He was barking orders for the others to lower their weapons. The guard reached out to shake his hand once he was close enough. "I know who you are, Jack, and we've been waiting on you. Please come with me, I have the key to your place and you can shower and change. I will explain everything to you when you are finished." Jack could only nod. This seemed to be a day full of confusion. He could only hope this man knew all the right answers.

Chapter 32

Chance was chewing the last bite of her dinner when Sylas' phone chimed, signaling a text message. He turned with a huge smile and showed it to her.

"Jack here. Did you miss me, Kitty?"

They gave a collective sigh of relief as Sylas sent him a text back.

"Sylas and Chance on this end.
We both missed your ugly puss!
Where the fuck you been?"

"In a cage. Big bad wolf had me.
He huffed but forgot to puff. Where r u?"

"Holed up. Sending directions.
Get a guard to bring you.
Use roundabout and make sure not followed.
Explain later. Good to know you're alive, Puss-n-boots.
BTW – Chance says it's about fuckin' time."

"Kiss that woman silly for me.
On my way, Sylvester."

Sylas put his phone down after sending directions and smiled at her. "He should be here within two hours. It gives me time to do as requested. Besides, dessert sounds good."

Chance grinned and took his hand when offered. He stood and pulled her tightly to him. He nuzzled her neck as he ran his hands slowly down her spine to her buttocks, pulling her up so she could wrap her long legs around him. Chance couldn't suppress a giggle when he started purring into her cleavage. The feel of his whiskers abrading her skin, along with the rumble, tickled. She took a handful of black hair and pulled his head up so she could kiss him. She poured all of her relief at having Jack back into it. Hell, they both did.

Lighter spirits cleaned up the dishes from dinner. When finished, Sylas went to the back to take a shower. Chance debated a whole minute before she stripped off her clothes and joined him. She'd never showered with a man before and this was one of many firsts to cross off her bucket list.

Sylas was standing with his back to her when she opened the door and soundlessly closed it behind her. She pressed up against him and heard him moan at the feel of her skin against his. He reached back and pulled her around him, placing her under the warm spray. Chance reached for the bar of soap and started washing him down with it. His muscle definition was more pronounced with the slick soap and water and she enjoyed learning his body this way.

His cock was standing erect and swollen with her ministrations and she sunk to her knees to wash him up close and personal with her lips and tongue. Sylas pulled her hair loose from the bun she had it in and then sunk his hands deep into the strands. He watched her suck and lick him and she dared him with her eyes to look away. She could feel his legs trembling and it excited her to know she held this much power over him.

Sylas leaned his shoulders against the shower wall to keep standing upright. He guided her with his hands and hip thrusts into her willing mouth. He came in quick bursts when she ran a fingernail down the sensitive skin behind his now tight sack. She swallowed every drop relishing the taste of him. Sylas groaned watching her and she smiled when he instantly grew hard again. He pulled her up and kissed her like there were no more tomorrows.

"Shit baby, I could watch you do that all day, but Jack will be here soon. It's my turn to wash you, love."

Sylas washed her slowly, enjoying the fact that his hands were making her squirm with need. He turned washing her tresses into a sensual massage. She moaned and melted into his hands. He turned her to the wall to brace her hands against and placed his still hard shaft between the cheeks of her ass, grinding as he slid his hand down her front and found her throbbing nub waiting for him. For once, Chance was grateful for a plump behind. Feeling him grinding against her like this was an erotic overload. She reached behind her with a handful of long silky pleasure and held it against him as he moved. Chance couldn't tell if Sylas growled or moaned as his pleasure increased from the feel of it against his cock and legs.

"You're so perfect for me, baby. Goddess help me, I want you," he whispered in her ear, driving her closer.

Sylas kept a hand busy pulling and tweaking her nipples. When she was close, he extended his fangs and bit down on her shoulder, bringing them both to exploding climaxes. Sylas held Chance up when her knees tried to give out and waited patiently for her regain control. The water was getting cooler, so they finished rinsing off and got out.

Sylas toweled her dry, kissing all the exposed parts he could reach. "I love you, Chance Cadens, and I can't wait until I can make proper love to you and claim you as my mate."

"You already have me, Sylas Taiken. I was yours the moment you waited for me to speak that night at the bar. But I understand and hopefully we can make it official soon. I want it as much as you do, my sweet sexy cat." She kissed him and helped him dry off too.

"Your eyes are glowing, baby. That ought to give old Jack a start to his already over active imagination."

Sylas chuckled and shook his head. "I can't believe he made it out in one piece. I can't wait to hear this story. He will be here soon and as much as I enjoy looking at you naked, I don't want that tomcat pawing after you."

Reaching into one of the drawers under the bed and drawing out a pair of brown leather pants and one of her matching corset tops, Sylas grinned as he handed them to Chance. He remembered her penchant for going commando and commented he loved knowing she was always dressed that way. He grabbed boxers and sweat pants for himself. They dressed quickly, needing to clear and make the other bed for Jack to use.

"I wonder if he's eaten? Should I make him something?" Chance asked as she watched Sylas tuck the last corner of the bedspread into place.

"I don't know, he didn't say, but maybe we could put a couple bottles of beer on ice. I know he won't turn that down."

Sylas grinned and then patted her on the behind as she went to put the beer in the freezer.

Twenty minutes later they heard car tires crunching outside and Sylas asked her to stay inside while he made sure it was safe. Chance watched out the window and as soon as she saw Jack getting out of the car she forgot her orders. She ran outside to jump on Jack, giving him a full body hug with her legs wrapped around him tight.

"Whoa! Missed me that much did you, Chance? I like it but not so sure your man does." He chuckled and gave her another tight squeeze before letting her down. Chance felt the tears falling as she blushed and stepped back to let Sylas in for a fist bump and a playful cub-like head-butt and nuzzle.

"Don't you ever scare me like that again, Jack. My heart can't take it." She gave him another quick hug and let Sylas pull her into his arms. She stared at Jack, unable to look away now that he was back. She noticed his eyes widen as he looked at her. Then he looked up at Sylas' grinning face.

"I think I have lots to catch up on, little miss glowing eyes! Got a cold beer? Food? I'm starving!"

Chance laughed as they went inside. She grabbed him a beer and set about making him dinner, while Sylas caught Jack up on all he missed. She broiled him a thick cut of steak and nuked a baked potato. She set it on the table in front of him with other sides and trimmings.

"Rare and still sizzling, Jack, and there's more if you're still hungry."

From the best they could figure out, the Beta grabbed him from the bar right before it exploded and took him away without being seen. It seemed he was missing about four days. Time was starting to mesh together with all the excitement. Jack told them how he got away and his shock at finding armed guards on his property.

"That was Chance's doing. She wanted to make sure they didn't ruin your home like they did the bar."

Chance chimed in, no longer able to contain her thoughts, "Your bar is gone, Jack. I thought I lost both of you. Sylas went in to find you and almost didn't make it out."

The tears fell again with the fresh reminder of almost losing the family she had come to know and love. She stood up, suddenly self-conscious about the tears.

"I'm sorry. I don't mean to cry like this. You both mean the world to me. I'm going to take a walk for a few minutes and compose myself."

Jack reached for her arm and pulled her down into his lap. He looked at Sylas and dared him to say anything. "I know she's your gal, but this old puma needs another hug and I think she needs a Jack hug too."

Sylas smiled at them both. He knew it was something they both needed. He got up to clean up Jack's now empty plates and Chance knew it was his way of giving them a moment to sort out the rush of emotions she was going through.

"This old man will always be here for both of you, Chance. I consider you part of my family now too. Besides, I would much rather look at you than his ugly puss any day of the week. No more worries now, okay?"

Chance nodded, giving him another hug. Sylas came back to join them. She smiled at Jack, kissed his cheek, and moved over to Sylas' lap where she belonged. She heard Jack chuckle when she closed her eyes and nuzzled his neck. Thirsty, she got up to get them all another beer and this time chose to sit in a chair next to Sylas so she could admire both her men.

Sylas filled Jack in on the rest of their plans and then relayed what his mother had said. Jack was shocked that Lachesis told him to leave the old Beta alone. He agreed to abide by her rules because he didn't need her upset with him, but that was the only reason.

Chance smiled while they talked. She spoke up a couple of times adding her two cents here and there. Jack went into a conniption fit when Sylas got to the part about her being used as bait. Sylas stopped him with a hand on his arm when he went to stand up sputtering, "Oh, hell no!"

"Trust me, Jack. She has this. Chance showed me right quick she can handle it." She smirked when she saw Sylas unconsciously cover his balls with his hand. She started laughing when Jack noticed and raised his eyebrows.

"She got the better of you, eh pussy? It's about time she beat your ass!"

"She did catch me off guard…" Chance punched him in the arm, effectively cutting him off.

"Okay, okay. It was my fault, *but* she will not be put into any kind of danger until *after* we mate. Our time is getting closer every day and I'm hoping by the end of this week, it can happen. Once we mate and she can shift, I'll feel much more comfortable letting her bait them in. Once her eyes continue to glow and not fade, it will be our cue to set things into motion."

"Yeah, I see they are already fading. How long is the glow lasting now?"

"This time it was about four hours. It extends by about an hour or more every time I give her a nudge with my bite."

"Well, don't let me keep you. Go get your bite on, Morris." Jack smiled at them both with a goofy lopsided grin.

Right as he spoke the words, Jack inadvertently let out a long yawn and Chance took the cue to show him to his room.

"Everything here is yours to use, Jack. I bought this motor home to keep all of us safe until Craven is no longer a threat. What's ours is yours and I hope you'll be comfortable. If you need anything else, just make a list and I'll make sure we get it for you."

Chance gave him another quick hug before she stepped away.

"I'm just glad you're okay, Jack." She gave him one of best smiles and turned to go be with her man.

Things were finally as they should be. Jack was alive and safe and she was another day closer to becoming the mate of the most powerful earthbound immortal ever. She wasn't going to let anyone hurt another hair on either male. She would die before she let that happen. She raised her head and vowed it silently to Lachesis and hoped she heard it, because she meant every word.

Chapter 33

Dakota stared at his phone in disbelief before putting it back to his ear. Hell, he still didn't believe all he was hearing from the person on the other end of the call. He needed to sit down to listen after the first minute of the conversation. If what was being said was true, then his life just changed for the better. Now all he had to do was figure out how to fix the problem before it was too late. He ran once, he wouldn't do it again. It didn't matter what his reasons were at the time; he was a different person now. He was a better man. He had years of street smarts and life experiences on his side this time. He would make it right somehow.

Dakota said his goodbyes and hung up. He needed to find this girl and fast. There were things to take care of, but he wasn't one for leaving a job undone, no matter how crazy his employer was. He shifted and stepped out of the cave to sniff the air. His black wolf form kept him hidden in the shadows and it was needed today. The sky was void of clouds and the air was clean and crisp from the small shower that rolled through the night before. The sun burned off the last of the mountain mists and if he wasn't careful he might be seen.

The girl's scent was everywhere on the land near the construction. They didn't clear-cut the trees and he was thankful. He could get closer than normal to the humans working on the site. He got a good whiff of a male wolf shifter too; in fact, his scent was very strong near the digging. Alpha males had their own scent and this one was exuding an Alpha scent that seemed strangely familiar. Dakota knew this because he was also an Alpha. *Was he here working with the humans?* Dakota backed away from the area carefully. Last thing he needed was trouble. He was close and he could feel it all the way to his bones. His instincts were telling him to stay here. She would come back and he would be waiting.

* * * *

Trey spotted the black wolf just before he pulled back into the tree line. *So the tracker is still here.* He didn't expect to see him, positive he would have left by now. He wondered if they were both on the right track waiting for Chance to show up here. He was still worried he wouldn't be able to get to her before the tracker did. The construction was progressing much faster now since the digging was completed. They poured all the concrete for the lower floors and added the steel infrastructure for it. The towers were completed, along with the mill down at the stream. He was now working on digging the cable ditches, which was taking longer than expected due to terrain and tree roots.

Trey had been sleeping in his vehicle offsite, but gave that up and moved it onto the property in a secluded area of woods near the entrance. There was still no sign of the pack, but it didn't mean they weren't there or watching. He wasn't getting much sleep these days. Between working and staying up at night looking for pack members, he was snatching four hours a day at most. He was starting to get paranoid, which was affecting his decision making.

One slipup and he was caught. The nightmares were not helping either. He kept dreaming snatches of the night his parents were killed. He was too young at the time to remember much, but bits and pieces would come in his sleep. It was mostly the screaming he remembered, and when they came, he would jolt awake, shivering with fear.

Trey knew he was a survivor of a terrible tragedy and he was bound and determined to find a way to avert another with his old pack. He saw what was happening and feared they would pay the price for Craven's doings. Get his female and save the pack was the mantra keeping him straight or at least he hoped it was. He wasn't so sure any more. He had way too much time on his hands to think while running the backhoe. Things were coming to a head sooner than later and he could feel it. Just like the tracker though, he would have to wait.

With his workday over, Trey struggled to get to his car. He felt like he was going to pass out from the lack of sleep. He seemed to be hallucinating, hearing voices in his head or was he? Through sleep deprived eyes, Trey glanced around warily. He saw the shifter but it was too late. He felt something sting the back of his neck as he started to shift. Then everything went black.

* * * *

Craven was ecstatic for the first time in weeks. Ryder had found and brought him Trey. He'd lost weight and looked like shit, but he was alive. Seeing everything starting to come to fruition after all this time was a major head rush. He told his new Beta to carry him to the basement and together they manacled him to the wall.

Craven made sure Ryder knew he had done well by shackling him, facing the wall, next to Trey. He whipped the man from head to toe, and he was still begging for more. He took advantage of the man being restrained and had his way with him for the next hour. Yes, life was good.

Later that evening, Craven patiently waited for Trey to come to his senses. He wanted to make sure he knew why he was there and what was going to happen. Then he would tranquilize him again and keep him under until Dakota brought in the bitch. He saw Trey finally stir and stood up from the chair he was relaxing in.

In a soft voice laced with venom, he called to him, "Wake up, Trey. It's time find out what happens to traitorous wolves in my pack."

Craven laughed as Trey raised his head in confusion. He was chained to the wall with his hands stretched apart and manacled above his head. There was just enough slack for his feet to touch the floor, but that was all. He wouldn't be able to lie down or move from the spot he was in. There were spikes in the cuffs, and they were embedded in Trey's wrists to prevent shifting.

"What the fuck do you think you're doing Craven?" Trey started to shift and stopped when he realized he was trapped with the cuffs.

I am enjoying this way too much, but it is so worth it to see his face. Craven laughed again at the thoughts racing through his mind. "You're here to watch your precious bitch get her rewards for attacking me.

What's the face for, Trey? Did you seriously think I didn't know what you were doing? All those things I promised to do to her? You'll now have a front row seat. I will strip her, beat her, and fuck her while you watch and I'll keep doing it until I break her. Get my drift, traitor?"

"You touch one hair on her, and *I will kill you*, Craven. I'll make you wish for death before I end you."

"Those are idle threats coming from a man with no way of escape, don't you think? Maybe I will share her with the rest of the pack too. Hmmm… now that's something to think seriously about. I don't imagine there's a man in this pack who'd turn down a naked and restrained woman, do you?"

Craven laughed again as he watched Trey struggle to free himself.

"Careful Trey, you don't want another permanent injury do you?"

Trey let out a string of useless curses and Craven tired of the game. He hit him with another tranq dart so he could leave to hatch more plans for his revenge.

* * * *

Jack woke up feeling much better than the day before. There was nothing like friends, food, and beer to set things right again. He mourned the loss of his bar, The Den, but the insurance would take care of it. He wasn't sure if he wanted to rebuild it in the same place though. He liked the area Chance was building on and considered finding a spot nearby to build instead. Out in the country was always better than the city in his book. Better clientele was a major selling point. He also knew most of his employees would have no problem making the move with him. He spent the morning calling all of them so they could stop worrying. He also set it up with the bank to make sure they all received pay while the bar was in limbo.

Jack used his afternoon to restart training with Sylas and Chance. Sylas made sure he gave her a booster bite before hand and she matched Sylas blow for blow after. It did his soul good to see her becoming his equal. He would never say it to the man, but Sylas needed this for far too long. Even though they weren't related, Jack thought of him as a brother.

Jack met Sylas at the beginning of the Revolutionary War and fought together again in the War Between the States, both times as medics. It was during the latter Sylas saved his ass the first time. Sylas shielded him from a cannon blast by pulling them both out of harm's way just before the cannon ball struck. The second was when he kept him sane after the loss of his wife and cub in Montana.

Since he wasn't in the greatest shape since his capture, he watched them spar and pointed out things he thought needed improving. He also volunteered to cook meals for the day and he worked on the bait strategy while they trained. He wasn't going to allow anything to go wrong this time.

The way he worked it out, the best place to do this was on her property. The terrain was perfect to set traps and now that her road was in, they could drive into the property and effectively close down the entrance with a downed tree. If they were to get to her first, they would have to carry her out and that alone should allow enough time to catch up to them and retrieve her.

The hard part would be to draw the Alpha out. Jack brainstormed some ideas but he would have to run them by Sylas and Chance first. He still had the standby crew waiting in the wings. He'd made sure as soon as he woke up this morning.

Jack used a SAT phone Chance had with her. Having no trace on the phone meant no one tracking back to where they were. He also timed Chance's eyes this time, and it lasted eight and a half hours. By his calculations, if Sylas boosted her three times a day, in two or three more days, she should be finished with the change.

Sylas told him they needed to move again by day's end, so Jack took the list Chance made and picked a campground in northern Alabama. It was near Cloudland Canyon State Park and would make a good spot to start the return to her property. It would be all back roads from there and less chance of being discovered until they were ready. It was the quiet before the storm keeping Jack on edge. Something was not right. It was too quiet and going too well for his comfort.

When their training finished and had sated their hunger, Chance begged off strategizing in favor of a shower and sleep. Jack knew she was letting the men have some needed talk time. They really needed to talk about this without her present and Jack made sure he let her know his appreciation with a quick hug as she left the room.

"You have a special gem in that one, Sy. Best not let anything happen to her, or this old cat will have to pull out the claws. Catch my drift?"

"I caught your drift a long time ago and trust me when I say, I will go down first before I let anyone hurt her. She finally told me about her childhood, Jack. It wasn't pretty. I know you've seen her flinch at loud noises. Trust me when I say she had good reason. I've never wanted to kill a human before, but the abusive pricks she lived with as a child, deserve very painful deaths."

"I feel you, Bro. She's still a tough cookie. I sure as hell don't want to be on her bad side. I like my boys hanging healthy and I mean to keep 'em that way. I'll drive us to the next camp if you want to take advantage of your not-so-empty bed back there. But I suggest you get some sleep, because tomorrow we need to teach your wildcat the intricacies of shifting. I know she can't shift yet, but I'm thinking we need to give her pre-instructions to ward off the worst case scenario."

"You're getting the heebeegeebees too, I see. Something isn't kosher in shifter land. This has been too easy and it's making my hackles rise. My cat hasn't stopped pacing for 2 days now and I'm not sleeping. Waiting for the ax to fall makes my balls itch. Just glad you're here, Jack. I feel better knowing I have my back covered. I'll chat ya in the AM, Bro. Keep it locked and batten down the window covers before you crash. Oh, and thanks again for being alive, Jack."

Jack waited until Sylas crawled in with his lady before cranking up the house on wheels. The next few days were going to be hell. Jack was going to make sure they all made it through in one piece, come hell or high water.

Chapter 34

Chance was still awake when she felt Sylas crawl into bed with her. She was facing him when he pulled her close and she opened her eyes to look into his. He was humming to the radio he turned on before closing the door and coming to bed. He held her face gently with his hands and sang to her along with the music.

It was a popular Bruno Mars song and the words and his voice stroked her in ways hands could not.

"I'm not Bruno Mars, but the words mean the same. I love you, Chance Cadens."

"I have the person I want, Sylas Taiken. I love only you, forever and a day."

He pulled her in closer, brushing his lips to hers. It was feather light and the kiss made her melt. Something was different with him tonight. It was as if this was their last time together and he was expressing how he felt through this one kiss. It wasn't desperation, just love. Chance wrapped her arms around his neck and moved as close as she could, molding her body to every inch of his. Closing her eyes, she let her mind feel every breath, heartbeat, and muscle that was Sylas. Their heartbeats and breathing synchronized as they lay there holding each other.

Chance had no idea if it would work, but she projected her thoughts at him. She concentrated on the dream they both shared in the past. She put all her love into it and knew she was successful when she felt his breath hitch with a small gasp. She wrapped a leg over his and held him tighter, not wanting him to distract her.

Chance pictured them in cat form in the forest and she rubbed her muzzle and body down his. She manipulated the dream to fast forward to where they shifted back to human and made love amongst the trees. He was behind her, holding her breasts and entering her with his hard shaft. As they mated, he reached down and bit into her shoulder. Her dream self looked over as if looking into a camera and mouthed "I love you, Sylas." just before they both climaxed.

Just as in the dream, Sylas leaned down and bit her in the same spot. They climaxed at the same time as their dream selves and they never moved other than the bite. They both lay on the bed quivering from the mutual orgasm and power behind the dream she sent him. It was the strongest orgasm yet and she nearly fainted.

"Holy fuck, baby! I'm not sure what you just did, but I'm… speechless."

When Chance finally regained some semblance of control, she asked, "Sylas, can mated pairs talk to each other in their minds? I mean the paranormal romance novels all say they can but those are just made up stories, right?"

"I have no idea, love, but you just talked to me. I was there with you Chance. I love you too."

Sylas kissed her on the nose and smiled. "You know once we mate the bite mark won't disappear like it does now. It's a way of marking your other half as taken and our scents will mix. Other shifters can see and smell mated pairs. The only difference with us over other shifters is we don't emit a scent, at least I think it will work the same. Since I can shift into many animals, I don't carry a scent that shifters can identify. The same should go for you as well and the difference between our dream and reality is we will need to mark each other for the mating to be official."

"Sylas, you do have a scent. It's very unique and I've always loved it. It's a cross between dark spices and a pine forest. If I can smell your scent, why can't others?"

"Maybe it's the mate thing, Chance. You have a distinct scent to me as well. You smell and taste like honey and wine mixed with a hint of summer flowers. I bet if we asked Jack, he wouldn't know what we were talking about."

Chance watched as he got up to get a warm wash cloth to clean up. He carefully washed her down before cleaning himself. He crawled back under the covers with her and this time he turned her and pulled her back to his chest. His hands roamed her body absentmindedly as they both recalled the power of the dream. Her curiosity was in full bloom and was laden with lots of questions.

"What if I hurt you with my bite? I won't know what I'm doing and it scares me a little, Sylas."

"Trust me love, you will know when the time comes. It's instinctual and natural. It will be the first of many such bites. Only the first one will scar. The rest will fade like they do now."

Chance could feel his arousal poking into her back. She took a fistful of hair and reached back to rub him with it. She heard his sharp intake of breath when the silken strands brushed his body.

"You really don't play fair, woman. Do you have any idea what you're doing to me?"

Chance had only one thought on her mind now. *Fuck the questions.* "Show me."

Sylas growled before he got up and pulled her to her hands and knees. He moved behind her and grabbed on to a thick strand of her locks, effectively keeping her still by pulling her head back, taking advantage of her exposed neck, His free hand played with her breasts for a moment before moving down her back to her sweet spot. She was dripping with need and she heard him growl again as she grew wetter in anticipation. He eased her down on her stomach and pulled her to the end of the bed. He slid down to the floor on his knees still behind her. "I want to be right here buried so deep it makes you scream my name." She felt his tongue lapping up her running juices and moaned, with her leg muscles already starting to quiver. He wrapped both of his arms under and around her legs, trapping her and spreading her wider. His shoulders pushed her ass higher in the air, giving him perfect access to her honey pot.

His long tongue and fingers tortured her by bringing her close and then backing off. Her virginity was more important to both of them than him getting his rocks off, so he stayed clear, careful not to break her hymen.

"What do you want baby?" He whispered to her. She begged him to let her come.

"Then come for me Chance, I need to taste more of you." She felt him lick higher as his fingers played with her clit. Just as she was ready, she felt him insert a wet finger carefully in her ass. That did it. She stiffened and cried out his name as promised. He continued to move his fingers in both spots as she rode the magical high. She heard him moan and growl as her juices flowed. Sylas didn't let her up until he made her scream his name again.

Sylas wasn't finished with her yet. He got up and straddled her, pulling her higher onto the bed and turning her over onto her back.

"I love your breasts, baby. They are more than a handful and perfect."

Reaching down, Sylas took hold of his cock and rubbed himself between her breasts. Chance caught on to what he was doing and moved her hands to press her flesh together over his now rock hard cock. He moaned when she reached her tongue out to lick him as he rocked back and forth over her. She wanted more than just a taste and pushed him back on the bed to finish what he started. He was still straddling her legs but she didn't care. She wanted to satisfy her man the only way available to her for the moment. When he came, Chance fell back on the bed, worn out but at least they both were satisfied.

Sylas rolled them both over, spooning her again. This time they left the mess, too tired to wash.

"Bite me again, Sylas, before you sleep. It comforts me." His hands cupped and massaged her breasts as he complied, biting her shoulder and sucking the tender skin. Unexpectedly, she came again with the pleasure of his simple but loving movements.

"I love you, Sylas." She fell asleep almost as soon as the words left her lips.

They awoke the next morning starving and in a new campground. After a much-needed shower, and more steamy shower fun, they joined Jack to eat the breakfast he cooked while they were playing. Thoughts of the night before played havoc in Chance's brain. She started twenty questions with the both of them over some hot coffee.

"Jack, do Sylas or I have a scent that you've noticed? Sylas said other shifters can't smell his scent, but I can."

"Now that you mention it, no, you don't have any scent other than that perfume that I caught wind of in the bar. I've never been able to catch a scent on Sy either."

Chance remembered the dream and that brought up the next question. "I don't want to bring up a bad memory, but when you were with your mate could you to speak to each other with your minds?"

"First, there is only one bad memory of her, sweetness. The rest are beautiful thoughts that I will cherish until my time is done here. Sy showed me the reality of our life together and that is how he kept me sane after her loss. There was only the one bad one, to the millions of good, and the good were what he kept me focused on. To answer your question, no, we were never able to speak to each other in our heads. Why?"

Chance let Sylas tell him what she had been able to do. She watched Jack's eyes widen as he told the story. He kept looking back and forth between them in disbelief. She just blushed and smiled.

"Chance, when was the last time Sylas bit you?" She glanced at Sylas and shrugged. He didn't bite her in the shower this morning and she hadn't looked in the mirror. Sylas was looking at her strangely now and it was making her nervous.

"Maybe an hour or so after Sylas came to bed? Why? Do I have a wart on my face or something? You two are scaring me, so spill it."

It was Sylas who answered her after glancing at his watch. "It was about midnight when I went to bed last night baby. I bit you around one. It's about noon now. Usually, your eyes glow bright for the first hour and then they noticeably fade over time until there is just a small spark of light that eventually disappears. Right now, your eyes are as bright as mine and they are showing no sign of fading after approximately... um, 11 hours."

Sylas held her hand while relaying the news and now she had a very tight grip on his.

"Do you think...?" Chance was at a loss. She was excited and scared all at the same time. She sure as hell didn't want to jinx it. Sylas squeezed her hand, watching as the emotions warred over her face. She looked down, afraid to see what he was feeling and finally whispered her thoughts out loud.

"Could it have been the dream? Did I change things with it? Sylas, could it really be happening this time?"

"The only way to be sure is to wait until later to see if anything has changed. In the meantime, we need to train more. Jack and I also want to walk you through the shift process. Even though you still are technically human, you need to know what to do when the time comes in case I'm not with you."

Chance gasped at his words.

"What do you mean if you're not with me?" She was getting upset now and she stood to pace. It was Jack who stopped her this time.

"Chance, he is only talking about the worst case scenario. If this goes bad, we need to know you will be okay. Both of us agreed on this.

We can't let you go through this blind, especially if neither of us can be with you. Please relax little Thomasina. We're not going to let anything happen to you."

Chance collapsed in her chair and then giggled, her nerves getting the best of her. "You just called me Thomasina. I really feel like I'm part of a family now."

Sylas kissed her and Jack chuckled at her confession. "You've been part of us since the day we met you, Sugar. You'll always have a family, if you can stand us that long."

Sylas huffed.

"Speak for yourself, Jack. Now let's change and go train, baby. I've got plans for us later." He winked and they left to change, leaving Jack still laughing at their backs.

Chapter 35

Dakota watched in the distance as the other wolf was tranquilized and carted off. He recognized the Beta's voice among those taking him away. He followed at a distance in the chance they would take him to the wolf den. When they arrived at what appeared to be a cabin and Craven joined them, he knew this was where he needed to be for now. It bothered him that they were so close to the build site. He backed off a few miles and made a quick call.

With his arrangements made, Dakota settled in to keep watch. The plans he made previously had to be modified. The man he spoke to on the other end of his call would guard her property. He would stay here between the two, so he could be at either within minutes. He wanted to avoid patrols, so he shifted and shimmied up a tall tree to wait.

Morning rolled around without much excitement. He saw a patrol off in the distance, but they never came close enough to catch his scent. Dakota decided to use the daylight to catch a quick nap up in his tree. After a couple of hours he heard talking off in the distance. It was two patrols passing by each other. It was another close call but neither of them came near his spot. He made another call to check in and settled in for more waiting.

* * * *

Jack couldn't believe Chance's eyes were still glowing. It was up to 18 hours now and they were just as bright as when she woke up at noon. He was waiting on them to get out of the shower from their workout so they could talk her through the art of shifting. He hoped they would be around for her first shift, but after what he'd been through, he wasn't taking anything for granted. She would be the first human in their long history to change into an immortal. It was instinctual with born shifters and Sylas was made as a full grown adult. Chance needed all the instruction she could get before the time came.

Chance was already showing abilities that other shifters didn't have. She could project her thoughts to Sylas and she could smell his scent. She could match Sylas blow for blow in training, and that was something even Jack couldn't claim. In all the years together, he never could keep up with the man, but that's as it should be. Jack was never jealous of Sylas. He respected him and loved him as a brother. There was nothing he wouldn't do for him, including keeping his future mate safe.

Sylas and Chance finally joined him at the table and he fed them a quick meal. Jack wanted a beer but he needed to be sober for this. They didn't need for her to get misinformation or get any more confused than she already was. He also needed to make a quick trip into town once they were finished. He needed clothes and a few other items that Chance didn't have available.

Chance spoke up first. "Sylas said earlier you two want to train me in the basics of shifting. How can you do it without my change in place?"

"We can help you visualize the change and what should happen when the time comes. By the way Chance, your eyes have not dimmed and it's been over 18 hours. The sooner the better for this talk."

Sylas spoke next, "Baby, you will have many animal choices to pick and choose from. I want your promise you will stick to four feet until I can coach you through the flying process, okay, love?"

Chance nodded and he gave the same to Jack so he could begin.

"Chance, I want you to close your eyes and see your inner cat. You will not feel her presence until you're immortal, but Sy told me you've dreamed about her on many occasions."

When her eyes closed, he continued. "It's not painful to shift. It can be uncomfortable the first time, but not painful. You'll need to allow your cat to take over your mind and body. Giving control of your mind can make you anxious. Now I want you to relax. Breathe in and out slowly. Let every muscle go slack and clear your mind."

Jack waited until he saw her shoulders slump a little. When she was almost in a trance like state, he continued again, "Visualize your cat, Chance. Feel her muscles and her heartbeat. She will speak to you and ask permission to take over. When the time comes, you will feel your consciousness being nudged aside. You'll still be there and will know all that is happening around you. Just know that she has as much invested in you as you do. If she loses you, she loses herself. Trust in her and you'll be able to give her control."

Chance suddenly gasped and turned pale. Sylas jumped to her side within seconds.

"What is it, baby?"

She stayed silent and unmoving, but as they watched, Chance started to smile and her skin turned a healthy color again.

"Chance, I need for you to let me know what's happening. Please, baby, talk to me."

She slowly lifted her hand and touched Sylas' face, but didn't open her eyes or speak.

Jack turned to Sylas with a question on the tip of his tongue when he saw his eyes glass over. "Okay, both of you are starting to spook this old man. Someone please tell me what the hell is going on!"

Sylas must have heard him because he shook his head before looking up at Jack.

"Jack, you're not going to believe this. Hell, I don't believe it and I just saw it. Chance is communing with her cat. She can see and talk to her. Her cat is in control for the moment. She's been talking to me through Chance. She touched my face just now. She told me she has waited centuries to tell me she loves me. She wanted me to know that the change would happen very soon. It was her love for my cat and I that led her to pick Chance as my mate. She collaborated with my mother when they chose Chance, as a team."

Chance came out of her trance and looked up at Sylas with tears in her eyes.

"She may have chosen me as your mate, but she's not the reason I fell in love with you. I did that all on my own. She never influenced my feelings for you, and I do love you, Sylas, with all my heart. Our leopards are soul mates that have waited hundreds of years for each other. Now our human halves have found each other, making our combined souls complete."

Jack cleared his throat to remind them that he was still sitting there.

"I see this lesson's over now." He chuckled and shook his head.

 "You never cease to amaze me, Chance. I don't think you'll have any problems relinquishing control since you've already done so, and while you are still human-ish!" They all started laughing, effectively releasing the tension permeating the air.

Jack finally remembered his chores and asked, "I need to make a store run. You two need anything while I'm out?"

Jack heard Chance clear her throat and he turned to look at her.

"I have one last confession to make before you go, Jack. I wanted to talk about this the other night, but it seems I was distracted." Chance giggled and looked sideways at Sylas.

"This is probably not news to either of you, but do you remember when I said I was permanently unemployed?" She waited until they both nodded.

"I am unemployed because I will never need to work, and that is because I am apparently very lucky and not just in my choice of friends."

They looked at her with confusion. Sylas piped up first, "What are you trying to tell us exactly?"

"You remember that rather large lotto from a few months back that had only one winner and topped nearly $400 million?"

Chance grinned and pointed towards herself, then reached in her pocket and handed Jack her black American Express card. "Whatever you need... just get it, okay?"

Jack whistled and looked at her, stunned. Sylas could only chuckle. "We knew you were spending a lot of cash, babe, but now everything makes more sense. Jack and I are not exactly poor either. Since we've both lived over 500 years, we've built up really nice bank accounts ourselves."

In synchronized fashion, they both reached into their wallets and showed her their own black cards.

Jack handed her card back, laughing at the shocked expression on her face. "Actually, I built my account up. Your man over there gets an allowance from his parents, but he never spends any of it."

"Never had a reason until lately," Sylas said winking and reaching over to hug Chance.

"Time to get my show on the road. Have fun while I am out!" Jack said still laughing.

"Jack, can you hold up a minute? I want to talk to you first." Sylas squeezed the hand of the woman he loved and then walked with Jack outside.

* * * *

Sylas waited until he knew they were out of earshot of the motor home. He turned to Jack with a grin from ear to ear. "She is ready Jack. Something rotten is in the air and I don't want her first time to be rushed or ruined by this madman. She deserves her first time to be filled with love and not anger. Do you mind staying here and keeping the place on lockdown while I take her away from here, some place special to create a good memory?"

Jack's face was plastered with that crooked smile he used when he was in conspirator mode. "You go get the two of you dressed for hiking. I will hide the necessities in the Jeep. Tell her I decided to wait until later and I suggested you show her Cloudland Canyon since we are here."

"Thanks a million, Jack. Owe you big time for this!" Sylas felt like he was walking a tightrope with the bad guys on both sides trying to push him off, but for once he didn't care. This was for his girl and he was going to do at least one thing right for her.
He walked inside and took Chance by the hand, guiding her to their room in the back. When they got there, he pulled her to him and breathed her in.

"Jack changed his mind about making a store run, baby. How would you like to do a small side trip with me to see the canyon? I've never been but Jack has and he said it is something we should see. Besides, I think we both could use the break to get away from all this, even if it is only for a few hours."

Chance smiled and nodded. "I think it'll be fun, Sylas. Do we need to change?"

"Maybe some sensible shoes, babe. Your boots are not the best for climbing." He swatted her behind when she turned to find her tennis shoes and she gave him a proper squeal for his efforts.

Chapter 36

Sylas drove the Jeep to the canyon but stayed out of the park since it would be dark soon and the park closed the gates at 10pm. He drove in as far he could without drawing attention of any forest rangers. When they got out, Sylas went to the back and found a picnic basket full of snacks and a blanket stuffed between the handles. *Leave it to Jack to think of everything*, he thought chuckling to himself. Chance looked at him and raised her eyebrows but didn't say anything.

Hand in hand, they headed down into the canyon, wanting to get towards the bottom before it got too dark. Not that it mattered, since they could both see perfectly no matter the time of day. An hour later and they found a perfect spot near one of the waterfalls. The view was spectacular. The sun was starting to set beyond the walls of the canyon causing the light to streak across the sky. There were woods right behind them and a large open area to set the picnic out on. The forest was full of animal and bird sounds and the air was crisp, smelling of fresh pine.

Sylas opened the blanket and spread it out and moved the basket to one side. He opened it and took out an array of cheeses, meats, and crackers. He found two wineglasses and a chilled bottle of light Chardonnay. Jack even remembered to include a cork wine opener. Sylas opened the bottle and poured them both a glass. Turning to Chance, he smiled and handed her one.

"A toast to the most beautiful woman I've ever met. I love you now and forever, Chance Cadens. There is nothing I wouldn't do for you. This is for day one of forever."

Chance gasped, suddenly understanding his meaning of day one. She quickly touched her glass to his and took a swallow. Sylas could tell she was nervous and excited by the look on her face.

"Are you saying what I think you are, Sylas?"

"Chance, you have been through so much and I want for you to have a special memory to wipe out all the bad ones. My love for you comes from the depths of my soul and beyond. I think it's time to make a certain dream become reality."

Sylas took her glass and placed it along side his on the basket lid. He stepped closer to her and pulled her in for a world-shattering kiss. He reached back and pulled her braid slightly, exposing her neck. His kisses rained down her neck like gentle droplets. He savored every one of them. She tasted like honey and wine and he could not get enough. She leaned into him, wrapping her arms around his waist, moaning her pleasure.

Sylas leaned back and pulled the braid around so he could pull the silky strands loose. Running his fingers through it, waves cascaded over them both as the strands came free of their bonds.

"I love your hair, baby. Please don't ever cut it or change it. It is one of many things that are perfect about you." Chance sighed as he ran his fingers up to her scalp, tangling them there on purpose.

The last of the daylight faded from the sky while he kissed her again. He needed to feel her skin against his and so he began to pull up her shirt. She stepped back to let him pull it over her head. She was not wearing a bra as usual and her nipples were standing erect, waiting to be nibbled on. He pulled his t-shirt off and pulled her back into him, relishing the feel of her against him.

Chance's hands were roaming his back and one found its way down to cup his ass, pulling his erection into her. She was grinding her hips into him as if she was dancing and he soon he found he was matching her rhythm. He wasn't sure what song was playing in her mind until he felt her in his head. It was the song he sang to her first, On the Dock of the Bay, and they danced as he sang along once again.

When the song ended, Sylas pulled her down to her knees to the blanket and then gently laid her back so he could roam her body some more. He suckled and kissed each nipple in turn before moving down to her navel. His tongue circled the crystal in her navel before moving lower. Sylas reached down and pulled her shoes off and then used his teeth to pull down her zipper. His tongue was everywhere, tasting her essence and sweetness. As expected, she was commando under her pants and he could smell her arousal as he tugged them down and off. Every time he touched her, he could hear her moans in his mind.

Chance was mentally telling him what she wanted and where. He took his time, teasing her with his hands and tongue, running them up and down her thighs. He found all the spots that spiked her need. Deciding he could wait no longer he dove into her honey pot with his tongue and she was dripping and ready for more. He lapped up every drop and teased her for more. His tongue sucked her nub, readying her for him. Sylas finally let her come and the sound of it in his head was more than his beast could take.

Sylas was shaking, fighting the need to shift and let his cat take over. *Not yet! This is my time! You will have yours soon,* he told the beast. Chance sat up and reached for him. She could sense the war happening in his head. Her hands found his zipper and she helped him remove his jeans.

"I'm ready, Sylas. We both are. It is time for our souls to complete their journey."

Sylas moaned and leaned over her, no longer able to contain his need to make her his mate. He pulled her up to her knees. He sat on his legs between her legs and let her straddle him.

"Take me in hand, Chance, and guide me in. This is for both of us. I need this to know you are absolutely sure."

Chance reached down and took a gentle hold of him. She stroked him, all the while her eyes never looking away from his. He was already hard, but it was her way of letting him know this was what she wanted. Guiding him to her entrance, she eased down over him, letting the tip enter her.

Sylas held her still, wanting to control this to make sure he didn't hurt her any more than necessary. He lifted his hips and watched her face for any signs of discomfort. He eased in a little and felt the resistance he was looking for.

"This is the part that will hurt a little, baby. It will only hurt once and that will be the last of it. Pleasure will be yours thereafter."

Chance nodded and he eased back and then pushed until he broke through. He held still a moment, watching as a single tear traced down her cheek.

"It doesn't hurt, love. That was a happy tear. I love you so very much, Sylas. Make me yours forever."

Gazes locked on each other, Sylas increased his speed a little and drove himself deeper. She fit him like a glove and she was hot with need. When he finally drove himself in all the way, he groaned at the perfect feel of her.

Chance started to circle her hips and he could hold still no longer. They rose and collided in perfect harmony, both feeling the tingles building in their bodies. Sylas felt his fangs descending and noticed hers doing the same. She paid it no mind and moved her head closer to his shoulder. Sylas pulled her hair aside and they both turned their necks to give each other access. It was the first time their eyes were not locked on the other. Their motions increased as the need rose to release.

At the same moment, they each bit into the other and they both exploded in one mind-blowing orgasm. The world turned into colors and sparks flew through their minds as they became one entity, four souls finally together. Chance screamed his name as she released her bite, still in the throes of becoming an immortal.

Sylas shook with emotion and ecstasy. His thoughts were a jumble of his cat roaring his gratification over his mate, Chance's exultation, and his completion of a lifelong search. They sat wrapped in each other's arms, both trembling now. His joy was overwhelming and he became hard again.

Chance felt his desire growing inside and she smiled up at him. Her hips moved of their own accord, her need matching his. Sylas held her as he moved them both down to the blanket with her under him. He wanted control this time and he took it. She opened wider for him, letting him drive as deep as he wanted and he did. This time he didn't want careful or slow and she understood it, matching him stroke for stroke. They both came screaming the others name.

Sylas never wanted this to end, but he knew they had no choice. He reached for their glasses and they downed the wine in a few gulps.

"We need to go soon, but not before you shift, love. Our cats are getting impatient." He chuckled when she nodded her agreement a little too enthusiastically. Sylas shifted and sat on his haunches, bumping his huge head into her in encouragement. Chance closed her eyes and smiled. Her body vibrated less than a few seconds and then she was there in all her feline beauty and grace.

She nudged him and licked his face, purring her love for him. Sylas roared, reveling in her. They turned and sprinted into the trees, running with pure joy. She tackled him to the ground and he chuffed at her, laughing. His beast took over, needing to seal the mating process. Afterwards, they trotted back, shifting before they broke the tree line. Sylas made love to her again against the tree they were standing by, her back was to him and he entered her like in the dream.

He couldn't get enough of her. He wanted to make love to her and become one. He shared his thoughts with her and she with him. It enhanced every emotion and feeling that was coursing through them.

Love was the main emotion and it brought them both nearer to each other, if that was even possible. Sylas latched onto her shoulder and drove into her until they came together in perfect harmony. Their mutual orgasm shattering all thought processes. This time it was so intense Chance passed out and he had to catch her before she hit the ground.

Sylas carried her back to the blanket as she came to. She wrapped her arms around him and kissed him silly.

"You have taken every bad memory from me, my love. They no longer exist. Nothing will ever take this time and moment away from me, Sylas. The world could end tomorrow and I would die a happy woman. I never felt such love and tenderness from anyone before you. I don't think I have the words to express what this has meant in healing my heart and soul. I love you with all that I am and from deep within my heart. I am filled with it and it feels as if I could explode from happiness."

Exalted in Chance's declaration, he whispered in her ear, "This is what I want to give you every day, from now until eternity, and I will, Chance. I waited for this moment for over 500 years. You make me whole and yet, I still feel as if I cannot get enough of you."

Sylas helped her dress and then dressed himself. They packed up the picnic and finished off the wine. Just before they were ready to walk back up the canyon, he stopped and turned her toward him, dropping to one knee. "I know it is a human thing and we are already mated, but humor me for a moment. Chance, I don't have a ring yet, but once this is over, will you do me the honor of marrying me?"

Sylas scanned her face, watching as she bit her lower lip. Tears began to fall silently down her cheeks. He panicked for a small moment when she stayed silent. He relaxed only when she gave him a beautiful smile and said yes. He jumped to his feet and grabbed her, spinning them around and around.

"Goddess bless us, I love you, Chance Cadens!" Suddenly there was a golden shimmering light surrounding them, filling them both with warmth and love. Sylas felt his mother's presence and he thanked her aloud for the gift. He felt her touch his face and then watched, as Chance's eyes grew round and suddenly a large diamond engagement ring appeared on her ring finger.

Sylas drove back to the campsite content and happy. Jack was still awake and waiting on them. He'd already put a bottle of champagne on ice with 3 glasses waiting for them to get back. He popped the cork and toasted the newly mated couple after they both got teary hugs from him. After he refilled their glasses, he shooed them both to the back, telling them he would have breakfast ready in the morning and not to worry about a thing.

Sylas made love to Chance in the shower and then carried her to the bed to continue his ministrations. He licked and tasted every inch of her, bringing her to ecstasy over and over again until they both finally passed out from exhaustion.

Chapter 37

Chance woke up sore but extremely content and relaxed. She was wrapped in her man's arms and she felt like she was home for the first time in her life. He was the earth and the air all wrapped into one perfect being and he was hers. She was facing him with her head on his arm and her hand on his chest. She could feel his heart beating and it made her smile. She snuggled in closer, relishing the feel of his skin against hers. She saw his lips turn up in a smile and he pulled her up so she was lying on his chest.

"Mmmm, good morning, future wife of mine. Did you sleep well?"

"Yes I did, Mr. Taiken. Better than I can ever remember. Oooo, is that a pickle in your pocket or are you just happy to see me?" She giggled when his eyes grew big with feigned surprise.

Chance slithered down his body, but not before throwing thick strands of hair over him. She found her prize and quickly licked the pre-cum before it had a chance to escape her. She took him into her mouth and felt him shudder, his pleasure obvious. His hands found their way into her mane as she bobbed up and down over his perfect shaft. She took him in deeper and deeper into her throat, wanting to please him all the more. It wasn't long before he lost control and was shooting his seed into her mouth. She took it all greedily and when he was done, she crawled back up to share his taste in a deep kiss.

"If you are not too sore, my lady, I would love to show you my appreciation."

Chance grinned at him and then suddenly found herself on her hands and knees with him behind her. He drove into her in one fluid movement and she moaned, wanting more of him. She tried turned her head to watch as he drove his cock into her over and over, but he had one hand using her tresses as reins. She was nearing climax quickly with his passionate lovemaking. Sylas gave her a gentle tug, wanting her up so he could bite her. As soon as his teeth sank into her shoulder, her entire being exploded around him.

She fell back asleep with him still inside her. Neither of them wanted
to break the contact it gave them. She woke later in the morning to
the feeling of him growing hard again inside her and she could not
put the erotic feel of it into words. It was sexual in a whole new way
and it made her instantly wet with desire. She moaned when the
feeling overwhelmed her senses and he took his sweet time slowly
loving her once more.

After another shower, they smelled bacon cooking and reluctantly
left the bedroom to join Jack in the kitchen. He was cooking a feast
for breakfast and they made sure he knew it was appreciated by
eating every last bite. Who knew sex could make one so ravenous?
They skipped training after, figuring they had given each other
enough of a work out.

Chance knew Jack was antsy to go shopping and so she helped him
sort everything out. She hugged him and gave him a peck on the
cheek. "Thank you, Jack. You are like a brother to me and I want
you to know how much I care about you. Be careful and hurry home
okay?"

He smiled at her and she stood beside Sylas as he drove off.

* * * *

Sylas held Chance in his arms as Jack drove off in the Jeep. He had
an uneasy feeling and it was eating at him from the inside out. He
sniffed the air but couldn't smell any shifters around the area. They
went back inside and he turned to lock the motor home down. They
would enjoy each other some more, but not outside. This would be
as safe as he could make it. He locked the door and pulled the
shades on all the windows, including the ones over the windshield.
Chance was back in the shower and he itched to join her, but this
time she was trying to ease some very sore muscles in a steam bath.

Instead he called his mother, taking advantage of the small window
of time where he could talk to her alone. Lachesis shimmered in,
dressed in her flowing toga style dress. "Mother, thank you for

coming. I can feel trouble in the air and I need to know what you might know of it."

"The time has come son, and I can no longer help you. You know what to do. Now go to her." Sylas started to say more but his mother had already faded away.

It was then that Sylas heard them outside. He wasn't sure how many were out there but he knew there wasn't any time left. He ran to the back just as the first rock hit the windshield. The rock didn't break through, but did crack it. He got to Chance just as a scream was about to leave her throat.

Sylas put his hand over her mouth, startling her, but she knew who it was in an instant.

"We have to get ready now, Chance. No fear, baby, just our love."

She nodded and hurriedly dressed in her black leathers. She pulled on her special boots and checked her gun to make sure it was ready and loaded. Then she quickly braided her wet hair, not bothering to comb through it.

Chance rummaged through a drawer and pulled out a package she had bought special for this moment and handed it to Sylas. She tried not to panic when she felt the motor home shaking and more rocks hitting the glass. Sylas opened the box and inside was a matching set of leathers in his size. She also included some armbands and a full vest like hers. She intended to survive this with both of them in one piece.

They only had a few precious moments before the fight would begin and she took advantage of every second by pulling Sylas into her arms. They locked eyes and kissed, putting all their love into it. Sylas pulled back when he heard feet running down the hallway. He braced the door and then turned to her, whispering urgently.

"Stay in human form Chance. I need you to promise me you won't shift. Keep it a secret until absolutely necessary and do not, for any reason, shift to protect me. Remember they can't kill us, only my parents can do that. They won't know you are mated as long as you keep the mark covered. They won't be able to tell by scent either. Keep your shoulder covered as long as you can, baby. I love you no matter what happens. If they should take you from me, know I will find you."

Chance nodded and kissed him again as the wolves tried to break the door in. She was grateful she spent the extra money on a better home with solid oak doors. With tears in her eyes, they both stepped away from the door. It shattered as a man fell through it. Sylas took the first and Chance the next. She ducked a fist and nearly ripped his arm off as she grabbed it and spun. She reached up and grabbed his head, breaking his neck in a single move. As she moved to take on the next one, she saw Sylas shift. Blood and gore flew as he ripped his claws down his attacker's chest. He was alive when he hit the floor, but not for long.

They moved out into the hallway fighting everyone who came at them. Chance held nothing back, her training kicking into full survival gear. She slipped on some blood and started to fall, but Sylas was right there, shoving her out of the way with his body, when a knife hit the floor right where she would have been. They worked their way outside where they both had more freedom of movement. Bodies and parts flew everywhere. Blood covered her from head to foot and yet, she didn't notice it. She stayed as close as she could to Sylas, needing to be near him. She kept his words in her head and caught herself a few times wanting to shift.
Shifters kept coming at them. She had no idea how many they killed already and still they came. Some were in wolf form. She already had a few bite wounds seeping and she knew Sylas did too. They were getting smarter and coming at them in larger numbers. She grabbed her gun and shot two that were attempting to wrestle Sylas to the ground. She turned it on three more who were rushing her. She turned again when she smelled smoke and saw they'd set the home on fire. She heard other shots ring out and wrenched herself back into the fight. She used her last 3 bullets taking out two of the shooters, missing one.

She ran to Sylas when she saw two more trying to take him down. She pulled her knife and chucked it into one of them and used her toe knife to slash into the other's leg, effectively disabling him. Just as she turned to finish him off, she felt a sting in her thigh. She reached down and pulled a dart out of her leg, falling to her knees as it took immediate effect. She screamed for Sylas, but the sound never left her throat. Her last sight was of Sylas getting slammed to the ground by a volley of bullets. Her world faded to black before she could process another word.

Want more of Sylas and Chance?

Coming soon to a store near you!

Chance Found

Jo LaRue can be found on Facebook @

http://www.facebook.com/AuthorJoLaRue

and on Twitter

@JoLaRueAuthor

Or sign up on her Blog @

http://jolarue.blogspot.com/

Email Jo at: AuthorJoLaRue@gmail.com

See the next few pages for a sneak peek at Chance Found!!

Chance Found ~ Prologue

Jack had not seen this kind of destruction and carnage since the Civil War and as soon as he pulled up to the motor home, his mind flashed back to it in horror. There were bodies or pieces of them strewn all over the ground.

Glass and parts of the home he shared with his two best friends were scattered about like shrapnel. The motor home itself was a smoking burned out shell. Like a man in shock, Jack stood stock still, unwilling to believe his eyes. While he was out shopping for supplies and clothes, his world had been ripped apart.

Snapping out of it, he rushed around the site looking for Sylas and Chance. Of Chance, there was no sign, but he found Sylas on the other side of the home with several bullet wounds to the chest. Jack sank to his knees; his muscles no longer able to hold him erect. With shaking hands he reached to check Sylas' vitals. There was a heartbeat, but it was very faint. *This can't be happening again!*

Jack reared his head back and roared his pain. In his grief, he started flashing back and forth between his human and puma form. Reaching deep down for a calming breath, he screamed for Lachesis, Sylas' mother. He would not lose another person he loved or cared for. The deaths of his wife and child would be the last, else he feared for his sanity.

Lachesis shimmered before him and collapsed to the ground beside her son. Sylas was covered head to toe with mortal wounds, both man-made and animal. Jack could see the tears sliding down her cheeks as she held her hands over his body. They glowed with a golden healing light as they passed over Sylas from head to toe. Jack looked up to see Zeus standing behind her, lending her the energy to heal their son. Her hands went dim and they watched as Sylas took a deep cleansing breath.

With his eyes still closed, Sylas reached for his mother's hand and shot up into a sitting position. He pleaded with his mother. "They took her, but I can't sense her! Please tell me she is still alive."

Sylas opened his eyes slowly and took in his surroundings. Jack finally released the air he had been holding. He looked around the site again and was shocked to see other shifters standing in a loose circle just outside the tree line. They all were in human form with their heads bowed, as if in prayer. He could not scent all their animal forms, but he could tell that there were many different animals represented.

Jack tore his gaze back to Sylas and Lachesis when he heard her begin to speak. "She is alive, my son, but she has been drugged as you were. You will not be able to sense her or mind speak with her until allowed to come off them." Zeus helped them both to their feet and Jack followed suit.

Zeus looked at his son with love in his eyes. He raised his hand and motioned to all the shifters at the tree line. "I have called for all of the Alpha's from the immediate area clans to come here for you. It is time for this to end. This Alpha male and his Beta have pushed too far. We have done what we can. It is now up to you to finish this, Son."

Jack and Sylas bowed their heads in reverence. Lachesis stepped over and placed a hand on each of their shoulders. Looking at Sylas and then at Jack, she smiled and kissed them both on the cheek.

"I know this is hard on you both, but all will be well. Never give up your faith, either of you. Be well, my sons." They watched as Zeus took her hand as they slowly shimmered away.

Chance Found ~ Chapter 1

"How did they find us here, Jack? I don't understand it."

Sylas paced the ground in front of him, stopping only long enough to ask the question and scrub his face with his hands in frustration. When he removed his hands and finally looked up, he stopped. Jack was pale and slightly shaking, but from what he wasn't sure. He hadn't seen him this pale since his mate died and it suddenly dawned on him. In his worry about Chance, he hadn't considered what his best friend was going through. Sylas reached out a hand and clapped it on his shoulder.

"I get it, Jack. We will find her and we will both exact revenge on what they've done. I need you to help me keep my shit together. Okay, Bro? Remember what I told you long ago? I am truly immortal and so is Chance. Neither of us can die from mortal wounds. "

Sylas watched as Jack nodded and took a deep breath, pulling his thoughts together and back into the game. He could tell he was going to be okay when his color deepened, returning almost back to normal. They both seemed to remember at the same time they had an audience and as one they turned towards the tree line. Sylas stepped forward first, with Jack following as his Beta. Once they reached the tree line, the Alpha's nodded their heads in respect and waited for him to begin speaking.

"Thank you for heeding my father's call. I know by now many of you have heard rumors of the wolf Alpha, Craven, and his pack of rogues. Most of what you've heard is truth."

The other clan Alpha's shifted uncomfortably at this news and a few in the back were murmuring quietly. Sylas gave them time to let his news sink in. He wanted their full attention and this was the only way to get it. All shifters knew defiance of the Enforcer was an open declaration and a death sentence. One that 99 percent of the population did not want. Craven defied him and now would pay, and these shifters would jump at a shot to help bring him down. Bringing attention to their existence could mean a death sentence for all of them and they knew it.

"I need to enlist all of you to help me track this Alpha down. He took from me the one thing I care for the most, my mate."

More murmurs broke out, but this time Sylas didn't pause. "I need tracking specialists from each group. I know he will run. I was left for dead by his Beta, but I know Craven and he won't chance getting caught. I need the fastest of you to head to their compound in an effort to catch him before he can."

Heads turned towards the woods and Sylas heard movement as their companions left to do their bidding.

"I will need some to stand watch on her property and not disturb the construction there." More heads turned and more orders were obeyed.

"Mostly I need the word spread throughout the lower 48 and Canada that no one is to give him a place of harbor. I will consider those clans part of the enemy and justice will be dealt swiftly. I want my mate back in one piece. I'm sure you understand my meaning."

The birds hit the air and mammals the ground.

"I need her back as quickly and safely as possible. Craven is sadistic and it is not beyond him to try and use her as a shield. Keep this in mind if you confront him. Thank you again. Jack and I are heading to his compound first. Those that wish to join us are welcome."

Sylas turned to Jack and nodded. No words were needed. They both shifted and hit the ground running as fast as their legs could carry them. Sylas took a second to glance behind him. It appeared that all of the Alpha's were with him and he smiled inwardly. He would need them all to accomplish his goal. He could hear the beating of wings above him, but he didn't need to see them to know the birds were moving ahead of them at break neck speed. It had been centuries since all of the clans had come together like this and it gave him hope.

The miles between were covered in record time. Sylas didn't slow until he was almost to the compound. He caught a whiff of wolf in the air but the scent was familiar. As they rounded a stand of trees, he saw a man standing in a clearing apparently waiting on them. Sylas stopped and shifted. He motioned the rest to continue on without him.

Jack took the lead and the rest followed. As he moved closer, he took in his appearance. He was dressed in black western attire from his hat to his boots. He wore long black hair and his eyes were silver gray. The man raised his hands, palms up, in supplication but kept his eyes on Sylas. When he got within five feet of the man, he stopped and waited for him to speak.

"I know you, Enforcer, and I know for whom you are searching. My name is Dakota and we need to talk before you go to the compound. Please, spare me a minute?"

"You have two and I suggest you not waste them."

"To the point then. I just learned recently that you've met my father, John, the Indian dowser from the property next door. I also learned my children, once thought dead for many years, are still alive. Your mate, Chance, is one of them… my daughter."

Sylas looked at the man closely. He could see a resemblance. He also remembered what John said that day on the property. He called Chance his granddaughter. John was not a shifter, but a human shaman. He didn't understand how this could be. He could smell the truth in Dakota's words, but it wasn't adding up, because obviously the man was a wolf shifter.

"I can see your confusion, Enforcer, but I don't have time to explain everything now. We both have a common goal and that is to get Chance back safely. I am the best tracker in the country. Stick with me and we will get her back together. Deal?"

Dakota reached out his hand and Sylas took it. He would get his answers later. Sylas shifted and Dakota followed suit. Together they continued towards the compound, black leopard and wolf running in tandem.

Once they reached the cabin, Sylas took in the controlled chaos as he shifted back to human form. Jack was shouting orders to round up the rogues into a nearby barn. When he saw Jack's face, he knew they arrived too late to catch Craven. The anger and frustration he saw there was palpable.

Sylas turned back to speak to Dakota, but the man was running into the cabin and he couldn't help but follow. He watched as the man sniffed the air and literally followed his nose down a darkened hallway. He opened a door at the end and saw the man disappear down a set of stairs. Sylas took note of several cameras and put it in his mind to find the computer equipment in hopes of garnering more information. He heard a commotion coming from the stairwell and rushed down to help. What he saw in that room made his heart stop.

There was torture equipment everywhere he looked. Dakota was trying in vain to get someone down off the wall that was shackled there. Sylas looked around and finally laid eyes on a hook with some keys attached. He grabbed them and rushed over to see if any would unlock them. The shifter chained there was unconscious and of no help what so ever. Dakota held him up while he went through the keys. Finally on the fifth try, he found the right key and unlocked them. As the man slumped into Dakota's arms, he heard a quiet sigh of relief.

Dakota lowered him gently to the floor and then whipped out a phone. He made a quick call to John and hung up. Bending back down over the hurt man, Dakota started talking to him. Sylas had backed up to give him space, but he could still hear him.

"Trey? Can you hear me? Nod, if you understand."

Sylas watched as the man on the floor gave an almost imperceptible nod. In the state he was in, Sylas guessed that he had been drugged and had been chained in this room for days. Sylas went back up the stairs and found several unopened bottles of water in the kitchen area. He took them back down and handed one to Dakota after opening it.

"Give it to him slowly. There is no telling how long he has been without. He also appears to have been drugged. I'm a medic. May I look him over for major injuries?"

Dakota nodded his thanks and permission. Sylas checked him over and found nothing more than flesh wounds from the shackles. He had been trussed up with spikes to prevent shifting. Once he was able to shift, they would heal quickly. He looked at Trey's face and felt as if he knew him from somewhere, but for the life of him, he couldn't place him. His scent was familiar and it hit him suddenly.

This was the wolf that attacked Chance in her home. His scent was distinctive and he knew something was off. Sylas went back up the stairs and called for Jack. He asked for men to help carry this man, Trey, up the stairs. Jack went out and came right back with a couple of bear shifters. They went down and brought him up with Dakota right on their heels.

Sylas pulled Dakota to the side as they laid Trey out on a couch. He handed Jack the other bottle of water and nodded towards him. Sylas noticed the reluctance in Jacks demeanor. They both knew this was the one behind some of this mess. Jack took it and gave Trey more water while Sylas asked Dakota the burning question on his mind.

"Who is this Trey? I recognize his scent from my mate's home and if he's the man I think he is, then he has some major explaining to do when he comes around."

"Trey is my son and your mate's full brother."

Sylas kept waiting on the punch line that never came. He eyed Dakota for signs of deception and found none. He ran his hands through his hair and let out a big whoosh of air.

"You're telling me the man who attacked my mate in her home is her brother? She almost killed him! Hell, if he's who I think he is, I almost killed him! Could this situation get any more fucked up? Jack… JACK!" Sylas felt his last thread of sanity slowly unraveling and he needed to take a walk to clear his mind.

"Dakota meet Jack. Jack, Dakota. Dakota, please tell Jack everything you told me and everything you haven't. I'm going outside for air before I do kill someone. Jack…"

"I got your back, Sy. Just go. I got this."

Sylas walked away as Dakota started his story. He wanted to hear it, but right now was not the time. He wanted to try and contact Chance mentally. He needed a clear head for it and that was not going to happen listening to their conversation. Sylas walked outside and saw the Alpha's had everything under control, including interrogations of the prisoners.

Sylas pulled one to the side and gave him instructions that none were to be harmed. According to his mother, they were innocents and to be treated as such. Wrong place, wrong time scenario. After he was given the promise that all were being kept under guard, he wandered off to find a place to calm his mind.

Searching until he found a large boulder in the shape of a giant chair sitting under a large oak, Sylas finally sat down and crossed his legs in a meditative position. It took everything in him to clear his racing thoughts. It seemed like it took forever, but was actually only minutes later when he reached out a feeler for Chance. Nothing was coming to him, so he dug deeper and reached out farther. Next thing he knew, Sylas was assailed with excruciating pain and darkness. He gasped from the intensity of the feelings she was sending him. As suddenly as the pain hit him, it was gone.

Sylas tried for several more minutes to reach her and failed. Craven must have drugged her again and Sylas seethed with anger. He vowed that Craven would suffer before he killed him. If it was the last thing he did on this earth, the man would pay.

There are many people I would like to thank for making my dream become reality. First and foremost, my family, without whom any of this would be possible. Their patience and tolerance (most of the time) of my disappearing behind a computer to write has made this possible.

My Dream Team of miracle workers, Cristina Frey, Francesca Klinger, Amanda Graves, Amanda Hamlin-Maneke, Lisa Harkenrider, Barbi Rumfield, Tanya Hahn, Macee Fay, Jillian Reed Young, Shawn Proveaux, Lois Lane, Natasha Post, Erika McDonald, and Ken McBride. All of you may not have wanted credit, but you deserve it and so much more. Without all of you, this would not be happening. I Heart all of you with a capital H!

My real job co-workers, Clyde, Carey, and Sheila, who took the time to let me pester you into reading chapter after chapter. Thank you to Casey, Rick, Branden, Joyce, Lisa, and Ellie for allowing me to edit while working and for answering my 1000 & 1 questions about the book and covers. You all are the best people I have had the honor to work with.

Special thank you: To Hank Irwin for his publishing advice. To authors Karen A. Thompson and Elle Casey for all your help with advice on where and how to become my own person in this strange new world. Imoan Braxton, thank you for wanting to publish my book, and accepting my wish to do this on my own.

Ken McBride for volunteering to do my covers. Best almost stalker a girl could ever have. Thank you to Amy Wels for bringing his almost stalking self to me. I <3 you too!

Last but never least to my extended family for believing in me. You all are the best aunts and cousins a girl could ever have. I inherited my love of reading and writing from my late Grandma Drew. I know she is up there watching me with a smile on her face. She would never approve of the story content, but I know she would be proud of my accomplishments.

Index

Prologue

Chapter 1
Chapter 2
Chapter 3
Chapter 4
Chapter 5
Chapter 6
Chapter 7
Chapter 8
Chapter 9
Chapter 10
Chapter 11
Chapter 12
Chapter 13
Chapter 14
Chapter 15
Chapter 16
Chapter 17
Chapter 18
Chapter 19
Chapter 20
Chapter 21
Chapter 22
Chapter 23
Chapter 24
Chapter 25
Chapter 26
Chapter 27
Chapter 28
Chapter 29
Chapter 30
Chapter 31
Chapter 32
Chapter 33
Chapter 34
Chapter 34

Chapter 35
Chapter 36
Chapter 37

About The Author

Teaser: Chance Found

About the Author

Jo LaRue has kept stories in her head all her life, but never put any down on paper until recently. Her favorite genres are Fantasy Fiction and Paranormal Romances of any type, be they for teens (YA) or erotica (NA).

Jo lives in northeast GA with her hubby of 20 years, their son, and a small menagerie of neighborhood kids. They have an Amazon parrot, Honey, who will more than likely outlive the lot. They are also owned by a wonderful 80 lb. rescue dog, Calypso, who is afraid of her own shadow, except when it counts.

Jo still has many stories to share, so keep a watch out for more and hopefully they will pleasantly surprise you.

Made in the USA
Charleston, SC
21 January 2014